DEATH TO THE PIGS

Péret by Picabia, 1921.

Death to the Pigs, and Other Writings

by

Benjamin Péret

Translated by Rachel Stella and Others
Introduction by Rachel Stella
University of Nebraska Press
Lincoln and London

Published under the title *Death to the Pigs: Selected writings of Benjamin Péret* by Atlas Press, London.

© 1988, Atlas Press
© for translations remains with translators
© for French texts: Association des amis de Benjamin Péret
and Librairie Jose Corti.
All Rights Reserved.

Book design: Alastair Brotchie.
Printed by Antony Rowe ltd., Chippenham.
Published simultaneously in the United States
by the University of Nebraska Press.

Library of Congress Cataloging-in-Publication Data
Péret, Benjamin, 1899–1959
Death to the pigs, and other writings
/ edited & introduced by Rachel Stella.
p.   cm. – (A French modernist library)
Bibliography: p.
ISBN 0-8032-3685-9. ISBN 0-8032-8721-6 (pbk.)
1. Péret, Benjamin, 1899–1959 – Translations, English.
I. Stella, Rachel. II. Title. III. Series.
PQ2631.E348A27 1989
841'.912—dc19   CIP 88–27731

Contents

Biographical Introduction

1. Nantes to Paris

IN 1915, THE SIXTEEN-YEAR-OLD BENJAMIN PÉRET AND ONE OF his friends were caught by a local gendarme in the act of defacing public property. It seems that it was his mother who gave him a choice between reform school and the army. He chose the latter, enlisted and served from 1915 to 1919. He was sent to Salonica, where he caught amoebic dysentery and was evacuated. He finished the first World War in Lorraine.

Little is known of Péret's youth, spent in various parts of Brittany. He was born in Rézé in 1899; but he and his brother grew up in Nantes, where his mother moved after her divorce from Péret's father. We know something of Péret's feelings about her from *La Parole est à Péret*; and Guy Prévan* (asterisks indicate notes to be found at the end of this book) suggests that it was Péret and not Eluard who was responsible for the anti-maternal "Strike while your mother is young" in the *152 Proverbes mis au goût du jour* [152 Proverbs brought up to date].

He never went to college; indeed, he never graduated from his *lycée* in Nantes, he left school with only the *Certificat d'Etudes*, required by compulsory education laws.

His first appearance in print consists of some sugary symbolist verse with a slight *fin-de-siècle* cast. These appeared in *Les Tablettes Littéraires et Artistiques*, a small ephemeral review of no particular orientation—its poor quality can be judged by the fact that the young Benjamin Péret was

7

its most famous contributor. Three poems were printed in this magazine during the early part of 1919.* Charitable souls have called these early attempts "Mallarmésque," but this is no doubt a by-product of the anecdote reported by Claude Courtot, namely that Péret, during a transfer of his military unit, came across a book of Mallarmé's poetry on a bench in a train station in Compiegne. Courtot adds that later Péret declared that this was a crucial event in his life.*

Dominique Rabourdin gives a different account of this discovery. In 1952 Péret was invited to speak on a radio show called *Les Armes Parlantes.* Rabourdin reports Péret's words at this time:

"During the war I wrote poems influenced by Mallarmé, in a Mallarmésque style, none of which I saved. But in 1918 I discovered Apollinaire through an issue of SIC* left on a bench of the Troyes-Praise train station, and the site of rather nasty memories. I still remember the shock that this publication gave me at the time, however harmless it might seem now. It was as if I had suddenly come across an unknown shore covered with flora and fauna I had never even imagined. This encounter was followed shortly after by the discovery of Rimbaud. It was reading Rimbaud, and then later Lautréamont and Jarry, which persuaded me to abandon the banal paths followed by my predecessors and to take off for adventure."*

Before Péret took off to become someone whom Max Jacob would describe as a "confirmed dadaist,"* he was, according to Robert Desnos at least, a stupid looking fellow whose "naive good nature and shyness made him for some time the butt of the group's jokes." Desnos described the provincial's move from Nantes to Paris in the following terms:

" . . . his mother took him to see Breton, who was well known in their hometown, and who was at the time living on the Place du Pantheon, in the Hotel des Grands Hommes.

Having come on a night train, they arrived at Breton's around six in the morning. "Monsieur," said the mother, "I have heard all about you and I am told that you could do something for my son who wants to embark in literature."

Then, without another word, she left.

Péret stayed alone with Breton, who tried, in vain, to get him to talk."*

Péret's first public appearance with the Dadaists in Paris occurred on the 26th of May, 1920, during the Dada festival at the Salle Gaveau, where he came on stage shouting "Long live France and French fries!" By this time Breton, Soupault and Aragon had already been publishing *Littérature* for

Outside Max Ernst's first exhibition in Paris: Breton, Soupault, Rigaut, Péret, Charchoune.

Péret as he appears in Breton's "Nadja."

several months. Péret's first contribution to this magazine was an article on Landru, which appeared in the fifteenth issue (July-August 1920). This same month finds *Importe du Japon* between the covers of another small magazine, *Action*. This poem, which has no rhymes, concerns both an opium-smoking Papuan who is actually a chimpanzee, and the activities of a white chrysanthemum and a royal blue goblet. Clearly, Mallarmé is now as far away as the railway station.

By the following year (1921), Péret seems to have been completely integrated into the Parisian Dada movement. He appears in the group portrait taken during the notorious visit to the church of Saint Julien-le-Pauvre on April 14th, 1921, as well as in photographs of Max Ernst's first Paris exhibition. He played a small but important role in the Barrès trial on May 13th, 1921. This travesty of a legal proceeding tried the establishment author, Maurice Barrès, for "crimes against the security of intelligence."* Needless to say, the press was, on principle, outraged by this event, but Péret's role as the Unknown Soldier was considered the most reprehensible of all. A. d'Estarbes, a dedicated anti-dadaist, wrote in *Comoedia:*

"It was a pitiful, grotesque event, made even more odious by the introduction into this humourless charade, of the character of the Unknown Soldier, a travesty of what this symbol represents for the great majority of French citizens."*

Another critic mentioned that "a grotesque travesty, both idiotic and indecent took place the other night in Paris . . . The vile, base evocation of the Unknown Soldier went completely beyond the pale . . . "*

Pierre Naville has described the significance of this event in Péret's life:

"He came out of the army furiously hostile to everything connected with it, and it is here that one can find the source of all of his imprecations, which never let up, against anything and everything which recalled military discipline . . . Partisan of life, it was at the top of his voice that he exclaimed his horror of society's murder machine, and he did everything possible to detach himself from it. By playing the role of the Unknown Soldier in the Barrès trial, Péret, wearing the uniform of the anonymous casualty, demonstrated the radical protests of those coming from the death trenches. Everything which related to the domain of military attitudes came under his categorical condemnation; there is no doubt that this intransigeant and unrepentant attitude earned him the hostility of others besides publishers and the press."*

10

But for Péret, the most important event of 1921 was probably the publication of his first book *Le Passager du transatlantique*. Robert Desnos notes that after this collection of poems Péret was no longer treated as a kind of "naive idiot"*. Soupault wrote that it was one of the most remarkable books to appear in ten years*. The collection contains sixteen short pieces, several of them dedicated to writers (Ribemont-Dessaignes, Fraenkel, Rigaut and Vaché) with whom Péret lost contact after a short while. Although none of this work is translated in this anthology, it is worth noting that all the texts in *Le Passager du transatlantique* contain the imagery and humour, as well as the use of found language, that is so characteristic of Péret's writing. However, other traits of his, namely his particular use of conjunctions and prepositions have not yet made their appearance. This collection also contains *Bar pour bar fumoir pour fumoir*, which seems to be Péret's first automatic text.*

2. Taking off Dada spectacles.

Early in 1922 André Breton wrote his declaration *Lachez tout*, which un-equivocally advocated: "Drop everything, drop dada." From then on, *Littérature* was published under a new cover, and became the mouthpiece of "a new current which is no longer stubbornly focused on destructive agitation." In other words, Surrealism. In the October 1922 issue of *Littérature* Péret wrote a text allying himself with Breton: *A travers mes yeux*, in which he takes definitive leave of Tristan Tzara's crowd* and their activities, stating: "I take off my Dada spectacles." Péret was the only early member of the Surrealist group, apart from Breton, to remain active within it until his death in the fifties.

A letter from Simone Kahn-Breton to Denise Levy (wife of Pierre Naville) documents Péret's new vision:

"Asleep, Benjamin Péret becomes a winged being, unattainable. And, at the same time, he is so funny and so happy, that you burst out laughing listening to him. Péret undertakes a marvellous journey . . . in a world without water, humans, animals. The air is rarified. Indeed it isn't air. There are plants like fur, which grow and grow, and great red eggs which fly, jump, fall flat and return to their original form.

But I am summarising and this is terribly demeaning and impoverishing. Péret, his head on his arms, answers questions with an ecstatic air, absolutely angelical, with a sweet, soft voice, ethereal, detached, far off."

Benjamin Péret in 1925

This letter is a description of "The period of sleeping-fits", when the Surrealists practised writing under self-induced hypnotic trances. Crevel had introduced the idea, and it was he, Desnos and Péret who employed them with the most ease and the most striking effects.

As a result, in part, of his exploration of automatism, it is during this period (the early Twenties) that Péret wrote most of his most characteristic short fiction pieces, as well as *Mort aux vaches et au champ d'honneur*, his so-called novel. Though many of these pieces did not see print for ten or twenty years, it was at this time that Péret took his place in the Surrealist movement both as a poet (his poetry was put out by publishers close to the movement), but also as the co-editor, with Pierre Naville, of the group's first important review *La Revolution surréaliste*.

The first issue of this magazine appeared on December 1st, 1924, two months after the *Bureau des Recherches Surréalistes* opened its doors. This office, at 15 Rue de Grenelle, served two functions: as headquarters for the magazine, and as a centre for gathering and disseminating information. The Bureau was open between 4:30 and 6:30 pm every day except Sunday; and two Surrealists were assigned to be present each day. According to the daybook, Péret and Paul Eluard were responsible for Tuesday afternoons.

A great deal of interesting trivia about Péret (and others of course) can be gleaned from a study of the daybook*. For instance, Péret's attendance was somewhat lackadaisical. He didn't always show up if he had some other preoccupation: on October 14th 1924, Eluard notes "When René is sick, Péret is not here." Moreover, there are numerous complaints in Breton's hand about the quality of Péret's work.

The Bureau's daybook, along with the appended letters, declarations, and the minutes of various meetings held early in 1925 give a clear picture of why Breton eventually closed the Bureau to the public (putting Antonin Artaud in charge), and then took over the direction of the magazine himself. Essentially, he felt his goals for the magazine and the movement were not being met. By October 30th, 1924, he had already noted:

"2) The magazine. All things considered, there are too many Surrealist texts . . . Cut them down or cut them out. Get one or several more poems by Eluard. Insufficient number of reports and chronicles. The Cami interview by Péret is hateful. And, as usual (but this time even more regrettable) there are no anonymous communications, no anouncements, no good advertisements, no finds whatsoever; nothing here bears witness to any real extra-literary life. The whole thing, as one might have suspected, is of an artistic character . . . Nothing which makes one want to wait for, or desire, a second issue. Nothing, other than some vague affirmations, to legitimise the existence of a research bureau . . . Without any exaggerated pessimism, one is allowed

13

to wonder exactly where the Surrealist spirit is amidst all of this."

Whether Péret was glad to be relieved of his editorial responsibilities is difficult to know. What is evident is his continued participation in the activities of the group.

By the end of 1925, one can say that the Surrealists have shed the last vestiges of the nihilism and anarchism left over from the Dada period. The declaration *Appel aux travailleurs** marks the beginning of a much more active political commitment. This declaration was subtitled "Do you condemn the war, yes or no." The declaration referred to the *Guerre du Rif*, in which the French government was giving aid to Spain so that the Spaniards could hold on to their colonies in Morocco. Henri Barbusse, editor of *L'Humanité*, drafted the declaration, which was signed by 52 intellectuals, a large group of Surrealists (of which Péret was one) included.

The importance of this document is twofold. For one thing, it marks the beginning of a dialogue between Surrealists and Communists, since the other intellectuals who signed included the entire editorial staff of *Clarté*, a magazine as left-orientated as *L'Humanité*, but which did not enjoy its official position as the organ of the French Communist Party (PCF). The document is also important for what it says. It not only declared an intention to revolt against History, it called for an opening towards Asia (that is to say, toward the east, i.e. the USSR) and anounced a firm commitment to a social revolution. The final paragraph takes a hardline stance: "We consider a bloody revolution to be the ineluctable revenge of all the spirits humiliated by your (bourgeois) works."

For Péret, this new liason with the Communists not only meant an opportunity to express his political opinions, but also a job. Marcel Fourier, the director of *Clarté*, was also, at that time, the editor of the cultural page of *L'Humanité*, and consequently managed to insinuate some Surrealist by-lines there for some time. Thus, Peret became a stringer, writing filler and human interest stories such as the *"chien écrasés"** and contributing movie reviews to *L'Humanité* for over a year.

According to a letter Péret wrote to E. F. Granell, it was in 1925 that he officially joined the Communist Party. However, most reference sources date Péret's joining to the publication of *Au grand jour* [Out into the Light], a manifesto written in 1927. *Au grand jour* consisted of several parts: a declaration, and five letters. These documents were signed by Aragon, Breton, Eluard, Péret and Unik. The main point of the declaration stated that the five undersigned had officially joined the French Communist Party (PCF). The letters were addressed to various people who might be interested in this event.

Shortly thereafter, Pierre Naville, who had left the Surrealist fold to become an editor of *Clarté*, published *Mieux et moins bien* in *La Revolution*

Surréaliste. This was in part an answer to *Au grand jour*, and the beginning of a dialogue concerning the quality of the Surrealists' political commitment. This dialogue was extremely complicated and wound up, by the end of Naville's life, as a series of monologues. In his memoirs, Naville comments on Péret's political activities in a very flattering light, but one should take into account that his tribute is also a way of getting back at Breton. Nonetheless, it is useful to consider Naville's assessment of Péret's politics in the mid-Twenties:

"Early on I noticed in him a political sense which was all his own, and which was unique among the circle of friends which clustered around Breton . . . And, as soon as it became clear that the movement was heading toward a confrontation with the Communists, he was one of the people who saw right away that there was an important choice to be made which had to do with the very nature of the Communist preoccupation; he realised this unease could not be reduced simply to some kind of background for poetic divertissements."*

3. The Left Opposition

Part of the explanation for Péret's political stance can be found in his friendship with Mario Pedrosa. Péret had married the singer Elsie Houston in 1927, her sister, Maria, was married to Pedrosa. That year, Pedrosa was sent from his native Brazil to study in the USSR to become a Party cadre. However, he fell ill in Germany, and cut short his journey in Berlin. Here he came into contact with Zinoviev, who was then forming the Unified Left Opposition.

Shortly after their marriage, Péret and Elsie Houston emigrated to Brazil. Through Pedrosa, Péret became active in the circle of people involved in Latin American Trotskyite activities, including Joachim Barbosa, Rodolfo Coutinho and Aristedes Lobo. These men were the instigators of the Brazilian Left Opposition. This movement originated in 1928 during conflicts between rank and file members of the Brazilian Communist Party and its Stalinist controlled bureaucracy.

By 1930, Pedrosa, who had returned from Europe a convinced Trotskyist, began editing *A Lucta de Classe* [Class Struggle] . This publication became the forum for discussions which eventually led Pedrosa and Lobo to join with Hilcar Leite and Livio Xavier (members of the Brazilian Communist Youth Organisation, who left the party because they did not agree with the nationalistic emphasis of Brazilian Communist Party activities) and form, in January 1931, a new political organisation, the Communist League (Opposition). This was the Brazilian section of the International Left

15

Photograph taken by André Thirion of Péret and his son Geyser in 1932.

Péret's membership card to the "Brazilian League."

LIGA COMMUNISTA (OPPOSIÇÃO)

(FILIADA Á OPPOSIÇÃO INTERNACIONAL DE ESQUERDA)

PAPELETA DE ADHESÃO   N.º 20

COMPROMISSO

Declaro acceitar o programma e a tactica da Liga Communista (Opposição), submettendo-me á disciplina revolucionaria e lutando, por todos os meios ao meu alcance, para que o Partido Communista, restabelecida em suas fileiras a liberdade de discussão e de critica, receba novamente em seu seio todos os verdadeiros communistas expulsos pelos golpes de força da fracção centrista. Assumo o compromisso de orientar a minha actividade revolucionaria de acordo com os ensinamentos de Marx e de Lenine, consubstanciados nas theses e resoluções dos quatro primeiros congressos da Internacional Communista. Reconhecendo a justeza do programma e da tactica da Liga Communista (Opposição), compromettome a lutar até o fim, sem desfallecimentos, pela victoria da Revolução Proletaria Internacional no sector brasileiro da luta de classes.

Rio de Janeiro 24 de abril de 19 31.

(Assignatura) Benjamin Péret

Opposition, part of the Communist International. During this period, the basic goal of these Trotsky-inspired groups was to change the official party and the International (either from within or without) in order to return them to a political line more in keeping with Bolshevik tradition.

During his stay in Brazil, Péret took an active, militant stance in the Left Opposition. He participated both with written contributions to Pedrosa's magazine and with militant activities. In 1931 he was appointed Regional Secretary (for Rio de Janeiro) of the Communist League. It was because of these activities that Péret was thrown out of Brazil by the government.*

Péret returned to Paris in the spring of 1932, accompanied by his wife and a newborn son, Geyser (born August 31st, 1931). Thirion, not entirely without an axe to grind, described their return in his memoirs:

"Péret acted as if we'd last seen each other the day before, just as easy in his skin, just as disarming in face of the world. Elsie was a bit more opulent than she had been in 1921, her nose was a bit larger, but she was still an attractive woman. . . The Stalinism of our group seemed to bother Péret a bit, but Péret was never a great proselytiser. He was a Trotskyist, he repeated it, but he signed whatever everyone else did so as not to annoy Breton with his reservations*. Besides, he was more unsubmissive than intransigent. He did not feel all that concerned by the manoeuvurings of his friends . . . His Trotskyism was not very well thought out. It consisted mostly of an attitude of moral hostility toward any compromise, an absolute non-conformism which one could find a little simplistic if Péret had not, on several occasions, accepted all the consequences. After two or three months of relative tranquility, the difficulties which always seemed part of Péret's life caught up with him. He faced them with a kind of candour, a kind of fatalism, the courage to make do with little, a total absence of ambition, even though he was just as sensitive as the next person. Once again, he took up being a proofreader. Elsie took a job in a cabaret. Péret would wait for her every night, to walk her home after the performance. One morning Elsie refused to follow him and went home with someone else. Péret became even poorer. Badly dressed, in poor sorts, he lived day by day, knowing very difficult moments, cadging a meal here, a fifty franc note there. This penury did not alter his stubborn good humour, indeed, it reinforced his attitude of generalised disobedience."*

This disobedience took the form, between 1932 and 1934, of Péret's membership in a militant organisation, the *Groupe Oppositionel du 15ème Rayon*, which his old friend Fourier had introduced him into. Péret had tried to join the French Communist League (i.e. the Left Opposition to the PCF) but had been turned down by the Executive Committee. His letter

17

protesting against this exclusion is printed in the "letters" section below. Consequently, he had joined the *Groupe Oppositionel*, which was, in effect, the opposition to the opposition. In 1933, however, there was an attempt to unify the various oppositional (i.e. Trotskyist and internationalist) tendencies and, in that year, Péret was active in the unification conference which took place in April/June. Among the tangible results was the fusion of the *Groupe Oppositionel*, the Communist Left (Alfred Rosmer, Kurt Landau) and the *Fraction de Gauche* of the Bagnolet Group (Henri Barre, Marc Chérik) into a new grouping: the *Fraction de la Gauche Communiste*, whose organ was *Le Communiste*. A few months later, on 2nd December, this group rejoined the ranks of the Communist Union which had been created the preceding month following exclusions from the Communist League. Péret and Fourier belonged briefly to this new formation, but left surreptitiously in March 1934 for reasons which are not clear.

After 1934, records of Péret's political affiliation are lost until his name is found in the membership list of the *Parti Ouvrier Internationaliste* (POI, or International Workers' Party), which he joined shortly after its founding in 1936.

The years 1932 to 1936 correspond to the period when the differences between the Surrealists and the PCF came to a head. From the time of *Au grand jour* (1927) until the early Thirties, Breton maintained frequent, if strained, contacts with the PCF. Signs of the rupture appeared, however, in 1930, when Aragon travelled to the USSR with Elsa Triolet and Georges Sadoul for the 2nd International Congress of Revolutionary Writers. There, he and Sadoul signed a declaration condemning Freud, Trotsky, and the Second Manifesto of Surrealism "insofar as they go counter to the teachings of dialectical materialism." A year later, Aragon published *Front Rouge*, a piece of Stalinist propaganda which caused the definitive break between himself and the Surrealists (see the notes to Péret's first letter in the "Letters" section).

Nonetheless, the Surrealists, led by Breton, did join the *Association des Artistes et Ecrivains Revolutionnaires* (AEAR) in 1933. This organisation was founded in 1932 by Paul Vaillant-Couturier and had a distinctly Stalinist orientation. Breton was even part of the organising committee, however, as a result of articles published in *Le Surréalisme au service de la révolution*, Breton and Eluard were expelled.

Despite this, the Surrealists were still members of the PCF. However, the situation became more and more strained as the Surrealists published more and more controversial (from the Soviet point of view) tracts and manifestoes. Examples of these include *La mobilization contre la guerre n'est pas la paix* [Mobilising for War is not Peace], which was written in 1933 in response to the PCF's favouring peace between Germany and the USSR. In this

18

tract, they made the statement: "If you want peace, prepare for civil war!" In 1934 the alienation of the Surrealists from the PCF became inevitable when they published a defence of Trotsky in *Planète sans visa* [Planet without Visa]. In May of 1935, Laval, now Prime Minister, signed the Franco-Soviet mutual aid pact which included an agreement to expel Trotsky from France, where he had been a political refugee for two years. That month, Péret and Breton visited Tenerife for an International Surrealist Exhibition, during which they spoke on "Art and Politics" and "Surrealism and Religion."

The most important event in 1935 for Péret's political life was the International Writers Congress held in Paris in August. The virtual exclusion of the Surrealists from this event resulted in the publication of *Du temps que les surréalistes avaient raison* [On the time when the Surrealists were Right], and in Breton and Péret's resignation from the PCF. With the outbreak of the Spanish civil war, Péret travelled to Spain.

4. Spain and Mexico

The Spanish Republic was declared in 1931 and governed by a coalition of left and centre elements. By 1934, the conflict between factions erupted in a general strike and a bloody uprising of miners in Oviedo, the capital of the province of Asturias. Although in 1936 the Socialists were strong enough to remove president Zamora, who was too catholic and conservative for their tastes, they were not strong enough to control a wave of strikes and political assassinations which then ensued. Spain had always had a tradition of the *pronunciamento*, or officers' revolt, and that is what happened in July 1936. The uprising started in the Spanish colonies in Africa and quickly spread to the mainland. By July 20th, Spain had been partitioned into those areas controlled by the rebels (falangists and franquinists in the north) and those controlled by the republicans (primarily Socialists in central Spain, Anarchists in the East).

In the first weeks of the war, the border between France and Spain remained open—Léon Blum's Popular Front government was supportive of the legal government of the Republic—and shipped war materials to it. However, on August 8th, Blum announced a ban on military aid to Spain.*

Péret had left three days earlier, on August 5th 1936, for Barcelona. (A few days later, the 11th, he sent the first of a series of letters to Breton, which are translated below). He had travelled to Spain with Jean Rous, delegate of the International Secretariat of "The Fourth", and the film-maker, Pierre Sabas. The three of them were to represent the International to the POUM.* Their mission had been defined by the so-called Geneva

19

Conference. Basically, they were to work out a relationship beteen the Trotskyists and the POUM, to see what could be accomplished in collaboration with the POUM in terms of political support, and to see what the possibilities were for military support (eventually, the Lenin column).

A month later, Rous left for Madrid. Péret's letters testify to his own activities, but another testimonial can be found in the words of Juan Andrade, member of the Executive Committee of the POUM:

"In my position as a member of the Executive Committee of the POUM in 1936 I was in direct contact with Benjamin Péret from the very first days of his arrival in Barcelona, i.e. three days after the military uprising. He offered to serve in military combat in any capacity, without reservations, accepting the life of a simple militiaman. He could easily, as did most of the participants in the Anti-Fascists Writers' Conference in Valencia, have asked to be housed at no expense in one of the grand hotels and then made a three or four hour tourist visit to the front in order to assuage his antifascist conscience. But Benjamin Péret was faithful to his political beliefs, and gave himself wholeheartedly to the fight. He shared the same dangers that the fighting workers did on the Aragon front, and participated completely in their life as a militiaman. Fighting the fascist army with only the rudimentary arms which were available, he was fighting both for Socialist freedom and confronting Stalinist terrorism. Those who lived through these great moments of Spanish political history know how much courage, will power and faith were necessary to fight both these battles at the same time.

I think I can speak for all of the militants in the Barcelona POUM as well as the numerous anarcho-syndicalists who were Péret's friends, regardless of the feelings which separate us now, when I vindicate Péret's memory and testify to his behaviour during the Spanish civil war."*

By the spring of 1937, the Stalinists in Catalonia were imprisoning and killing Anarchists and Anarcho-Syndicalists, and the POUM demanded more vigilance against counter-revolutionaries. Péret left the POUM early in March 1937 (see letters) as a result of the hostility he felt it was showing towards members of the POI. He decided to join the Anarchists on the Aragon front, for they, and Durruti's followers in particular, seemed most open-minded with regard to his own political stance.

Shortly after May Day 1937, serious altercations occurred between the Stalinists and the revolutionary groups. In Barcelona, the revolutionaries were no longer fighting the fascists, but each other. By May 4th, Barcelona was under a general strike. On May 5th the "Friends of Durruti" and the POUM were the only ones still fighting the Stalinists, the Stalinists gained control of the city on the 9th. On the 28th the "Friends of Durruti" and their political organ, *La Batalla* were outlawed, and in August 1937 Andres Nin, a leader of the Left opposition, was murdered. Meanwhile the Stalinists were smearing the POUM as "Trotsky-Fascists" in every political newspaper they could find. Peret returned to Paris.

Between 1938 and 1940, Péret's activities were affected by two main currents—the continuous redefining of anti-Stalinist communist positions, and Hitler.

Meanwhile, Breton had met with Trotsky in Mexico. Together they drafted a manifesto entitled "For an Independent Revolutionary Art"*. The basic premise of this document was that for art to be revolutionary, it must be independant of all forms of government. The *Fédération internationale de l'art révolutionnaire indépendant,* or FIARI, was also born of this manifesto, which Péret immediately joined. He wrote for the only two issues of its magazine, *Clé.* Péret was also corresponding with Breton in Mexico, keeping him abreast of the political situation in Paris: "There is open warfare between the revolutionary left and the Socialist party, which is facilitating a *rapprochement* between the Trotskyists and other extreme left groups." (18 April, 1938). In June he wrote to Breton to inform him that he, and Remedios Varo, the Surrealist artist he had met in Spain, were unable to get visas for Mexico. In September came the German invasion of Poland and the general mobilization. Most of the Surrealists were called up.

Péret was called up in Nantes. As a veteran, he was assigned to a job which included the registration and recording of suspicious persons. By day he devoted himself to this job, gleefully removing the names of all political suspects from the files and substituting those of all the priests in the area. (It is almost impossible to underestimate Péret's hatred for religion in general, and priests in particular. Numerous anecdotes testify to this passion,* and of course, there was the famous photograph in *La Révolution Surréaliste* . . .). By night he set about a more serious task, reconstructing the Trotskyist cell in Nantes.

In May of 1940, police raided the apartment of Jean-Claude Diamant-Berger in Paris. There they found information about the political activities of Péret, and his associates Léo Malet and Bruno Stenberg, who were all arrested and taken to prison in Rennes. Following the German bombing of Rennes, the new authorities destroyed many files, and let some prisoners leave. However, since Péret was already in uniform, a sum was demanded for his release. Péret describes in *La Parôle est à Péret* how he was released on July 22nd 1940, after paying a ransom of one thousand dollars to the Nazis.

He returned to Paris to resume his proof-reading work. The armistice was signed on June 22nd, 1940, and it was not long before Péret's name appeared on a blacklist in the collaborationist newspaper, *Le Pilori.*

Péret and Remedios Varo left Paris clandestinely, and headed for

"Our colleague Benjamin Péret in the act of insulting a priest." from "La revolution surréaliste," no. 8, December 1926.

Above: Breton, Eluard, Tzara, Péret, early 1930's.

Below: Péret, Remedios Varo, Breton in Marseilles, 1941.

Marseilles. From August 1940 to October 1941, Péret was living in the vicinity of the Villa Air-Bel, where many Surrealists had gathered in this house set up by the American Relief Committee for Intellectuals. With Char, Dominguez, Herold, Itkine, Breton, Serge, Bellmer, Brauner and others, he played Surrealist games* and worked for Le Croque-Fruit, the magazine of an anti-fascist cooperative.

Having been refused a visa by the USA because of his political history, Péret and Remedios Varo decided to move on to Casablanca. In December, they were finally allowed to board a Portuguese steamer bound for Mexico, a country particularily attractive to Péret since it had broken all diplomatic ties with fascist Spain, and had also given refuge to Trotsky.

Péret spent seven years (1941-48) in Mexico with Varo*. They joined up with a number of veterans of the Spanish civil war, including Grandizo Munis, whom Péret had known in Spain, and around whom a group of Spanish militants of Trotskyist persuasion had grouped themselves. Munis had, in addition, friendly contacts with Natalia Sedova, Trotsky's widow.

In the spring of 1941 Péret was making his living by giving French lessons, and working politically with Munis. Together they were instrumental in setting up the Spanish group of the IVth International in Mexico. Much of its work was devoted to the critique of the post-Trotsky IVth International, the French section of which seemed to be crumbling under the leadership of Naville and Pierre Frank.

They also pursued, however, other "educational" activities, including the publication of periodicals aimed specifically at the Spanish exiles. In February of 1943 Munis founded a monthly publication, Contra la Corriente. This bulletin devoted itself to keeping the Spanish exiles informed of the political positions of the IVth International on various issues. From November 1943 to December 1944, eight articles by Péret appeared, analysing the European situation, particularily in France; they were written under the pseudonym of "Peralta". Meanwhile Fourth International, the paper of the Socialist Workers' Party of the USA, was also publishing articles by Péret, Munis and Sedova, and there are letters from him in the same group's International Bulletin, one as late as 17 April 1946 (signed "BP for the Spanish Group"). Most concern internal problems of direction and organisation between sections of the IVth International, and its growing bureaucracy, which Péret felt was becoming "sclerotic".

In the same year, also under the name of Peralta, Péret published the Manifeste des exégètes [Manifesto of the Commentators], which is dated Mexico, September 1946. This was drafted as a response to the pre-conference of the IVth International, which had taken place in April, 1945. Here Péret roundly criticises the self-congratulatory tone of the pre-conference documents and proceeds to dismantle their approach to the

24

In Mexico with Leonora Carrington.

Early 1950's.

problems of the day, namely how to deal with the new socio-political situations created in the aftermath of the war. He also describes his main bone of contention with the IVth International, which concerned its relationship with the USSR. Péret's position was that the USSR was not a Communist society, but a Stalinist society based on State Capitalism. This manifesto pre-figured Péret's definitive rupture with the IVth International in 1947.

An open letter to the French section of the IVth International signed by Péret, Munis and Sedova, and dated June 1947, concludes with these words: "Down with Trotskyist conservatism. Down with fetishistic Trotskyism. An end to unconditional support of the USSR. For an ideologically firm and innovative International. Long live the French proletarian revolution. For the world revolution. Long live the IVth International." Soon after, however, the three of them publicly disengaged the Spanish Group of Mexico from the IVth International.

5. Return to Paris: ultra Left, solitary militant

On October 13th, 1947, Péret wrote to André Breton: "Because of financial considerations, I still cannot make plans to return." Breton responded by organising an exhibition of works donated by Picasso, Miro, Ernst, Tanguy, Dominguez, as well as manuscripts by various writers, at the *Galerie Rive Gauche.* The proceeds of this sale paid for Péret's boat ticket.

On his return to Paris he made contact with the PCI, and joined a small group aligned to the so-called Gallienne-Pennetier tendency. This relationship was short-lived as the points that had been troubling Péret in Mexico were still unresolved, namely the PCI line on the USSR and its increasingly entrenched bureaucracy. In 1949 a split in the PCI led to an Ultra Left wing, which included the Gallienne-Pennetier group, Péret and Munis, part of the Spanish Group which had emigrated from Mexico, and a Vietnamese group. These then formed the *Union Ouvrière Internationale.*

While Péret was deeply involved in form the UOI's platform, he was still engaged in Surrealist activities. By this time many of the members dispersed by the war had regrouped in Paris, and had been joined by various new members as well. Breton and Péret edited the *Almanach surréaliste du demi-siècle* in 1950, perhaps the last of the important Surrealist collections, which includes their *Calendrier tour du monde des inventions tolérables,* translated below.

In 1949 Péret had also begun working on a subject which, with his political committment, became the main interest of his life up to his death. This was the assimilation of his time in Mexico, where he had sensed a new relationship between myth and poetry. This research into myth is evident in two works of the period, the long poem *Air Mexicain*, and the prose texts which make up *L'Histoire naturelle*. After his death Péret's *Anthologie des mythes, légendes et contes populaires d'Amérique**was published.

Between October 1951 and January 1953, the Surrealists collaborated with the Anarchist weekly *Le Libertaire*. Among Péret's contributions was a six-part series *La Révolution et les syndicats*, essentially a critique of the reactionary and reformist nature of trades unions, as opposed to the revolutionary nature of workers' committees. The essays were an attempt to find an anti-authoritarian and fundamentally revolutionary structure for political organisation, which Péret felt was absent in the routine of militant activism as propounded by the IVth International.

In 1953 the UOI disintegrated, and the Surrealists broke with *Le Libertaire*. This left Péret outside any political organisation, which situation continued until his death. During this period, when as usual Péret was beset with financial problems, and seemed something of a solitary militant—he could act only through his pen. He wrote prolifically for various left magazines, and was behind many of the joint Surrealist declarations in their reviews *Médium* and *Le Surréalisme, même*. The last time his name saw print during his lifetime was as a signatory to the *Message des Surréalistes aux intéllectuels polonais*, dated 4th June 1959. He died of a heart attack on September 8th, 1959, his funeral brought out many of the most celebrated of his contemporaries, and instigated a reassessment of his works which continues today with the publication of the *Oeuvres complètes* by the *Amis de Benjamin Péret*.

●

This anthology was compiled with the aim of doing justice to Péret as both a writer and a revolutionary. It is this double dedication that makes him such a fascinating and admirable figure. It is this duality also which makes me view Péret's work as the Ariadne's thread leading to the centre of the Surrealist labyrinth. His influence on the Surrealist press starts at its very inception, when he co-edited *La révolution surréaliste*, and remained strong right up to one of its last sumptuous publications, the *"Almanach"*. The numerous political articles he wrote for various magazines, Surrealist and otherwise, constitute some of the most pertinent analyses that the Surrealists were to contribute to the discourse on Communism and Anarchism. And his prose collaborations are perfect examples of the innovations that Surrealist techniques such as automatism and language games brought to the literature of this century.

In the midst of all these activities, he wrote some of the best poetry of his epoch. Yet, I have deliberately chosen to under-represent it, since the only aspect of Péret's work which is at all available in English is precisely his poetry. The prose works presented here have not appeared in English before*. And only two of the "polemical" works have been previously translated, but in very small editions*.

There are a few works such as *Air Mexicain* and some other texts discussing the relationship between myth, poetry and the marvelous which would have rounded out these glimpses of Péret's contribution to Surrealist theory, but space prevented their inclusion. Similarily, some of the purely political texts, and his articles relating to the visual arts have not found a place here. I can only hope that this anthology will inspire someone else to translate them.

This project began when Professor Leroy Brounig was open-minded enough to accept that the translation of *Mort aux Vaches* could be an appropriate independant project. Later, Mary Ann Caws saw a section of it and was more than supportive.

The *Association des amis de Benjamin Péret* aided my research in all phases. I am grateful to Matta for introducing me to two of its members: firstly Jean-Louis Bedouin, and then to Jean-Michel Goutier, whose encouragement was heartening. Other members, particularily Claude Courtot and Jean-Marc Debendetti both gave their advice freely and set admirable examples with their work on Péret. Yet another member, Guy Prévan, must be particularily thanked, for he was generous enough to share not only the documents he will be publishing in volume 5 of Péret's collected works, but also the far more important aid of his knowledge of French Left politics. Elisa Breton provided valuable photographic documentation.

Marcel Jean kindly took the time to look backward for a few hours and told me about Paris in the Thirties and Forties. André Thirion remained courteous in the face of an unexpected interview in the middle of a dinner; Ethel de Croisset was the gracious hostess.

The time I spent in France working on this project was facilitated by a teaching position in the *Assistante de Langues Vivantes* program of the *Ministère de L'Education,* and also by a research grant from the Perimeter Products Foundation.

Alastair Brotchie and Antony Melville, editors of Atlas Press, saw to it that the English version of Péret reads better than any American could have hoped. Mark Rudkin also made valuable suggestions on these matters and provided invaluable moral support.

My friends, family and family-to-be showed remarkable tolerance during this whole endeavour.

Rachel Stella

This collection of the works of Benjamin Péret

is

ATLAS ANTHOLOGY FIVE

published by

Atlas Press
10 Park st.
LONDON SE1 9AB

Series Editors:
Alastair Brotchie
Malcolm Green
Antony Melville

Editor of this issue:
Rachel Stella

We should like to thank the *Association des amis de Benjamin Péret* for their assistance with this project, and in particular, Bertrand Filleaudeau of the "Librairie José Corti."
Atlas has an active mailing list which you are EXHORTED to join. We hope we will soon be publishing or distributing, as a companion to this volume, Péret's extremely "Sadean" novel *Mad Balls.* This will only be available direct from us, as are the limited editions of our publications.

Our thanks also to **The Elephant Trust** for their grant towards this book.

There is a casebound, numbered edition of fifty copies

––

Poetry

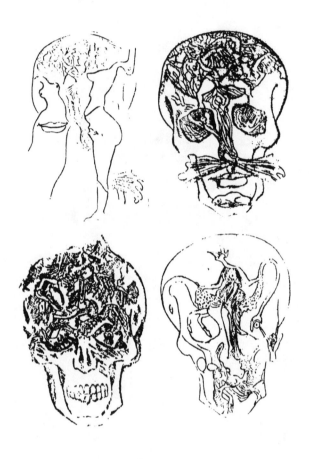

Four frottages by Max Ernst for "Je Sublime."

1.

André Gide's conversion

Mister Comrade Gide
sings the 'Young Guard'* between his arse and his shirt-tails
and tells himself it's time to flash his belly like a red flag
Communist
a bit a lot with all his heart
not at all
answer the balls of the choirboy he depilates
like a tomato rocked by the wind
Mister Comrade Gide makes a hell of a red flag
that no salad would want
a red flag which hides a cross
dipped in vitriol
good and French like no other concierge's dog
which bites its tail while listening to the *Marseillaise* being hiccupped
which gives birth to
Mister Comrade Gide

Oh yes Mister Comrade Gide
You'll have the hammer and sickle
the sickle through your guts
and the hammer down your throat

Life of Foch* the murderer

From a pool of liquid dung one day a bubble rose
and burst
From the smell the father could tell
He'll be a famous killer
Snotty filthy the vermin grew up
and started talking of Revenge
Revenge for what For paternal manure
or for the cow which made the manure
At six he was farting into a bugle
At eight two turds decorated his sleeve
From a pool of liquid dung one day a bubble rose
At ten he was commanding the lice on his head
and the itching let his parents know
he has talent
At fifteen he was raped by a donkey
and they made a lovely couple
they begot a pair of boots with spurs
into which he disappeared like a dirty sock

It's nothing said the father
his marshal's baton came out of the loo
That's the kind of career it is
The career was shining and the worker well up to it
Along his way vomit spurted like geysers
and spattered him
He is everything that's best in this type
bilious puke of military medals
and nauseating plonk from the legion of honour
which grew little by little

This puffy calf's lung* stretched out
and during the war provoked the bystanders to say
He's a fine lad He's wearing his lungs on his chest

Everything was going well until the day his wife picked up
the concierge's cat
Nothing could be done

34

the cat threw itself on the calf's lung
the minute it appeared
and finally it was fatal the cat swallowed it
Without a calf's lung Foch was no longer Foch
and like a butcher he died of a corpse wound

Joan of Arc

A cowpat haloed with flies
said one day to Joan of Arc
The little birds have no rollerskates
but Jesus has frozen feet
the cowpat was next to an old stick of rotten wood
which toads exerted themselves in jumping over
and each one as it leaped gave itself a name
Saint John Saint Paul Saint Louis Saint Theresa Saint Arseho

So Joan understood that she was before God
and swallowed the cowpat like a relic
Immediately God crystalised in the form of hemorrhoids
and all the dogs of Domremy licked her behind
But Joan knew that God inhabited her
and told her every night
I am here by the will of the pope
and I will suddenly come out by force of farts
Suddenly God spat so far that Joan could send kicks
into the backside of the horizon
God and the horizon cried out
King Charles VII hunts bedbugs under the staircase
but each crushed bedbug gives birth to two thousand lice
She also makes the sign of the cross over the rubbish bins
so that the lice hidden in them can follow her
like a dog on a scent
the one leading to the king

The king runs off chased by the swine
that the priests cover with holy water
they drink it and sanctify themselves
the swine go off to Jerusalem waving crosses
they want to suck Christ's bones like chewing gum
and the king flees

Joan joins him in a pissoir
and they love each other like urine loves damp slate

One day at Reims a rotten apple falls on the king's head
from it Joan makes him a crown
blessed by fourteen archbishops with putrescible gazes

A vengeful Altar-cruet hits Joan and suddenly she is wounded
the king devours her breasts and her feet
which smell foul like spoiled vegetables
and now she's cured

Meanwhile the English were raising their lice in France
and the English lice were beating the French lice
One day a piece of English louse clothing covered Joan's body
and suddenly she is a prisoner
For a long time she ate lice
hoping to resemble them
but she always remained a bedbug popping under the donkey's hooves
a foul bedbug so filthy and flaccid
that one day as oily as the Christ they had to
burn her to warm up the lice

Saint Joan of Arc patron of bedbugs pray for the French

The sixth of February*

Long live the sixth of February
grumbles the tobacco juice
dressed in a fleur-de-lis turd

How wonderful it was
The busses were burning like old-time heretics
and the horses' eyes
ripped out with our stilettos*
landed on the cops so lardy and revolting
that they could have been burning crosses*

Long live the sixth of February
I almost burnt down the maritime ministry
like a newstand
too bad the public urinals aren't burning

Long live the sixth of February
town councillors cretinized by their tricolour scarves
in order to rally all the lice and the bedbugs
made their blood run under the bludgeons
which suited them less well than the firing post*

Long live the sixth of February
Yellow green rotten priests
caressing the buttocks of teenage boys
while singing the *Marseillaise* and some canticles
while shooting at their brother cops

Long live the sixth of February
and long live the seventh
for two days I shouted
Death to Cachin Death to Blum
and I stole whatever I could from the stores
whose windows I broke
I even stole a doll I'll send to Maurras
so he can try to rape it
while shouting Down with thieves

38

The Fourway Pact*

The four of them all lice-ridden were dancing in front of a beefsteak
And as they danced their lice fell to the ground
I am French said one of them
light and sprightly as a cop beating a worker
and if I have blue blood and a pussy white wound it's because my nose is red

I am English said the second
and since the pound started dropping I feel my feet running like an old
    brie cheese

I am Italian said the third
fortunately I have the pope for a noodle
since the macaroni has been making machine-gun barrels

I am German said the last one
Fascist answered the echo from the latrines
and beneath each of these gentlemen
a little urine ran out
tracing for the German a map without the worm-shaped corridor*
for the Italian a horizon of greasy fasces
for the Frenchman the left bank of the Rhine
for the Englishman a missisippi of pounds sterling
Shit said the Frenchman who ate the Italian's nose
while the German was spitting into the Englishman's ear
and soon nothing was left but a little pile of generals
haloed by flies
which circled around the four flags
planted in their arses

The heroic death of Lieutenant Condamine de la Tour

For seven centuries Condamine de la Tour
his arms stretched like the hands of a clock
showing quarter past nine
standing on his red-white-and-blue canteen
commanded his fourteen lobsters
Through his pierced brain the breezes sang
Will you drop dead you pig of a sell-out
But from the sky as black as the forehead of his fathers
no crayfish came to the aid of his lobsters
Only the occasional splat of a fingernail
warned him that the cauldrons were changing sex
and the lettuces losing their ears
ran to ask him the secret of his pubic hair

Suddenly in the mouldy air
a nail bored with the noise of darkness
a nail blue and green like a spring morning
2, 437 bedbugs came out of his nose
4, 628 Chinese lanterns penetrated his ears

He cried out
I Condamine de la Tour am looking for the massacres
of children in the cloud-shoes
of the unknown soldier in the closet
But Jesus threw the unknown soldier into his rubbish bin
and the swine ate him
and the Alsations ate the swine

That is how you grew up Condamine de la Tour
how you grew up like a swine
and the unknown soldier's navel has become your own
But today Jesus put his foot in your strumpot*
which he used as a clog
both feet in the same clog
That's why we have a god
and why his priests have shoes
which look like their faces

Rotten Condamine de la Tour
The pope will make two hosts from your eyes
for your Moroccan sergeant
and your prick will become his marshal's baton
Rotten Condamine de la Tour
Rotten spineless filth

2.

Listen

If you sheltered me like a maybug in a cupboard
bristling with snowdrops coloured by your ocean voyage eyes
monday tuesday etc wouldn't be more than a fly
in a plaza bordered by ruined palaces
from which would issue an immense vegetation of coral
and of embroidered shawls
where one sees
felled trees depart obliquely
to blend in with park benches
where I slept awaiting your arrival
like a forest that awaits the passing of a comet to see clearly
in its underbrush whimpering like a chimney
calling the log it desires since it yawns
like an abandoned quarry
and like a staircase in a tower we would climb
to see ourselves disappear
in the distance
like a table swept away by the flood

Today

Let her smile surge up in the sky black as a slave escaped from a marsh
and the huge jack hammers that reduce my brain to rice paper
as likely to become a slag soup as a banana flower
cease their song of camels drinking in the mirages
because the oyster's cadaver has brutally leaped
on the potbellied osprey who demands an hour from passing women
in the form of R of O of S of A
who by the courage of the vulgar soapskin armchair
have turned to dust on a sheet of lava encrusted with eagles
blue as a racing car that will never finish
because the kilometres following the coasts
and the sharp turns preceding the descents
carry your name like a coat of arms
where one sees
that $4 + 4 = \text{ℬ}$
straight as a greasy pole whose summit I will attain
so that you may look at me not like a kilo of sugar
but as a night whose seam you have unstitched

Waiting

Battered by the huge plates of time
the man advances like the veins of marble hoping to spare their eyes
in a torrent where the fan-headed trout
dragging heavy chariots of champagne bubbles
which blacken your hair of fortified castle
where the pellitory doesn't dare venture
for fear of being devoured
beyond the great glacial plain where dinosaurs still brood over
their eggs from which will not emerge haemetite tulips
but caravans of blue-bellied porcupines
for fear of being swallowed by the fountain of sea lightning
created by your gaze where impalpable night moths whirl
dressed in closed train stations where I search for the key to open the signal
without finding anything
but frozen horseshoes
which leap up like an umbrella in an ear
and ducks of fresh nettles
solemn as oysters

I can't sleep

Tell me reflection of cobalt
why the flight of crows which surrounds you
as the coal clasps the fire which created it by swallowing red peppers
that have always placed red eggs on your Saint-George's lips
who goes up to Pigalle
swings in the hammock of the square
enlists like a bullet into a torso with balls
so resembling a gyroscope
one might think it was Pluto abducting Proserpine in his handkerchief
disappearing on the horizon like the two Channel Islands of your eyes
near the Channel of your nose
which is a moon-beam in the cellar I
burgle
hoping to find a snapdragon in the shape of a yes
without ruts from a dentist's chair
without a net to capture the mosquito-headed peaches
without mosquitoes asleep like a timer in the corner of a forest
without a timer gnawing the skeletons of my elders and hers
the way a head of garlic in the mayonnaise
truly projects
tonight
if only one sprinkles it with petals of bitter almonds
a strong bouquet of new wine
a little sour
a little sweet
sour and sweet
like a new volcano
whose lava will reproduce indefinitely your face

3.

One morning

There are endless screams
brayings of earth shaken like a fan dismantled
by jellied moles
sobs of planks being gutted
long as a locomotive which will be born
of the convulsions of rebellious trees which no longer want to let the sap run
that the metro refuses to carry ostriches
in its tunnel of badly shaven beards
there are screams
of vitriol spiders that I swallow unwittingly
near this dried-up river spouted from a pipe
which is none other than a long muzzle
a bit warm
a bit grumpier than a nearly empty kettle
this river you don't see any more than the dust of a Host
the wind has mixed
with the dust of the parish priest resembling copper sulphate
and with that of the church more twisted than an old corkscrew
for you are no more here than I am there without you
and the whole world is unkempt

Do you know

My sandpaper head rubbing so vigorously on a crystal goblet
made in your image of a bird a wild boar impedes from its first flight
is full of the spindrift of your eyes similar to two oranges no one will ever
    pick
your eyes which are perhaps a stone exploded like a lightning-struck tree
just like the little heart I have in my pocket
beside a stove redder than a burning zeppelin
resembling the budding of an aloe flower
that would be a red flag
more torn than hair in the wind
that wants to caress you like a newborn bird
and so blue it seems a dead leaf becoming green again
so shiny it seems a block of sealing wax in a bath tub
where you don't appear anymore than a water lily in the middle of the woods
no more than a wild strawberry in an inner tube
no more than my life around the corner

Where are you

I would speak to you cracked crystal howling like a dog on a night of flailing
    sheets
like a dismasted boat the foam begins to invade
where the cat meows because all the rats have left
I would speak to you like a tree uprooted by the storm
which so shook the telegraph wires
they seem a brush for mountains resembling a tiger's lower jaw
which slowly tears me with a hideous noise of a battered-in door
I would speak to you like a metro train broken down at the entrance
of a station I enter with a splinter in a toe like a bird in a vineyard
which will yield no more wine than a barricaded street
where I wander like a wig in a fireplace
which hasn't heated anything so long
it thinks itself a cafe counter
where the circles left by the glasses trace a chain
I would only say to you
I love you like the grain of wheat loves the sun rising above its blackbird head

Always

Nothing on the twisted horizon more worn than a rail about to crumble
and provoke the most sensational catastrophe of the year
the blond hairs of the horizon have gotten lost
like a boat of buttercups beginning to drift
along a coast bristling with elephant tusks
which bray like shops on the verge of bankruptcy
Nothing on the horizon when your two eyes of dry sherry
do not allow a single ray of this light to pass
where
miniscule
rushes along distorted by a thousand rival prisms
pin headed
cow headed
the blood which flows from me like a cat that has stolen a cutlet
and will leave me like a broken fork
in an empty lot where a few geraniums grow
so pitiful you would think them yellowed school notebooks
where you will only read I love you
on all the pages

A Lifetime

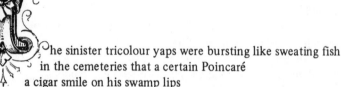The sinister tricolour yaps were bursting like sweating fish
    in the cemeteries that a certain Poincaré
        a cigar smile on his swamp lips
inaugurated his hands flapping like doors in the maple breeze that animated
    him
and already the voice of a blond hair carried off by the wind that arises from
    tikis
had made you leap across the streets in a St. Vitus dance
where Vaché was going to disappear like a sudden downpour in a living room
Nothing was said about words that kill harmful animals
not one sound breaking the bolts had been proffered
in the air loaded with epaulette dust
or slimy with familial haze stinking of incense
Nothing but an avalanche of laughs hurtling down well-groomed phthisic
    mountains
that flattened in passing the venerable flakes full of Sunday liqueurs
The artfully set table was invaded by the zoo
The heron pecked at the ear of the grandfather choking with rage
beneath the show window of his shirtfront that big blue flies were scaling
and the young girl of the house let herself get felt up by a lemur
which took her beneath the cataplasmic eyes of her mother reeling with
    vertigo
Art a champagne bottle knocked upside the head

50

dissolved into a mud of decorations and beards torn up like mobilization
posters
and expired with the squeak of a brand new shoe crushing the turd of a
Pekinese dog
Suddenly a fresh breeze of the year's first lilacs
swept away the factory's disgusting black animal fumes
and from the whole thicket the word freedom escaped with the scent of
hawthorns
while the beasts to be slaughtered under the heel
sacred heart gesture
present arms! look
punishment nose
keep moving! face
bank account smile
ministerial groaning
submissive half-wit
sell-out's hunch
false witness's mug
returned the truffle to the right-thinking slime
to simmer the ragouts of nourishing grudges in their shelters

But some beginning with the Carpathian rat
murmured freedom while thinking For the cops and my monocle
Others like the cross between the stoolie and did-you-come-dear
or the little broom of La Chapelle
took their cue from the trash can
and blossomed in filthy flowers to arouse dogs
Drop everything you said to set sail without compass or star through the
storms
toward the whirling agate shores and faces haunted by the opals' provocative
looks
Anchor long enough to fish in invisible water for the ghost of a cloud
a siren of the deep laughing like a forest
or a wing of palpitating fire escaped from a blunderbuss with a bride's
pennant
Go against the current carrying summertime goodbyes
to the virtues huddled in the alcove of snows awaiting the rape that creates
the hallelujah
Drop everything Now the gratifying prey and later its shadow
that dissolves beneath the eyes astonished by the next dawn galloping in
pursuit of a desire
that flies away in flames from hands grasping its ashes to dry up all the ink

spots in the world
Drop everything The dust of the day already yesterday must not darken the
      sun of tomorrow
Drop everything
fatherlands reeking of policemen
money foul with poverty
ideas decorated with a Crimean War medal
The only great men are those born to engender parricidal sons
and the rottenness of others would not even grow a nettle for whipping
      the priests of all religions
Everyone seemed to hear the skylarks' wake-up call
but they were hiding to repudiate the earthquakes of their dreams
      contradicting their sordid appetites
and while awaiting the celebration they were already measuring the side-
      walks of obscure streets where the customer drifts
calculating the cost in dollars or roubles of some well-aimed spit

Remember the receptions for buttocks blessed by righteous feet
remember the pates of sly callouses chanting anathemata
the symphonies of hands clapping on the rotting apples
the dripped cordon sentences if you please
when Anatole Crasse of the old residues of agricultural merit finally
      swallowed his beard and croaked
Automatic writing was going to multiply the marvels that the open eye
      dissipated
The soap orchid was going to bloom like a lamp humming black songs
the buttonhook the world's biggest practical joker began to pluck geese
for fun while awaiting the passage of generals going to expire on their beds
      made of the corpses of their men killed at the front
the inoffensive watchman in the square felt the noses reproduce by
      schizogenesis on his oystershell face
while thinking about scratching them against the trees to make them sneeze
and the grain of salt wrote its memoirs on the sails of a three-master that
      purred on its shoulder
But the horse between cart and feedbag
dreams only of the sun of the straw in the bourgeois darkness of the vast
      stables
The gallop that does not frighten the still-free butterflies
terrifies it like the martyrizing passage of a 40-horsepower straight 8
and the blasphemy of horse kicks repels it like the lobster repels cows
The weather belonged to the aurora borealis invisible in the dictionary's
      waiting rooms

You launched the Surrealist Manifesto
like a bomb exploding into a flight of birds of paradise clearing space in the
farmyard
and the sparks hit in passing some dignified old-timer with an elegiac mug
who sighed as he adjusted his pureed expression
Poetry is losing its guts and those hoodlums walk all over it
without imagining that his stuffed parrot was hatching all those moths that
strutted under his skull
The swallows words that open the venetian blinds of morning
suddenly took flight
crossing the deserts of skeletons polished by vultures
where the artichoke of the oasis raising its aperitif flower
bounded up like a rebellious lion as they went by
and every season they returned more agile than a shout and more sure of
announcing the birth of clear waters

The dream freed from the dungeon where Christ-faced spiders imprisoned its
gestures
ran through the house that was besieged by a vague anxiety
Were the chairs going to sob and the window play poker
Hurtling down the stairs like a torrent sweeping along its trout
the dream descended to the street for the Surrealist revolution
armed only with its rip-out-the-locks expression
and mixed with the nightfall-coloured passers-by
Where does it come from they asked this bench I'm sitting on this bench that
follows me like a puppy
That speaks to me in the trunk of this tree
to give me the time of the baths of lucidity in lightning waters
And dawn's rays tinted their miners' faces with dew

Freedom human-coloured freedom
you had already shouted right into the reinforced-concrete ears
that were planning new taboos to prop up the ruined barriers
erected between the man who takes and the woman who gives
For having betrayed the man who pulled them out of the bogs and chasms
glistening with horror
all the gods have crumbled to book dust that tries to tarnish the nascent corollas
and to block the fountains equipped with wings of morning wind
where the man of the woods and every variety of rebel the girl of the streets
and she who knows herself to be an entire world all come to drink
Consubstantial with man
love unceasingly dissipates the layer of gases bent on his destruction

Honour to the song of the slave rejoicing in the iron that brands him
crow caw sin shitting in the alcoves
prejudices throwing in the dark a dagger between two shoulders bent for a
    kiss
and always gold that doesn't even make good dentures for old men in the
    legion of honour
one after the other they threw the lasso that was supposed to strangle it
But always the lover would tear into them with her volcano teeth
for it is she who conquered with the tips of her breasts the fredom of its kiss
without any ceremony printed on civil imprisonment paper
without anything but the primordial sharing of the fire that no flood will
    put out
for all freedom exudes the whip and the galley if love has unfamiliar duties
Everything was said about love from onomatopoeia to formulas that
    condense it
or from the spark setting afire the lakes gilded by the sun
bowling over the unfathomable forest of hair shaken by the storm
magnetizing the flour bodies and the lemurian spirits hoisting themselves up
    the great trees
to the horizon draped in a piece of crepe of which each of them holds a
    corner
Everything was said except the words that rip the veils held by teardrops
and that clear the expanses with the thousand mirages that every step renders
    more palpable
More consciousness always more consciousness of love
From you like a bush exploding with all its birds
bursts forth this commandment that extracts love from the dark caverns
    oozing brains foul with incense
and tells it You the first one
As long as man his companion at his side has not explored your forests where
    no monster lives
travelled up your great rivers of silk or overheated boiler
climbed your peaks beyond dreams island birds floating on their backs
in order to contemplate from on high with an imperious glance the world
    that offers him the possession of its arms of fire mixed with darkness
freedom will be just another tomorrow fleecing will be free*

It would be useless to speak of the truth if one hadn't spat in its face so much
that its stubborn polar star gaze setting the tone
was not obliterated today like a city razed by the barbarians and already
    invaded by the bush
They've even handed the truth over to all the appetites of the troops

I name here the peat of the steppe as well as the underworld dressed up as a
   skyscraper and the scavenger with a holy water brain
sir handcuffs
the ground crewman with epaulette moustaches
the suitcase stuffed with keys that fit no lock
and its dog the blindman hypnotised by a jar of gherkins
You have always tried to distinguish its features as a rainbow above fields of
   buttercups
of the bruises that transformed a nose into an eucharistic snout
the beach of lips uncovering the dental lamé in the body of a guard infested
   with arms racks
and crushed with a dirty swelling the face like a garden after spring rains
Andre that's what joins us together like two kernels in the same ear of corn
that is unbent by any equinox of the rage of a rat held prisoner in its sewer
and unburnt by any solstice of flamethrowers devouring a singing landscape
   of free birds
repeated by the thousand echoes of streams of fairy eyes
since the brutal truth with its obvious stare that makes the gusseted bellies
   quiver
sings only hymns in gusts driving the cloud monasteries against the mountains
   that disembowel them
the songs in raised fists of the eternal rebels thirsting for ever new wind
for whom freedom lives as an avalanche ravaging the vipers' nests of heaven
   and earth
the ones who shout their lungs out as they bury Pompeiis
Drop everything

Ile de Sein, 15-23 July 1949

Prose:
Fiction

BENJAMIN PÉRET

LE GIGOT

SA VIE ET SON ŒUVRE

LIBRAIRIE LE TERRAIN VAGUE

23-25 Rue du Cherche-Midi - Paris-6ᵉ
1957

Several of these stories were reprinted in "Le Gigot."

Death to the Pigs and the Field of Battle (novel)

Nº 4 — Première année   15 Juillet 1925

LA RÉVOLUTION SURRÉALISTE

ET   AU

GUERRE   TRAVAIL

SOMMAIRE

Pourquoi je prends la direction de la R. S. :
 André Breton.
POÈMES
 Louis Aragon, Paul Eluard.
RÊVES :
 Max Morise, Michel Leiris.
TEXTES SURREALISTES :
Philippe Soupault, Marcel Noll, Georges Malkine.
Les parasites voyagent : Benjamin Peret.
La baie de la faim : Robert Desnos.
Glossaire (suite) : Michel Leiris.
Nomenclature : Jacques-André Boiffard.

CHRONIQUES :
 Fragments d'une conférence : Louis Aragon.
 Le surréalisme et la peinture : André Breton.
 Note sur la liberté : Louis Aragon.
 Exposition Chirico : Max Morise.
 Philosophies, L'etoile au front : Paul Eluard.
 Correspondance.

ILLUSTRATIONS :
 Giorgio de Chirico, Max Ernst, André Masson
 Joan Miro, Pablo Picasso, Man Ray, Pierre Roy, etc.

ABONNEMENT
les 12 Numéros .
France : 45 francs
Étranger : 55 francs

Dépositaire général : Librairie GALLIMARD
15, Boulevard Raspail, 15
PARIS (VII')

LE NUMÉRO :
France : 4 francs
Étranger : 5 francs

Chapter 5 first appeared in this issue.

1. Loof Smart

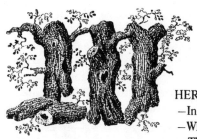

HERE ARE YOU STANISLAUS?
—In the water.
—What water?
—The water of the sky, of the earth, of the clouds, the trees, the birds, and the animals which crawl like eiderdowns.

—How bored you must be!

—Not always! Yesterday, for instance, I went to Paris and, like everyone else, I strolled along the boulevards, in the hope of meeting a woman. I didn't find one to my taste; I did, though have the good fortune to meet the 'last Abencerage'.* He was naked as usual, wearing the French flag draped diagonally over his chest. We were alone: I could not avoid talking to him. Off the top of my head I asked him,

—Were you coming back from Fez?

—No, he answered. For quite some time now my travelling has consisted of going with the fishermen who set out every night for Newfoundland, where they find boats of fresh cod to bring back. But we didn't have any luck. The poor fishermen I was accompanying didn't catch a single fish. Instead, each time they pulled up their nets, they brought in sealed bottles, each containing identical slips of paper on which were always written the same verse:

The masks with butterfly teeth
roll in the dust

61

which only makes up one mouthful
like a straightbacked armchair
on which my grandfather might have sat
with the pope's head on his knees
And he would have pulled its ears
to give himself something of an air
in front of his hot-springs mirror
which no one drinks from anymore
except mountains too old to be able to spit avalanches
like a grasshopper
a pine-cone

The boat's captain thought there had been a shipwreck. I didn't agree: I insisted that it was all an ingenious publicity ploy used by some shoe polish manufacturer or other. Nonetheless, the captain wanted at all costs to set his mind at rest.

Renouncing fishing, which, until now had given him only disappointments, he gave orders to search for soup tureens which he imagined existed in the area. After three days and two nights of sailing, during which we saw by day only radishes emerging from the sea and flying off with cries of "help, help," and by night, tongues of fire rushing to the water to quench their thirst, we saw at dawn, a few lengths away, a magnificent formal flowerbed covered with the most astonishing flowers one could imagine and, in the middle, a pathetic baby, hardly a year old. A fat red-white-and-blue fly was watching over it lovingly, and growled at our approach.

The captain ordered the flowerbed be tied to the ship, and the foundling and his guardian picked up. With a boat hook, a sailor tried to catch the drifting flowerbed. Hardly had the hook touched the flowerbed when a huge watch spring burst out of the corolla of a flower, wound itself with mad speed around the hook, and following its disorderly course, stuck into the right eye of the sailor and emerged immediately from his navel. A second later, the sailor had disappeared and the hook froze in space, its tip barely resting on the flowerbed. In the sailor's place only a delicious chocolate pastry remained.

The captain burst out laughing, although inside he was quite frightened. The baby was still asleep. Another sailor wanted to grab the hook in order to try to pull in the flowerbed; but, at the very moment he grasped it, the ship jumped backwards, and losing his balance, the sailor fell onto a fan which had taken the place of the fly and was turning crazily. He disappeared, evaporated, and was never seen again. Nor was the fan, for that matter. In its place appeared a bomb whose lighted fuse would not ignite properly.

The captain decided to make a third attempt. A lifeboat was lowered and two men prepared to get in, but nobody had noticed that where the life-boat had been let down, the sea stiffened like a thickening sauce. Once in the lifeboat, the sailors saw, all around them, rising from the surrounding solidified waves, hundreds of women's shoes in which spiders made of red sealing wax appeared. One after another and then all at once, the spiders started to hop and cried out to the sailors: "I am from the country of crap. Please sign your name on your forehead, hit your left knee with your right hand and your right knee with your left hand for ten minutes and listen."

The two sailors followed the advice they had been given and, closing their eyes, heard:

"Timbucktoo bark contains quantities of poisonous oil often used in the preparation of veal. But one shouldn't assume that this is the only reason Timbucktoo exists, that beautiful window which so many trample dis-dainfully in the Bois de Boulogne. When it is fresh, one can extract a mustard from Timbucktoo which is very good for burning and even for eating. Timbucktoo skin powdered and washed to eliminate its bitterness makes an excellent aperitif. You must let the powder marinate in pope's blood that has been changed daily for fifteen days. On the last day, you put the powder in a trumpet, sound the charge, and you're left with a completely un-acidic soap which is easily as good as snail's slime. That's not all. The water from these washings can be used to stuff geese, which as a consequence become magnificent evening gowns. In Germany, Timbucktoo is used by fire-men to burn down public monuments. The Turks combine it with cheese and gum the locks of nuptial chambers with the mixture. Rheumatics, etc."

When the voices quieted down, a medieval knight in armour appeared in front of the lifeboat and said to the dumbfounded sailors: "Twenty-five."

—Multiplied by two equals fifty, replied the sailors. And the horseman left at full gallop, prey to some terrible emotion, crying: "Fifty plus one equals fifty-one . . . fifty-one . . . fifty-two . . ." But he was dragging the life-boat without giving the two sailors a moment to collect their thoughts.

The 'last Abencerage' fell quiet and saluted me respectfully with the information that he was going to fight a duel with Monsieur Poincare whom he expected to crush like a horse-fly.

I was quite out of sorts because I'd planned to spend the evening with the 'last Abencerage' and I already felt a certain pride in this: not every-one has the honour of spending an evening with a personage of such importance. Disappointed, I went back to my original project of looking for a woman; but none were to be seen, neither old nor young. Where were they? If there were no women in the streets, perhaps they'd all stayed home. I walked into the first house I came to by gently pushing on the door, but obviously not gently enough, since a bunch of grapes fell on my head and left me all dizzy. To take revenge, I picked up the grapes and ate them. Hardly had I swallowed the last grape when I felt myself endowed with amazing strength. In truth, I felt myself able to leap in such a manner that in a single bound I could have crossed all of Paris. I was in a very dim corridor where I searched vainly for a staircase. A few hours walk in the shadows brought me to a turning in the corridor, in front of a mirror. I still didn't know how I was in front of a mirror, as it wasn't my image which I saw reflected, but rather a luminous rain which, on the glass, took up half as much space as my normal image. I turned around mechanically, assuming that the luminous rain was falling behind me. All I saw were three forks and two knives arranged in a bundle a few metres from my feet. And, under this strange bundle lived a family of white mice who were in no way disturbed by my presence. I had nothing better to do than go on my way, but little by little as I moved forward, the mirror backed-up, in such a way that the distance between the mirror and myself stayed constant. I was as if hypnotised by it, I walked like an automaton, without questioning where I was going. Suddenly, I felt the ground give way under me, and I fell. I fell for hours and hours. Naturally, I had given myself up for lost, never imagining for an instant that I might come back from this adventure. The darkness was total. My fall stopped as suddenly as it had begun and I started up again without realising what kind of ground I was walking on. But, was it really the ground I was walking on? No doubt I'll never know. Nonetheless, after walking for several minutes, I spied a luminous vertical ray intersected perpendicularly by four dotted lines about five metres apart from each other. These gleams intrigued me, and I thought that they must somehow have to do with a sign whose interpretation would perhaps permit me to get out of this hell. What a mistake! At the very moment I was going to touch this strange luminous figure, a mouth detached itself slowly from the vertical line and came towards me in a burst of laughter. Then all of the teeth from this mouth jumped at my face and remained stuck there. The mouth disappeared. The luminous figure separated itself into two equal parts. One of them turned a quarter circle. I passed under the other half and felt myself being stripped of my skin. I felt myself: I was nothing but a skeleton. An arm grabbed mine. I say arm because the only thing next to me was this single limb, the rest of the person being absent. A woman's voice said to me: "You're looking for a woman? Here I am." And the same laugh I'd heard a few minutes earlier burst in my ears. All the teeth which had been clamped to my face slid down my left arm and came to align themselves along the length of my radius bone. The woman's voice took up:

A woman dressed by my aunt
is always so elegant.

The mouth then returned to my side and said: "What poetry! And you find it amusing, idiot? I can write this kind of verse all day long. I am satisfied with writing some every year on Bastille Day and sending it to the President of the Republic. That why I've been decorated with the Legion of Honour like a stuffed sausage. Speaking of stuffed sausage, I met Gambetta last week. He was trying to shave with his ear. But this reminds me of a story about him:

"Gambetta had just, as he did every morning, taken his coffee with milk. He was going to go back to bed and sleep till noon unconcerned with national defence ("National defence is me," he would say, "and I want to sleep.") when a snowflake penetrated his room—although it was well sealed. For a moment he feared that the Germans were entering Paris and waited, his ears pricked. As nothing else happened, he relaxed and stretched out on the bed. He got right back up with an awful scream: his bed was full of water and he felt a fish rubbing against his left thigh. "After all," he told himself, "this is nothing." And he turned his mattress over. Alas! On the other side, his mattress was covered with mussels. Astonished and anxious, Gambetta started to pace up and down his room, his forehead furrowed by flights of crows . . . After having crossed the room a dozen times, he sat down and noticed that he was at the foot of a banana tree, petting a sheep. He thought he was on vacation. He pushed away the sheep and shook the banana tree. At first, false beards fell from it; then, a few seconds later, the bunches started to melt and transformed themselves into a kind of whitish gelatine which gave off a strong smell of musk. When in this manner, a hundred kilos of bananas were spread out on the ground, a sort of creaking sound was let out. The gelatine boiled and a little girl appeared, laughing out loud. She disengaged herself from the gelatine and started to dance in circles around Gambetta. Champagne goblets appeared under her feet. After a few turns, she stopped in front of Gambetta and said to him; "You'll learn eventually, you and your cronies. You'll be able to carry off women, if they consent, when you have found respectable reasons to convince them with. Unanimously, the people have proclaimed it; there is no appeal. They will always abandon a group of women to violence. It's such a firmly entrenched notion that nothing will ever budge it. You are listening here to the clear discourse of a free mouth. Hurry, quickly, out of my sight."

"And the little princess, for she was the daughter of the king of England, pushed herself, head first, into the banana tree. She was not to emerge until the signing of the Treaty of Frankfurt when she came out to read Gambetta's palm. But let us not get ahead of ourselves. After the girl's speech, Gambetta got up and boxed with an imaginary opponent. It is always more dangerous to fight with an imaginary person than a real one, because with the former you never know what can happen. Indeed, Gambetta took a crab right in the face and his efforts to get rid of it were fruitless.

"You see how edifying this little story is: so I recommend that you watch your words, gestures, writings, etc. Beware, not very far from your head there is a large snake waiting for you to go "oof!" so he can swallow you. And, if by misfortune, this were to happen to you, don't even think of the kind of risks you would be running. Take heed! Here he is."

I felt myself in mortal danger. Gunshots cracked from all sides. Impossible to go three steps without having one's face showered with blood. The heat was suffocating and it became harder and harder to walk. I was on the verge of deciding to stop when a tremendous explosion occurred and I immediately felt a sensation of glacial cold. A green liquid ran abundantly from my eyes—chlorophyll, no doubt—and I started to rise up into the atmosphere as fast as the liquid streamed from my eyes. Suddenly I felt myself emerging into the sunlight.

I opened my eyes which, until now, I'd kept shut out of fear. I was in a huge garden, unbelievably luxurious, a garden sprinkled with fountains, waterfalls, beds of colourful flowers. To recuperate from the emotions I had just been through, I sat down on a bench in the shade of the arbour. Meanwhile, I still didn't know where I was, and despite the satisfaction that I took in strutting about such a place, I left the arbour and took off for adventure in the hopes of meeting someone who could give me some information. After a few minutes walk, I came to a balustrade and saw below me a multitude of other gardens similar to the one I had just crossed. Suddenly I understood. There was no doubt: this splendid terraced park, these marvelous gardens could only be those of Babylon. The astonishment I felt walking through this celebrated place made me burst out laughing. A hand touched my shoulder and I heard someone asking me confidentially: "Why are you laughing, young man?" I turned around and found myself face to face with an old gaffer whose face was practically obliterated by an immense white beard. I greeted him politely:

—With whom have I the honour of speaking?

—I am the broom-seller, any old broom-seller.

Once again I acknowledged him respectfully and said:

—Please excuse my presence in these gardens. The truth is, I have no idea how I got here.

And I recounted my story to him.

—That's nothing, he said to me when I had finished. Come with me. You shall rest, and then I shall see how I can be useful to you.

We went down the gardens and after walking in silence for more than an hour, we arrived at a tiny train station on the bank of a river. On one

66

track I noticed a locomotive which seemed not to have run for a long time, but there were no wagons or railwaymen to be seen.

—Come in, said the broom-seller, make yourself at home.

We entered the lobby of the station and, pushing a little door next to the ticket window, we came to the foot of a staircase. It had seemed to me that the building had only one floor, yet we climbed thousands of steps. It was pitch black when the broom-seller murmured: "Finally, we have arrived."

—You live quite high up, I said, out of breath.

He pushed open a door and we entered a luxuriously appointed dressing room. At the end of this room, occupying an entire corner, was a huge scarecrow covered with stuffed parrots. The broom-seller whistled and then crawled over to the bathtub which he plunged into. The wall which the scarecrow had originally been in front of began to rise like the metal shutters of a shop. The sound of singing wafted over.

—You were looking for a woman, said the broom-seller, here are mine.

We passed into a vast room whose floor was covered in furs with here and there multicoloured cushions in all shapes and sizes. About fifty women were there, some dressed in sumptuous evening gowns, others naked or in nightdresses; some stretched out, slept or daydreamed, and the others were strolling about as if they were in the lobby of a theatre on opening night.

One of them was dancing, her outstretched arms covered with little birds of various species. Sometimes one of the little birds slid surreptitiously between her legs. She then began to shake with a redoubled frenzy. For a few moments her chest would rise more rapidly, her breasts swell, then the bird would emerge from her mouth shaking his wings and another would start all over again.

The broom-seller undressed and invited me to do the same.

—Choose one, he said.

I had already noticed a barely pubescent brunette of striking beauty who was lolling in a basin in the centre of the room. She seemed quite occupied with catching the fish which passed within the reach of her hand, and she would introduce them into the aquarium of her body. Seeing that I was looking at her, she signalled me to come near her. She had small, well-shaped breasts and I felt a tremendous desire to bite them until I drew blood. She swooned from this with little cries of pleasure.

—Oh, how beautiful the sea is! she said to me.

And, since I was chasing away a fish that wanted to haunt her, she added:

—Long live Lake Garda!

We made love in the position she had chosen. I almost suffocated her with my embrace and bit her. Sometimes I took her breasts in my hands and pressed them with all my strength. Other times, it was her neck which I

67

squeezed with the same violence, until she lost her breath. Suddenly the basin filled up with children's boats and we stopped, exhausted. After a few moments of silence and rest, she clapped her hands and a young woman whose breasts were cleft vertically and decorated with pendants representing the Tennis Court Oath bent over in front of us.

—Give us some storm liqueur, some earthquake wine, or some dew milk to drink.

The girl with the pendants went off and I remarked that her backbone was luminous and seemed, in the half-light, like an enormous glowworm. She came back a few moments later bearing a tray with decanters so malleable that they swayed and bent according to the movement of the liquid they contained.

We drank several glasses of these liqueurs whose flavour recalled that of damp moss and my companion who, in the meanwhile had confided that her name was Salade, once again clapped her hands. The serving maid with the cleft breasts reappeared.

—Bring us some Jupiter turkeys, emancipated crustaceans and singing fruit.

The serving girl came back a few minutes later accompanied by three colleagues so similar to her that they appeared to be each modelled on one another, and it was impossible to distinguish the first from the new ones. All four were carrying trays of multicoloured feathers filled with strange victuals giving off a mysterious smoke, but whether it was related to the odour of new suitcases or to a tunnel through which a train has just passed, was impossible to tell. We did justice to this superb meal, which nonetheless did not proceed without a few complications. Indeed, the truffled turkeys were still chanting mass when they were carved, and the lobsters took wing in order to flee the plate, so that we were obliged to go after them with revolvers.

We began, once again, to feel alert and strong like a shell fired from a cannon. Salade had invited to join us one of her companions who held a fistful of seeds in her hand and declared to whoever wanted to hear that her greatest pleasure was having them germinate inside her. And, according to this woman, it only took a few moments, during which she experienced incomparable satisfaction. She undertook to initiate Salade, within whom she deposited several wheat seeds. Almost immediately, Salade was taken with a vibratory motion which reached all her limbs. Even her hair was vibrating! And this movement was so intense that all the people around her participated despite themselves. Soon Salade left the ground and remained suspended ten or fifteen centimetres in the air. From all the evidence, it seemed that she was experiencing extreme pleasure, and her companion appeared to be in the same circumstances. We had the presentiment that some phenomenon was about to take place. Salade called out in the dying voice of an echo: "Volatile, my darling!" But already she could hear nothing. From the furs which she was stretched out upon, a monkey wrench burst forth as if projected by a hidden catapult. I then noticed that a jellyfish had lodged itself between my legs, where I was beginning to feel an immeasurable arousal, a voluptuousness such that I suddenly had nothing left to desire. Finally, I in turn rose into the air and quickly reached the level at which Salade and Volatile were floating. They started to drift like a barge carried off by the current, and hardly had I noticed this phenomenon when I felt myself being carried off in turn. A voice screamed:

−The flood! Save the furniture. Bring the candles, the hurricane lamps and the locks. The giraffes are upon us . . .

We were going faster and faster and, after a few minutes, we found ourselves outside the room, slipping between the trees in the garden. The voice of the broom-seller came to me softly:

−Have a good trip! Enjoy yourselves.

Despite my extreme arousal, I found the strength to wave goodbye and shout:

−Thank you! Goodbye. See you soon . . .

We travelled for a long time like that in mid-air. The jellyfish was tireless and I did not tire of feeling it there. Two days and two nights went by. At dawn on the third day we saw several miles ahead of us a snow-covered mountain surrounded by a belt of parrots which fluttered all around crying "ours is all the joy" at regular intervals.

As we reached the mountain, the sun came up behind us. Barely had we touched the snow when the parrots rained down around us, all talking at once in different languages. They were greeting us in their own way. Salade and I had no idea how to get away from this mass of birds. With great difficulty, we cleared a path through them, and after having gone several hundred metres we reached a platform overlooking a vertical drop whose bottom remained invisible. A sinister howl interspersed with sobs rose from the abyss. We did not know what to do, being caught between the cliff and the parrots, when a weighing scale which seemed to be brandished on the end of someone's arm, appeared out of the pit. A stream of white feathers blew off one of the pans of the scale, and the atomiser which occupied the other pan was spraying non-stop. When the pair of scales reached our feet, the feathers streamed back into the pan and the atomiser stopped to say to us:

−Too many cooks spoil the broth, when you are trying to mix business with pleasure. This may not be altogether new but it cannot be very well known as most people are still intrigued.

The feathers covered up the atomiser and snow began to fall so thickly

69

that we soon lost sight of the scales, and forgetting that there was a precipice in front of us, we got lost and fell into it. In fact, we descended, rather than fell, at the same speed as the snowflakes. Finally, we reached the bottom of the pit and having taken a few steps, we noticed it was not snowing anymore, and indeed, was quite hot. We attributed the unexpected heat to the presence, in a crack in the rock, of a clump of giant dandelions. In fact, one had only to move the slightest distance away to feel the heat diminish, and it was impossible to put one's hand closer than three centimetres to those plants. We were about to go away when a flower that looked like a carnation sprang up from the ground and fell at our feet making a hole that could easily have held a cow. One of the dandelions nodded ceremoniously as if taking a bow and, after several startled jumps, turned toward the right as if it wanted to draw our attention in that direction. But there was nothing there except a half-rotten tree-trunk blocking a narrow path. A single one of the main branches remained. As we questioned the meaning of the dandelion's gesture, we realised, not without some fear and surprise, that what had appeared to be a branch was none other than an enormous snake emerging from the under-side of the trunk where it was still partially hidden. It rose upright in front of us and began singing:

> *There was a rat*
> *a rat on a boat*
> *There was a rat full of soup*
> *with bottles floating in it*
> *One evening at the theatre*
> *a piano tried to strangle it*
> *In front of the jetty*
> *a champion was dying*
> *while hats*
> *were budding in the valley*

It swayed for a moment and added:
—What is left of Greek civilisation? Just some marble rubble. If that is the case, what do you expect to be left of the moon except a little bit of butter?

The snake fell silent and disappeared under its tree, which tried to rise and stand upright against the rocks, and sweating profusely, succeeded. The path was clear. We set down the path, but we were not to get very far. A few hundred paces further on was a cavern from which came a suffocating stench of sulphur and innumerable humming-birds. When we came to the entrance of the cavern the smell of sulphur dissipated and the humming-birds fluttering about were swallowed in the rock. At the same time, a voice cried out:

—Watch out for the landmine! Watch out for the mine!

This warning was not entirely useless; for a few seconds later we were deafened by a massive explosion, then a huge bale of straw burst out of the cavern, flew over our heads and crashed to the ground with an almighty ruckus. The echoes in the mountains had not yet died away when a woman of great beauty dressed in a sumptuous evening gown came out of the cavern and said:

—Do you want to see my legs?

And she gave us her card, on which I read a name, Vagabonde, and the address of a beauty parlour.

We in our turn introduced ourselves, although we declined the services indicated on the card. However, as she insisted, we followed her into the cavern. The walls were covered in big white mushrooms with red spots, which moved with a continual gyrating motion. From time to time one of them opened up and a newborn baby's head popped out, fell to the ground and broke like an egg. A colourless liquid oozed out of the skull into a little pool, while at the same time a light steam rose from the closed eyes that shrouded the whole head. When the steam cleared all that was to be seen was a fat snail which set off towards the nearest wall of the cavern and hid behind a mushroom.

Seeing that we were interested by this performance, Vagabonde smiled and said: "This is nothing. You will see some stranger things in a little while."

A small glass door at the back of the cavern opened. Having crossed the threshold and descended several steps, we found ourselves in a vast kennel where hundreds of dogs all of different breeds were barking silently. We practically ran across the kennel since it seemed that the dogs would break their chains at any moment and then surely they would have devoured us, for they looked absolutely starved. We came out in a long and winding corridor which ended at a platform resembling that of the Paris Metro, but between the two sides a stream of lemon-coloured water flowed rapidly. A motorised launch came alongside, and Vagabonde invited us to step in.

We boarded, and Vagabonde, who had stayed behind on the dock, gave the departure sign with a friendly wave goodbye. No one was piloting the boat, which nonetheless glided swiftly along, and soon we were plunged into complete darkness relieved by fleeting glimmers of blue. From time to time we could tell from the angle of the boat that we were making a turn. No sooner had this dawned on us than we were blinded by an intense flash of light; and then it was night again, with its vague blue gleams. Several long hours passed in this way, then the darkness lifted and the day broke; but was this crepuscular light, reminiscent of the long hallways of old fashioned houses, actually the dawn? However feeble it was, this pale light did allow us to distinguish, on the walls of the tunnel we were sailing through, many inscriptions apparently in Hebrew, our ignorance of this language precluding us from deciphering them. In the distance, a pier on which flowered an oleander near a stuffed zebra on whose head hung a squirrel-fur coat. Finally we emerged in an arena so vast we could hardly see the other side. Thousands of white swans with top hats on their backs were swimming in every direction. Here and there an islet housing an umbrella pine in whose shade lived bands of squirrels as white as the swans. White carp, too, occasionally sprang out of the water.

—Are we at the North Pole? Salade asked me.

—I don't think so, I answered, though I would like to know why there are so many swans.

Barely had the words slipped out of my mouth when a violent wind whipped up enormous wave. All the swans gathered and came toward us. They were still a few metres away when they called out:

—Tear out your hair for heaven's sake. If you do not, your ears will drag in the water and you will drown.

I protested that this advice was idiotic and refused to tear out my hair. The swans insisted, but I remained immovable. Faced with my resistance, the swans made off with our boat. A few moments later we were floating rapidly down a wide river edged with womens' eyes wearing long made-up lashes which fluttered as we went by. I was intrigued and asked the swans where we were going.

—To find the Golden Fleece, they replied with enigmatic smiles.

2. Hand in Hand

 – THE 'LAST ABENCERAGE' RUNNING ON A ROOF BE-
tween the chimneys planted with orange tree branches laden
with fruit.

2. – He picks an orange.

3. – An orange falling from the sky plops on his head.

4. – The 'last Abencerage's' head turns.

5. – Faster.

6. – The head turns so fast that one can't see it anymore.

7. – The head stops short.

8. – A magpie above the head of the 'last Abencerage'.

9. – The 'last Abencerage' falls into the street on his back, his arms crossed.

10. – His beard grows.

11. – Oh! The beautiful beard!

12. – He has bloody hands.

13. – His heart comes out of his chest.

14. – Behind his head a bush emerges from between the cobblestones.

15. – Something rustles in the bush.

16. – Salade's face.

17. – Nude as usual.

18. – She approaches skipping (two steps forward, one step back), holding
her handkerchief with both hands.

19. – She leans her head toward that of the 'last Abencerage.'

20. – Why does she cry?

21. – She wipes the dead man's face with her handkerchief.

22. – Oh! The beautiful landscape in the handkerchief!

23. – Salade dances around the dead man while holding her handkerchief with both hands.

24. – She places her handkerchief on the dead man's knees.

25. – Two rabbits.

26. – They slowly approach the dead man.

27. – Each one holds a corner of the handkerchief in its mouth.

28. – They back off dragging the handkerchief which they place on a pipe.

29. – The pipe grows in front of your very eyes.

30. – Ten metres high.

31. – Salade stretches out next to the dead man.

32. – She yawns.

33. – What is she dreaming of?

34. – Ah! Those dratted flies.

35. – And now the butterflies!

36. – Salade with a butterfly net between her breasts.

37. – What a marvel!

38. – Better and better.

39. – Ecstasy.

40. – The 'last Abencerage' is nude.

41. – He leaps up.

42. – This woman swoons.

43. – He gnaws Salade's hair.

44. – He gnaws Salade's right knee.

45. – He gnaws the other knee.

46. – He flees howling.

47. – Four butterflies at the end of his nose.

48. – A glass car in the shape of a porcupine and travelling at full speed.

49. – Two teats at the front of the car.

50. – They spurt a jet of red wine.

51. – A horse atop a bicycle arrives backwards.

52. – The collision.

53. – A geyser.

54. – In one direction a horse and an empty car out of control.

55. – In the other direction, a horse and an empty car out of control.

56. – The geyser disappears.

57. – On the road a troop of priests marching in step.

58. – A cow precedes them.

59. – The pope, a phallus tattooed on his forehead, is perched on a cow.

60. – He has hands fifty centimetres long.

61. – Everyone is on their knees.

62. – Eat the earth.

63. – Beautiful eyes.
64. – Where are those eyes going?
65. – Hesitation, indecision.
66. – On the hands of the pope.
67. – The hands shrivel like burning paper.
68. – A mailman, his hands in his pockets.
69. – A letter, for whom?
70. – For Salade.
71. – The envelope lengthens inordinately in Salade's hands.
72. – Why is Salade undressing?
73. – Why is she getting dressed again?
74. – The mailman capers in the neighbouring field.
75. – What a beautiful sheep!
76. – Salade is so happy, so happy . . .
77. – The priests sit down in the road.
78. – Wallowing in the dust, they play, like young dogs chasing their tails.
79. – The priests are killed one by one.
80. – The last one has his belly ripped out.
81. – A dog runs, crazed.
82. – It goes right through the dead priests.
83. – It grows a white feather for each priest sniffed.
84. – The parade of orange trees.
85. – Here they are on the road.
86. – One per priest.
87. – The priests disappear in the trunks of the orange trees.
88. – The fall of the orange trees.
89. – The orange trees swell.
90. – Orange trees march off goose-stepping.
91. – "What an apalling smell," says Salade.
92. – It's intolerable!
93. – Salade on the road.
94. – Where the mailman is found again.
95. – He is eating a live bird.
96. – The clear water.
97. – A dive.
98. – Good will reign with the fish.
99. – With the toads as well.
100. – Impossible to get back to the fresh air.
101. – Appearance of the gills.
102. – Of the fins
103. – And off you go!
104. – Toward the source.

105. – It's raining.
106. – The drops of water run like mice.
107. – What a downpour!
108. – It's raining torrents.
109. – The torrents run in herds, bite each other and fight.
110. – The flood.
111. – Salade in a barrel carried by mice.
112. – At sea.
113. – The storm: waves of Swiss cheese shake the barrel in all directions.
114. – An enormous barrel of boiling cheese.
115. – The barrel is thrown on the shore.
116. – A wave of Roquefort.
117. – The barrel breaks against a Parmesan rock.
118. – Salade: "Where am I?"
119. – Off to adventure.
120. – A field planted with spurs.
121. – Salade plucks a spur.
122. – The spurs grow in front of your very eyes.
123. – The spurs bloom.
124. – Bowler hats: what beautiful fruit!
125. – We pass.
126. – A stream.
127. – It's mint!
128. – A shadow on the stream.
129. – It's a basset hound.
130. – Salade in the stream.
131. – The basset hound glides along the surface.
132. – Salade glides downstream propelled by the basset.
133. – The stars around Salade.
134. – She eats them.
135. – Salade walks in the night.
136. – Falls into a tree-trunk.
137. – Salade falls asleep.
138. – She dreams: I must go away, my husband will be back soon.
139. – She is in a soft bus.
140. – The bus crushes a turkey.
141. – The crushed turkey crawls like a lizard.
142. – The ambulance moves forward in fits and starts.
143. – The turkey is put on a stretcher of cigarette paper.
144. – The turkey at the hospital.
145. – At dawn: 25 turkeys in a hospital bed.
146. – Salade wakes up.

147. – The 25 turkeys emerge from her mouth.

148. – The turkeys dance around Salade.

149. – Salade afraid.

150. – She flees.

151. – A cloud of hair.

152. – A cloud of foreheads.

153. – A cloud of eyes.

154. – A cloud of noses.

155. – A cloud of mouths.

156. – A cloud of necks.

157. – A cloud of torsoes.

158. – A cloud of arms.

159. – A cloud of phalluses.

160. – A cloud of legs.

161. – The impact of the clouds.

162. – The clouds back off from each other.

163. – They throw themselves at each other.

164. – A thimble falls to the ground.

165. – A goat falls to the ground.

166. – A coal bucket falls.

167. – A pearl necklace.

168. – A flute, a handful of nails, a multitude of plates, radio receivers, eye-glasses, cakes of soap, packages of tobacco, a pumpkin, Newton's corpse, flames, elephant tusks, fall on the ground, surrounded by lightning in the middle of a torrential rainstorm.

169. – The 'last Abencerage' falls feet-together on the pumpkin.

170. – He is embedded in the pumpkin.

171. – His head still shows.

172. – The pumpkin seeds sprout.

173. – The 'last Abencerage's' head is surrounded by a forest of pumpkins which multiply incessantly.

174. – Fall of a goose onto the head of the 'last Abencerage.'

175. – The goose eats his hair.

176. – It eats his ears.

177. – It eats his eyes.

178. – It smashes his skull.

179. – It eats his brain.

180. – It sows pumpkin seeds in the empty skull.

181. – The seeds sprout.

182. – The pumpkin fills the empty skull of the 'last Abencerage.'

183. – The 'last Abencerage' frees himself from the pumpkin which holds him prisoner.

184. – Standing up.
185. – Swedish gymnastics.
186. – A narrow-gauge railway.
187. – The 'last Abencerage' jumps into a dump-truck.
188. – The virgin forest on the horizon.
189. – The train enters the virgin forest.
190. – A hillock of treacle.
191. – The train plunges into it.
192. – It emerges full of club-feet.
193. – Between the club-feet, balls of string.
194. – An outbreak among the club-feet.
195. – Glowing eyes.
196. –
197. – The wall crumbles.
198. – Enter the broom-seller.
199. – The train stops.
200. – The beans are ripe.
201. – A pallet.
202. – Two pallets.
203. – A coat burns.
204. – A salt cellar.
205. – The broom-seller's chin is wounded.
206. – A tragedy in a stomach.
207. – The mirrors on strike.
208. – Fear.
209. – Under a dump-truck.
210. – The 'last Abencerage' is under a dump-truck.
211. – He frees himself and stands up again.
212. – His skeleton leaves him.
213. – He runs off pursued by his skeleton.
214. – The broom-seller follows him.
215. – The 'last Abencerage's' skeleton gets winded following him.
216. – His forehead is all sweaty.
217. – The skeleton collapses, exhausted.
218. – The broom-seller picks him up and carries him on his shoulders.
219. – He catches up with the 'last Abencerage'.
220. – He returns his skeleton.
221. – The 'last Abencerage' is furious.
222. – He refuses to take back his skeleton and breaks it into a thousand pieces.
223. – The train comes off the rails.
224. – The train pursues them through the virgin forest.

225. – A dolmen in front of St. Lazare railway station.
226. – They arrive at the station.
227. – The dolmen breathes deeply.
228. – He coughs.
229. – In coughing he spits up a reindeer.
230. – A fit of coughing, a herd of reindeer.
231. – A reindeer race in front of St. Lazare station.
232. – A general trampled by reindeer.
233. – The reindeer are gone.
234. – The general has become a greasy priest.
235. – The 'last Abencerage' lies down on the dolmen.
236. – The broom-seller lies down underneath.
237. – Three policemen.
238. – They arrest the 'last Abencerage' and the broom-seller.
239. – Arrival of Salade disguised as sealing wax.
240. – A policeman swallows her.
241. – The policemen assault the 'last Abencerage' and the broom-seller.
242. – They have nothing but beefsteaks in their hands.
243. – They grind them up.
244. – They mix them with duck eggs and season them.
245. – They eat them.
246. – They fall asleep.
247. – They rot.
248. – Return of the reindeer.
249. – The reindeer eat the policemen.

3. No Charge for Fleecing

T THE CHAMBER OF DEPUTIES.

THE SPEAKER.* — Miss Lantern has the floor.

MISS LANTERN. — I'm not only thinking of the attitude the legs of mutton may take. I also note that certain Israelites who had put their names down to discuss the bill concerning the opening of a case of Camembert have postponed their comments to a later date, now that you have chosen today for the snubbing of pug noses. Nonetheless, we must snub these noses whose memory haunts the listeners in the gallery; and model them artistically so they take on the harmonious shape of a polishing brush. Meanwhile, gentlemen, there are two ways to refurbish noses. The simplest way consists of rubbing them with a cheese grater until a few dozen ants crawl out; but this method is not the most rational. I am of the opinion, shared by a certain number of our colleagues, that by rolling them first in flour and then marinating them in vinegar, we will obtain polishing brushes of a very superior quality.

MR. BROOM-SELLER. — But ever since we started using vinegar to varnish cobblestones, it has fled the moment we attempt to seize it. Could the Honourable Minister of Drawers briefly indicate to us the measures he intends to take to stop the vinegar?

THE HONOURABLE MINISTER OF DRAWERS. — The requisitioning of butterfly nets should suffice.

MISS LANTERN. – Which butterfly nets? The vulcanite ones?

THE HONOURABLE MINISTER OF DRAWERS. – No, ma'am, ones made of dried eels.

MISS LANTERN. – But this is not the entire story; above all, the vinegar question raises the issue of alcoholism among antique furniture. In the course of the preceding legislative term, some colleagues succeeded in making this assembly adopt a bill limiting the yearly consumption of alcohol by an antique to a single litre. But since this bill's publication, the well-diggers of the South have come up with an ingenious method of circumventing it; and thereby–as in the past–have been able to inebriate all the pieces of antique furniture which so desire. You could not but have noticed with some astonishment that, since the first months of the past year, our imports of flea preserves have increased by enormous proportions. Well gentlemen, it is thanks to these fleas that the law is constantly broken, for you must be well aware that fleas become drunk in the same manner as . . .

LOHENGRIN. – Surely, you are confusing them with geraniums.

THE SPEAKER. – Night has fallen.

MISS DEMOLISHED. – Yes, the night is filled with prune springs which must be trapped in order to feed our locomotives of dead leaves swept by a contrary wind. But first we must direct the money-forging leaden winds, however obstinately it remains deaf to the objurations of corned beef, buttocks, and the performing dogs who soive second degree equations while duelling on a turntable whose rotational speed is exactly proportional to that of a hair chasing a bicycle. The hair will catch up with the bicycle on some day when carnival tents rain into sausage skin. *(hearty applause.)*

A voice from the left. – Sow bagpipes! Sow bagpipes! The people are hungry and demand white wood lights.

THE BROOM-SELLER. – We will never get to the end of this if the reinforced concrete awaits the passers-by at the corner of deserted streets in order to stab them in the stomach with cherry trees. We absolutely must scrape the camels' chests until they sing a Viennese waltz.

THE SPEAKER. – The 'last Abencerage' will take the floor to present his observations.

THE LAST ABENCERAGE. – Gentlemen, I will get straight to the point. Garden-hoses represent a permanent danger to the peaceful populace of our countryside who–sheltered from manufacturers' trade-marks–are constantly exposed to the danger of being hit on the head by solidified lemons fitted with such sharp tips they resemble nozzles of everlasting bronze. Believe me, gentlemen, an effort is needed here to bring wood fires back to the hearths which have for so long shaved the skulls of the flooded forests. And, if you do not take appropriate action, you can be sure that, sooner or later, the dead trees will hunt the ears which, afflicted with dry-rot, chase after mangy dogs. Then, the trolleys will come off their tracks and crush the concierges beating rugs on the sidewalks, while rains of savages overrun the mineralogy museums, electric sauces restore to soles the agility of butterflies crazed by neon signs which grumble like secret drawers. What will you do then? Will you decide to plunge a newly ripped-out head of hair into an oil drum, so the Prime Minister* hears that the laundry-boats have served their country well; or will you ask the high-grade corks about the genealogy of the tin which escapes as ancient ruins from coaches assassinated by fanatics armed with harpsichords?

THE PRIME MINISTER. — You remind me of the road-mender who, when he picked a death's head off a milestone, called his grandmother to suckle him. No matter what he did, he could get no more from that stale breast than a trickle of bad coffee for the milk, which she drew from her roof of thatch so soft it seemed like an oyster mourning for its pearl, not knowing it is searching the whole world for a ravined path or an old flag forgotten in an elevator.

MR. COAL. — You don't mince words. I see the issue moves you as much as it does all of our colleagues, and I am glad. However, I don't know if the brutality of the acorns crushing feverish gazes will result in a more speedy regularistaion of a situation during which the rebellion of beets re-fusing to make sugar has impeded the snow's melting.

LOHENGRIN. — I propose that we preserve, in candle holders, the wheat found in Pharoanic tombs. *(Various commotions.)*

THE BROOM-SELLER *(sobbing)*. — Why do we torture the string-beans?

THE SPEAKER. — I beseech the Honourable Broom-seller not to cry. If he will restrain his tears until the arrival of the shipment of flat-irons, then I am sure that all our colleagues will experience the same mixed emotion in which is found—so intimately linked that the flint will not recognise the mushroom bed from which it has sprung—the beard of the patriarch, the *curule* chair, the toothless porpoise, and the cockaded mouse who goes by the name of Henry IV in grade school history books.

"The Honourable Minister of Clog Noises may take the floor."

THE HONOURABLE MINISTER OF CLOG NOISES. — Some of our colleagues have supposed that I am shying away from explanations. For instance, we saw, during the previous session, Mr. Coal demanding that the government divulge its reasons for purchasing a herd of trunkless elephants. Now I am ready to discuss this question whenever the assembly so desires. If I have not demonstrated undue haste, I will tell you, it is because I feared that imprudent words would be uttered from this side *(at the extreme left)* of the assembly. *(Vigorous applause from the centre, the right and various benches on the left.)*

MISS LANTERN. – And what about your subsidies to businesses using potter's clay to produce motor power ? . . .

THE SPEAKER. – Would you please allow the Minister of Clog Noises to explain himself.

A voice from the extreme right. – You are an abominable scoundrel.

THE HONOURABLE MINISTER OF CLOG NOISES. – Have we not gone so far as to invoke furnace sneezes to condemn the laying of rails on the lawns of the Bagatelle? These proceedings are barely worthy of pillowcases ripped by artichoke flowers which let beribboned trumpets escape. It is impossible to continue without a singing compass.

THE PRIME MINISTER. – The government demands a vote of confidence. May your mother-in-law fall asleep!

LOHENGRIN. – Fear nothing. The silk stockings are starting to blossom, and we can no hope for a good harvest of metal soap-cakes. The people could not ask for more.

MISS DEMOLISHED. – Look at the walls. They are covered with banana peel posters on which every guild and union is protesting the restrictive measures you have imposed on the traffic of granite. In the old days, that is to say the days before the trolley company was allowed to transport baby fish made of lemon which, it should be noted in passing, provoked the suicide of all the pheasants in the department of Ain—the department I have the honour of representing in this Assembly—in the old days, champagne glasses would knit during their spare time. It was all profit for the nation, which no longer needed to buy cloves abroad: hence a perceptible strengthening of the currency. And now, what do we find? All the children between the ages of five and six limp. Is this not horrifying? I demand that from now on, champagne glasses be cultivated in hothouses.

Various voices from the centre and the right. – Enough of champagne glasses, the hothouses are full of cannons . . .

THE SPEAKER. – I will not permit this business of cannons in the hothouses to be discussed again. The agenda calls for the questioning of Mr. Grotto about the restriction of abortions for the Equidae. The floor is open to Mr. Grotto, so that he may defend this point; but I must remind our honourable colleague that regulations prohibit the use of Homeric laughter during the discussion.

MR. GROTTO. – Grotto! I mean a cave filled with tins of sardines! When the pelican returns from a long journey, what does it do? Some claim that it goes to sleep without even unpacking its suitcase. I know very well this is stupid slander. The pelican would never behave in such a fashion; it is much too sensitive of appearances. No, I say this unhesitantly, the pelican, returning from a long voyage, does not simply go to sleep like a retired policeman; rather, he notices that his domicile is covered with a thick coat of dust, that blind dust that haberdashers are so fond of. He carefully gathers it into a soup tureen. Soon he will have a barrelful and will be able to corner the dust market in his neighbourhood. Isn't this a sign of the times? In fact, if there were no blind dust, how would the mares abort ? . . .

A voice from the right. – Between five and seven years?

MR. GROTTO. – I am well aware that this discussion concerns limiting abortions by mares to one per week. But it is important that these abortions take place under the best possible conditions, so that our rose doesn't lose the qualities which make French wine the best in the world. My challenge has no other goal than to ask the Minister of Toothaches to take all necessary measures.

THE HONOURABLE MINISTER OF TOOTHACHES. – Whip the eggs! You only hurt the one you love, tee hee! *(Various commotions.)* Besides, the deep sea divers will soon call to order the owners of flying snuff-boxes who are allowing them to roam the highways where they uproot trees in order to feed their fishbones. This intolerable abuse must cease, otherwise France will soon be bereft of crockery.

LOHENGRIN. – Since you tell us about the misdeeds of the flying snuff-boxes, why, then, conceal the reason? Would these boxes be so ill-fated if they didn't contain tricoloured tobacco which, under cover of the rapid flight of the boxes, escapes into the air and attacks the swallows which die by the thousands? How will you replace the swallows? This is the question you must address.

THE HONOURABLE MINISTER OF TOOTHACHES. – I will discuss it shortly, and I will not leave the podium without proposing to the Assembly the necessary measures for replacing dead swallows by aluminium tongues, which are far more efficacious and durable than swallows subject to hay-fever. *(Applause from various benches to the right and centre.)* But the principle obstacle impeding this project consists of the screwdriver, whose abolition is urgently needed if we are to avoid the clocks being rapidly over-run with moss. They have already stopped chiming seven o'clock, and regardless of how much they are bathed in currant jelly, we had no success: they obstinately continue to whimper pathetically like sputtering candles instead of chiming seven times. This might seem insignificant. But since we know this silence has caused the railroad tracks to soften— a softening as yet quite negligeable but which could be aggravated if the screwdrivers continue to wreak havoc—then we must anxiously ask ourselves what is going to happen to our railways on the day when no hours are chimed at all. It is obvious that the completely liquefied tracks will flow toward the sea and cause catastrophic floods. I realise that the abolition of screwdrivers will have dire consequences for our mining constituencies, which will experience serious unemployment. But we have not allowed the situation to go un-remarked, and the government intends to present, in addition to the law abolishing screwdrivers, an amendment destined to mitigate its consequences . . .

Voice from the right. — If we hadn't arrested the East Wind, matters wouldn't have come to this . . .

THE HONOURABLE MINISTER OF TOOTHACHES. — . . . they should not be exaggerated.

LOHENGRIN. — Stop hiding in the cracks between the floorboards. The weather is mild this December and the flies graze peacefully on the park benches. Nothing more is needed to start the cobblestones yawning from boredom—a very serious matter for the future of wheelbarrows. It's true that an escaped wheelbarrow attracts tuna fish, and the fishermen have no objections to that. However, it would be simpler to distract the cobblestones, and more economical as well. Financially speaking, the State has everything to gain. The Assembly must, without delay, assume responsibility for this question.

MR. BROOM-SELLER. — Sole and brisket of beef! You are entirely right; but I am equally correct in demanding that we cut off the ears of the chamber-pots to prevent them from singing. Their monotonous chants exasperate the newborn babes who are dying by the thousands during the spring when females sing night and day to attract mates. The muteness of the chamber-pots—whether it interferes with their reproduction or not—is an insignificance compared to the lives of our children!

THE HONOURABLE MINISTER OF DELICATE INSTRUMENTS. — I hold at your disposal a curved needle for knitting circles. *(Applause.)*

THE SPEAKER. — The white wine will take the floor.

THE WHITE WINE. — The beard which grows in the brains of corpses wears away faster than Capuchin-beard clogs, that's why it's used in the confection of women's clogs. If I bring this up, it's only because, in the past few months, smuggling corpses' brains has become increasingly frequent along our northern and eastern frontiers. This situation requires immediate action or else our producers of corpses' brains will soon be ruined; and an entire French industry will be overrun by foreign interests.

THE HONOURABLE MINISTER OF DELICATE INSTRUMENTS. — I have already ordered production of clothes-pegs to be speeded up so that they can be applied to all smugglers. The hellish noise of the clothes-pegs will betray any clandestine passages across the border. *(Applause from many benches in the centre and on the right, and a few on the left.)*

THE WHITE WINE. — That's not all. Leaves are falling from the trees with exceptional abundance this year. There are places where more than ten times the usual amount of leaves have been gathered: so many that commodity prices have fallen catastrophically and our manufacturers of

85

dead-leaf cheese are threatened with destitution as they can no longer find a market for their products.

THE SPEAKER. – The Honourable Minister of Drifting Boats has the floor.

THE HONOURABLE MINISTER OF DRIFTING BOATS. – I can assure the white wine that the government has already considered the problem and is preparing, in the near future, to submit a proposal for the Assembly's consideration. At this point, I can affirm that the government has envisioned the possibility of using dead leaves in the production of the floating lighthouses which were so useful to our navy during the last war.

THE WHITE WINE. – As of now I see the future with glass eyes. *(Applause.)*

THE SPEAKER. – Mr. Gatekeeper has the floor.

MR. GATEKEEPER. – Since the beginning of the world, the spoon has been employed to eat soup. To be sure, there are many kinds of soup: honeysuckle soup for marriageable girls, flag soup for retired officers, window display soup for children, weathervane soup for chimneysweeps, and plenty of others. Nonetheless, all of these are ingested with the aid of a spoon. But, for more than a month now, all the spoons on the market have been afflicted with a nervous spasm the moment they are dipped in soup, and they prefer to turn inside-out rather than fulfill their task. To force them to comply, they must first be plunged into a bucket of sawdust which they forthwith ignite. However, this operation causes them to deteriorate, and infections— often benign, but sometimes quite serious—do occur in soup lovers. I know one can do without soup, but are we in a free country, yes or no? Have not our peaceful citizens, the right, for instance to consume chasuble soup?

THE HONOURABLE MINISTER OF OVERHOT BATHS. – Our honourable colleague is getting upset for no reason . . .

MR. GATEKEEPER. – No reason! Not a single day goes by without bringing news of accidental deaths provoked by sawdust ignited by spoons. Yesterday, in fact, we learned of the horrible fate met by an entire family from Lyon who ingested a bowl of paralytic soup. They must have just passed their spoons through the sawdust when, having barely swallowed their soup, they were overcome with nausea, vomiting forks whose points tore the oesophagus, resulting in horrible suffering and then death. Quite the contrary, I think the Honourable Minister of Overhot Baths is wrong to underestimate a state of affairs which gets worse day by day. The time is ripe for action.

THE HONOURABLE MINISTER OF OVERHOT BATHS. – I share the feelings of Mr. Gatekeeper, and I haven't waited until his intervention in order to act. Tomorrow the *Journal Officiel* will publish a decree forbidding the production of these spoons and substituting double-shelled spoons which will be able to invert without causing the soup any inconvenience. Thus, the sawdust treatment will be avoided. That is why I persist in my view that Mr. Gatekeeper is quite wrong to upset himself about the future. *(Shouts and agitation from the extreme left.)*

Voice from the right. – You are abominable scoundrels . . .

MR. PLASTER. – The attitude of certain of our colleagues proves that . . .

Voices from the left. – Hush yourself, spinach . . . And what about boomerang-bicycles? . . .

MR. PLASTER. – I would like to take the floor to explain my position on boomerang-bicycles.

THE SPEAKER. – Mr. Plaster has the floor.

MR. PLASTER. – Ladies and gentlemen. People have considerably exaggerated this affair while at the same time underestimating–in the interest of political considerations which are no secret–the services that Boomerang-bicycles rendered this country during the World War. It is undeniable that the adjunction of a boomerang to the handlebars of a bicycle was a great innovation, since the well-launched cyclist needed no effort to return to his starting point, which prevented a great number of soldiers from being captured by the enemy. Is it our fault, now that peace has been re-established, that evil-doers make use of this device to further a reprehensible aim? . . .

Voice from the left. – Haven't you called often enough for the sale of boomerang-bicycles to be de-regulated? *(Applause.)*

MR. PLASTER. – I have asked for de-regulation, yes. But under certain conditions, only, not a complete de-regulation. It is enough, by the way, to put highly-resistant counter-boomerangs on the market which are strong enough to suppress, whenever necessary, all the advantages the device gives to bicycles. The counter-boomerang, striking the boomerang on the bicycle, provokes–thanks to the rupture of the boomerang–the immediate immobilisation of the bicycle, and the evil-doer riding it can easily be stopped and arrested. Let the Honourable Minister of Delicate Instruments decide.

THE HONOURABLE MINISTER OF DELICATE INSTRUMENTS. – The government accepts the suggestion of Mr. Plaster.

Uproar from the left. The Deputies stand up and revile the right.

MR. KINDLING. – Bulldog! This business is vital for the counter-boomerang business that you control, Mr. Plaster. With all our might, we oppose this solution; we consider the strict regulation of boomerang-bicycles to be the only equitable solution, whether your business suffers or not.

MR. PLASTER. – It will be mandatory for boomerang-bicycles to be sold with their own counter-boomerangs.

Voice from the left. – Inquiry! Export! Inquiries! Exports!

THE SPEAKER. – The Honourable Minister of Delicate Instruments has the floor for a rectification.

THE HONOURABLE MINISTER OF DELICATE INSTRUMENTS. – The govenment specifies that, from now on, boomerang-bicycles will be sold with an automatic alarm system to warn everyone of their approach, and to allow the population to prepare its counter-boomerangs in case of criminal attack.

MR. KINDLING. – The inhabitants of the big cities are already protesting against the innumerable sounds which make their existence so painful: yet you want to add even more. No! We cannot accept this solution. We insist that the sale of boomerang-bicycles be forbidden.

Voices from the left. - Bravo! Neither boomerang-bicycles, nor covered church fonts.

Uproar from the right. From one end of the room to the other, the Deputies rail at each other. The Speaker stands up. The session is suspended.

4. Loser Takes All

GREAT BIG AUTOMOBILE STOPPED IN FRONT of the house, facing us, on the opposite bank of the Marne. A woman in riding costume descended from it and entered the house, while the car left immediately, capering like a goat.

From one of the low branches of a tree which was shading us, a bird flew off, let out a few small piercing cries and came to perch on the end of the bench upon which Mr. Coal and I were sitting. It had an alarm clock in its beak which it placed on the bench, the face turned towards us; then it executed a few pirouettes and disappeared.

The alarm clock chimed twelve times for the hour of noon.

—Oh! said Mr. Coal, it's lunch time! And, lifting up the bench, he plucked a tuft of sage, and so discovered a roast chicken, cooked just right. He grabbed the chicken by the feet, split it open and, presenting the two halves to me, asked me to choose one.

The chicken eaten, Mr. Coal went down to the edge of the river and headed into the water, then, spreading his legs, made motions as if to get rid something behind him. A basket full of fruit sprang out of the river and came to rest at my feet.

At this moment, a fisherman, who, from a small boat, was raising his nets, caught an ear and a lock. His discomfiture made me smile and the furious fisherman threw the lock at me, which, as it broke against my lips, nearly drowned me with milk. Milk is a very healthy food, I thought to myself, and I wrung my clothes in order to extract it. But, instead of milk,

I found myself drawing out rancid butter. Well, perhaps the milk was of poor quality!

Mr. Coal was perplexed. He had unleashed the fruits which, already covered with tiny dogs no bigger than walnuts, had rolled on the grass. It was quite obvious that milk spontaneously turning into butter disturbed him. Suddenly he smiled:

—I see, he said, it's the heart.

—What heart? I asked, astonished.

—The great heart of nature, the one sometimes found under fresh mushrooms after thunderstorms.

—And . . . What has it done?

—Undoubtedly a horizontal movement.

—What?

—It's simple: vertical movement determines the growth of animals and vegetables, and horizontal movement that of vibrations. If the heart did not have horizontal movement, silkworms would never make cocoons. This heart is hard to recognise. Sometimes it looks like a gas whose analysis would reveal the presence of pepper particles.

Our conversation was interrupted by the apparition of a man with a crab in his hand, who was making a parachute landing not thirty metres from us, on the very edge of the river.

—Who is that? asked Mr. Coal.

Hardly had he uttered this question when the man came running at full tilt and threw himself on his belly in front of us crying out:

—No, you won't find the house.

—We'll see, answered Mr. Coal.

And the man disappeared, as if swallowed up by the ground.

We remained dumb for a few moments, then I proposed to Mr. Coal that I help look for this house we were defied to find. He accepted enthusiastically:

—It will be much easier if there are two of us, he said. But what we need before everything else is to discover the secret.

—What secret?

—Of the heart. Without the secret of the heart we will not find the house.

—Where and how to discover the secret?

—From an aeroplane it is easier to see the steam the minute it appears over Menilmontant. I will then parachute down and grab it.

We decided to rest until dusk, and we stretched out on the grass. I was just falling asleep when I was yanked out of my reverie by the sound of a trumpet. An elephant in this neck of the woods! I got up and looked around; not a single elephant! On the other hand, ten paces away, I saw a huge crystal comb with a magnificent snake curled in its teeth. Barely awake, I was none-theless astonished that a snake should be combing itself. But he raised his head and said, spitting out his words:

—I am the father of matchboxes.

—That's not true, I replied, since you are combing yourself, and the father of matchboxes has no need of a comb as he is bald.

—I am also bald, but this is not a comb, and I am not combing myself. This is my wife. Salade. Look.

The comb did, as a matter of fact, take on a beautiful scarlet tint, hop up and down very quickly like a sparrow, then stop suddenly, and I saw Salade wearing a dress of transparent tulle, which left all her charms open to admiration. The snake was coiled around her neck.

Bringing her index finger to her lips, she said to me, with a smile:

—I am the mother of matchboxes.

Then, suddenly becoming serious, she added in a low tone:

—Don't you hear blood calling? I swear this is your father.

—I will kill him.

Salade caressed the snake's head amorously and said in an undertone:

—Take care. This is my lord and master.

—Capucine, answered the snake.

I was going to abandon these affected lovers and stretch out once again on the grass when for a second time I heard trumpeting close behind me. I turned around and saw a small car, a real child's plaything, coming full speed toward me. A little girl of five or six got out and said, lisping:

—That old woman who drags herself along the Seine leaning on a crutch has appointed herself an important mission. She cures sick animals. She goes along to all those noisy stores along the riverfront from which the sharp call of the parrokeet mingles with the meowing of the imprisoned cats, and where ferrets paw through the straw and monkeys bite at their bars, and she asks: "Any sick animals?"

"And they give her all the afflicted animals in the place. She opens the sharp beaks, the little jaws with quick teeth, lifts half-closed lids, carries off each invalid and treats him in her own way. She cured a magnificent rooster who now calls to her when she goes by his cage. She then requests a quarter hour's freedom for him and takes him to the neighbouring cafe. There is always a little mulled wine for the rooster who drinks solemnly with little sips, like a connoisseur.

She smiled and acted as if she wanted to go off, but she retraced her steps and said to me gravely:

—Listen: behind the horse, on the sidewalk which borders the iron garden, there is a pile of fine sand. Beautiful white sand, shiny and soft to the touch like rice powder. A man wearing a frock coat and carrying books under his arm came up to it yesterday and filled up a little box with sand. He chose carefully, wanting it clean, and blew away the remains of the leaves and branches that were mixed in with it. And he gave this explanation to an officer who was watching his actions with amusement:

"You understand, you can't find coloured sand to dry your handwriting anymore. Nowhere, do you understand! I've been to all the stores in Paris, all the bazaars. It isn't sold anymore: I was lucky no one laughed in my face. This sand is perfect for what I want. If only you knew how pretty it is on damp writing, once it has been dyed! Don't talk to me about blotting paper, it stains and takes up all the ink."

"And he left dragging his feet somewhat, still muttering:

"No, don't talk to me about blotting paper."

The child had suddenly become very sad and looked at me with eyes full of tears:

—Just think that I could . . . , she whispered. And she added, speaking to herself:

—I would like a cup of coffee.

Then, making a gesture which could have meant 'too bad', she passed her hand over the hood of her car, and disappeared as fast as possible.

Once again, a trumpet call rasped my ears and Mr. Coal woke up screaming:

—The heart, quickly! The heart!

And he took off at a run in the direction of the trumpeting. I followed as fast as I could; but it was not nearly as fast as he.

After running for an hour, we reached a telegraph pole which was oscillating oddly in all directions. A crow was flying around the pole, aiming to land on it. But the pole was oscillating so fast that he could not. Each time the crow managed to make the slightest contact with the pole, the trumpeting, which had so intrigued me and which had seemed to Mr. Coal to be a manifestation of the heart we had resolved to find, would sound.

In any case, either because it tired of its vain and repeated attempts, or because our arrival frightened him, the crow did not tarry, but flew off and disappeared. The pole stopped oscillating almost immediately. Mr. Coal undertook to climb up to the top in the hopes of finding some kind of clue that would help us find the heart. In fact he discovered a little tin fish armed with a fish-hook. But, the moment he touched the fish, it diminished by half.

—The heart has been by here, said Mr. Coal, showing me the fish.

—How do you know that?

—Hasn't the fish diminished in size? And look at this line which is beginning to appear on his back.

A thin black line was tracing itself down the back of the fish. It soon took on a brilliant black hue and grew to be two millimetres in width.

We considered this phenomenon in silence. Suddenly, Mr. Coal let out a cry: "It bit me!" And he let go of the fish, which flew off and disappeared in less than a second.

Mr. Coal lamented:

—We have let the heart escape. Now we will not see it here again, and it will be more difficult than ever to catch it tonight; it will be on its guard.

After a few moments of silence, he sighed and said:

—Just as the little snail shows its horns after the rain and takes its bath, so has the little fish, which was none other than our heart, flown off.

It was around four o'clock in the afternoon, Mr. Coal hit the ground three times with his forehead. From a cloud high overhead, a rain of strawberries beat down.

—It's the heart again, said Mr. Coal. It feels safe now and is making fun of us.

I was looking down at the ground around us and I realised that the strawberries had traced out letters. I read them: Life is short.

I communicated my discovery to Mr. Coal, who said to me:

—It is a warning. Someone has suspicions about our project. We are being watched. We must be cautious.

A gust of wind suddenly rustled the trees. A Japanese flag came down from the sky, stopped in front of us for a few moments, and returned from whence it came.

The sun was beginning to disappear over the horizon and there were long lines of kangaroos led by young girls who sang a delicious song:

The lady is on the tower
The tower is drunk like a steer
a bleeding steer
which eats acorns
while getting up
and spits blood
while lying down

The lady is on the tower
The tower was so high
the lady was so small
that one made a mistake
it was payday
in the willow grove
all the turnips
coddled themselves

the lady was so small
the tower was so big
that the almonds
and the ᴗnamoratas
were loving each other under the staircase

One of the kangaroos, an old bald female, stopped for a moment, and screeched at the top of her lungs:
— Last stop, everybody off.
She stretched out on the road. An egg slid from her abdominal pouch, rolled along the ground, and stood up on one of its ends, then split down the middle, letting out a small silk handkerchief which an evening breeze chased down a gully.
— The heart, he sighed. Take the handkerchief, I'll take the egg. I caught the handkerchief easily and Mr. Coal succeeded in taking the egg. But as he grabbed hold of it, Mr. Coal became the broom-seller. Out of surprise, I almost let the handkerchief escape.
I was very sorry about Mr. Coal's misadventure, especially since I wasn't yet sure if he had got hold of the heart. I asked him:
— Yes, he said, I even swallowed it, hence all my unhappiness.
But the heart was not complete, since I had the handkerchief, which I called to his attention.
— No matter, he answered, I am going to swallow the handkerchief as I swallowed the egg!
And he did so on the spot.
We set off again for the Marne. A hundred paces further on, Mr. Coal suddenly dissolved. From this liquid, spreading out at my feet, there instantly arose a little pine tree of the kind usually chosen as Christmas trees. The pine tree shook in all directions as if it were being shaken by violent gusts, although the breeze was hardly moving the leaves of the neighbouring trees. A clock struck seven. Dogs barked furiously, I could hardly make out the echo of a patriotic song, and, at the very moment I decided to look again at the tree, I realised that it was covered over with a metallic cloth like the kind found in a larder. A pestilential smell continued to exude from the tree, but it dissipated suddenly, at the moment when a stream of clear water poured out of the metallic cloth. This collapsed all at once and I saw Mr. Coal crushing grandfather clocks with hammer blows. Seeing my astonishment, he burst out laughing and ordered:
— Sprout some beans.
Mr. Coal had obviously lost his mind. I left him grinding his clocks and fled at a run. At the turn in the road, I found an enormous pebble, three metres high. I lunged toward it headfirst, and plunged inside. I was safe. I

could think about the future calmly. I settled in.
And that is where I wrote this story.

5. The Parasites Abroad

HIS IS HOW IT HAPPENED:

"I had gotten a ferrous[1] on the round[2] and was sliding into white[3] when I felt my stems being squeezed[4].

"I thought: "It's getting dry!"[5] but I was too far to express myself[6]. When there was some air[7], I found myself with the flutterers[8], at least fifteen pipes[9] above the dung[10], but you know, I never did like to play with smoke[11]; I had only one wish:to find myself back on the dung. I said to myself: "This isn't deaf[12], all I have to do is glide down the shootings."[13] But it was easier said than done. As I made the attempt I saw that the shootings and I were but one. It isn't funny to find oneself all of a

1. Ferrous: shell shard.
2. Round: head.
3. To slide into white: to faint.
4. To squeeze the stems: to take by the limbs.
5. It's getting dry: things are turning out badly.
6. To be too far to express oneself: to be too giddy to defend oneself.
7. When there was some air: when I came to.
8. The flutterers: the birds.
9. Pipe: metre.
10. Dung: soil.
11. To play with smoke: to find oneself up in the air in an unstable position.
12. Deaf: difficult.
13. To glide down the shootings: to slide along the branches, or a tree.

a sudden on the black payroll[14], particularly as there was no reason for it to end. I tried once more to leave the shooting, but it was all wind![15]

"I was shooting, and very shooting. I felt the knocker[16] going crazy in my suitcase[17]. I thought I had reached the last line of my chapter[18], I was biting[19] myself: a chatter[20] positioned itself on my occ[21], rolled onto my cornute[22], from there to my suitcase, descended to my perker[23] and burnt one of my stems.

"I cried like a Siren, unaware that, since my stem had been burned, I was no longer affixed to the shooting. I made a bowl[24] and fell on a flasht[25] which, instead of being tussed[26], plunged into my suitcase. It was not love![27] He, especially, exploded[28] and I didn't know how to make him leed[29].

"I had a blow[30]—I must have been a real balooka[31] not to have thought of this earlier. I set myself to making flowers[32], and after a few big tulips[33], the flasht's round emerged from my piston[34]. And he sang, how he sang; it was worse than La Chenal.·

"I kept pulling on the flasht's round, and after about ten rattles[35] of effort, I succeeded in disencumbering myself of the flasht. Free, he had nothing better to do than to play the sap[36]. As for me, I was in the floating woods[37], and yet, I take the geezer[38] as my witness, I hadn't had anything in my pouch[39] for two sets[40]. I had air stems[41], no doubt because I hadn't

14. To be on the black payroll: to be the leaves which create shade.
15. Wind: impossible.
16. Knocker: heart.
17. Suitcase: chest.
18. The last line of my chapter: my last moments to live.
19. To bite oneself: to deceive oneself.
20. Chatter: mouth.
21. Occ: forehead.
22. Cornute: nose.
23. Perker: stomach.
24. Bowl: movement.
25. Flasht: cat.
26. To tuss: to crush.
27. It was not love: it was not pleasant.
28. To explode: to be furious.
29. To leed: to leave rapidly.
30. Blow: idea.
31. Balooka: fool.
32. To make flowers: to excrete.
33. Tulip: excrement.
34. Piston: anus.
35. Rattle: minute.
36. Play the sap: to flee.
37. To be in the floating woods: to be drunk.
38. Geezer: God.
39. Pouch: the stomach.
40. Set: day.
41. To have air stems: to tremble on one's legs.

sacked[42] in such a long time; after ten pipes I melted[43] and didn't waste any time in balancing[44] myself. I came back to the air[45] smelling strawberries[46] falling on my round.

"–Good God, here's the discharge![47]

"This slap[48] had a magical effect, and the burner[49] reappeared. It could have been salty[50] and, as it was summer, the burner should have been above me. It was on my left and was approaching at full speed. Five or six rattles later, it was between my legs and my radish[51] was ready.

"Ah! What sweetness my pape![52] It was like a new blast[53] and everything blasted[54] inside me. I never would have socketed[55] this. And now I assure you it's all finished with bloomers[56]. You don't know! You don't know.

"After this the bloomer disappeared in a shooting.

"I felt that I had galled[57] a blast, and I blasted alone, and I blasted alone for straws[58] and straws. I left in the direction of the burner which had returned to its place in the hat[59], but after a few rattles, I felt that I could never get there, I fell again on the dung and plunged myself in entirely; but it was therm[60] and it thermed[61] more and more.

"Finally, I surfaced from the dung, but I noticed that I had galled a swan on a portfolio[62], and I had my buckles[63] to the wind. On the dung was a gilded fatty[64] in complete misery[65]. He made me a little sign with the dish[66] and yelled to me:

42. To sack: to eat.
43. To melt: to fall, to cave in.
44. To balance: to sleep.
45. To came back to air: to awaken.
46. Strawberries: large drops of rain.
47. Discharge: downpour.
48. Slap: word.
49. Burner: sun.
50. Salty: noon.
51. Radish: sexual organ.
52. Pape: friend, comrade.
53. Blast: dance.
54. To blast: to dance.
55. To socket: to imagine.
56. Bloomer: woman.
57. To gall: to become.
58. Straw: hour.
59. Hat: sky.
60. Therm: warmth.
61. To therm: to heat.
62. Portfolio: pond covered with lily pads.
63. Buckles: feathers.
64. Gilded fatty: general.
65. In complete misery: in formal dress.
66. Dish: hand.

"—Hey Lohengrin! Proceed to the rallying-point!

"—Shut up, I answered accomodating[67] him as best I could.

"—I am General Pau, do you understand. You will be shot. False Frenchman, traitor!

"—Shut your trap, you poop-grower.

"—Swearing at an officer . . . Oh! you rascal, it's courtmartial and public works! Oh! You rascal!

"I ran toward him and pointed[68] him on the stems. He slid into white, galled a swan, and I a gilded fatty. It was my turn: I seized him by the tubes[69] and boom! he was black[70]. . .

"I changed gleam[71] and crussed[72] for a long time: five straws at least. I had just gone through a shoot-grove[73] and I was walking along a moist[74] when, from an old shooting—black now for paws[75], the flasht that I had had so much difficulty getting rid of, emerged. It stood up straight on its hind stems and said to me:

"—I knew a little Japanese girl who wore claws on her nipples. She was a wicked little thing. She had a cage full of birds which also contained two hollow spheres of equal size, made of an extremely thin sheet of brass. One was completely empty and the other contained a solid sphere which was a few centimetres smaller. The little Japanese girl called the latter the male. When she held the two spheres next to each other in her hand, she experienced a sort of shiver which lasted a long time and repeated itself at the slightest movement.

"This little shiver, this gentle but prolonged tremor, was her delight. First she introduced the empty sphere into her vagina and touched it to the neck of her womb, then she inserted the other sphere. So, the slightest motion of the thighs, of the hips, or even the slightest tumescence of the internal reproductive organs instigated a voluptuous titillation which could be prolonged at will.

"So, would you believe it, I couldn't see her doing this without feeling the irresistable urge to eat a canary.

"Good day, Sir."

"And he left leaving an enormous compass on my round.

67. Accomodate: insult.
68. To point: to peck with a beak.
69. Tube: neck.
70. Black: dead.
71. To change gleams: to leave a place.
72. To cruss: to walk.
73. Shoot-grove: forest, woods.
74. Moist: river.
75. Paws: years.

"What does this mean? I wondered. Surely this flasht is fire[76] and I was going to grout[77] when, from the top of a shooting, a would-you[78] dissolved from shootlet[79] to shootlet and came to position itself on the north end of my compass. The magnetised needle, which was pointing toward the therm country[80], turned sharply and stopped clack[81] at due North.

"Divvy[82], I said to myself, what's going on?

Yet it wasn't deaf to my grip[83]: my round had galled a compass, or rather, the compass and my round were so well united that they were but one. I was very touted[84]. You see what a descent[85] I would have had on the Boulevard with such a round: the rebs[86] would have entramped[87] me, they would have said I was fire.

So, I was quite touted. It was then that I had the blow to shift[88] myself. For a blow, it was quite a blow, and I congratulated myself at once. I had barely shifted when I found myself behind the wheel of a taxi parked on the 'Toile[89]. I wasn't gripping anything anymore and I was russeting[90] around as if I was fire. The gogs[91] were russeting at me and seemed to be asking themselves what I was doing there and why I had such a fire look. Finally I resigned myself. I let out the clutch and took off at full speed towards the Porte Maillot. I hadn't gone a hundred pipes when I realised that the road was blocked.

"A herd of pules[92] moved out of a shell[93] located to the right of the Avenue de la Grande Armée, crossed the avenue at full gallop, re-entered a shell on the other side, re-emerged through a second-floor large[94] and, climbing on the backs of their papes who were arriving from the opposite direction, returned to the shell on the right side of the avenue, entered by a second-floor large, then came out again through a large on the third floor,

76. Fire: dead.
77. To grout: to leave.
78. Would-you: eye.
79. Shootlet: branch.
80. Therm country: the south.
81. Clack: immobile.
82. Divvy: exclamation expressing agitation.
83. Deaf to grip: difficult to understand.
84. Touted: bored, anxious.
85. Descent: bearing.
86. Rebs: policemen.
87. To entramp: to stop.
88. To shift: to undress.
89. The 'Toile: The Place de L'Etoile, in Paris.
90. To russet: to look.
91. Gogs: people.
92. Pules: horses.
93. Shell: house.
94. Large: window.

once again crossed the avenue on the backs of their papes, entered the shell on the left side of the avenue and so on and so forth so that the entire avenue was completely blocked.

"I was ponnered[95]: how could I continue on my way? I couldn't dream of passing over this herd of pules; they were too numerous and formed an insurmountable wall. I had a heroic—or brilliant, whichever you prefer— blow. I backed up a hundred pipes, started up in third gear, then, flooring the accelerator, gave it all the gas and came on the obstacle with all the speed of my twelve pule power.

"I got through without accident. When I say accident, I'm speaking for the cutlet[96]; for I killed two pules, and I'd barely cleared the wall when a horrifying explosion resounded, making the dung tremble and shaking the shells like houses-of-cards.

"I turned around, and there wasn't a single pule left. Instead, there was a pond full of mercury; but the strangest thing was that the Arc de Triomphe had disappeared. Above its place was the U.S.[97] holding a saucepan in his hand in which he was batting his lashes[98], saying: "I am Doctor Voronoff, listen carefully!" And he started telling this little story which I find quite stupid:

"—With the heads you can make fabulous furs which imitate pheasants.

"But it's mostly gardeners who use them, not only as reservoirs, but for intensive farming as well.

"One can, in she-wolves, find the means to make rustic living-room furniture.

"The bottom makes the bottom, the beans the backboard, and the legs and the mass are so constructed, it looks like a piece of bentwood furniture.

"With two bottoms and three handles one can have a little end table that's both elegant and rustic; similarly, one can build some very pretty strangers. Barrels and kiosks can be constructed by using circles covered in silk which one sows seeds on.

"Finally, the old, cut in half, can be used by those who have no tubs, to take baths."

"After these slaps, he emptied his saucepan full of lashes[99] over the head of a reb who was just below him and who I recognised as General Joffre. the hero of the Marne, as he is known. (And what about me?) One can't say it wasn't funny: Oh how one can cuffle[100] with people!

95. To be ponnered: to be undecided.
96. Cutlet: me.
97. U.S.: Unknown Soldier.
98. To bat one's lashes: to urinate.
99. Lashes: urine.
100. To cuffle: to have fun.

"I left at full speed. That's when I met you in the Boulogne Shoot-grove, cracking[101] with a bloomer who was screaming: "Oh the wonderful mushrooroooroom!"

"—And so, what do you think of that?

"—I think we could scratch the salt[102] and spend our holidays at Deauville.

"—You're right, let's grout to Deauville."

.

101. To crack: to make love.
102. To scratch the salt: to take a train without a ticket.

6. Lovely Stories Continue but Don't Stay the Same

ETTER FROM THE HONOURABLE
MINISTER OF DELICATE INSTRUMENTS TO MISS LANTERN

My dear friend,

Believe me that I was sincerely afflicted when I learned of the loss you suffered: a steam powered urinal is not easily replaced. Yours, which had, among other precious peculiarities, the ability to sing the *Marseillaise* when in use, was certainly worthy of the esteem you bestowed upon it. So, it is easy for me to understand the despair that your sister felt when it became evident that the urinal was definitively lost. Nevertheless, from that to suicide is quite a step! And, although I know that many fond memories were associated with its possession, I cannot but condemn such a fatal resolve. But this censure does not prevent me from profoundly deploring her sad end. A suicide is always, for those close to the deceased, a tragic and agonising event; but when it is accomplished by means of jam, one cannot be less than terrified. Never would I have believed that your sister could resolve to die embedded in a vat of jam! And yet, all those unlucky enough to befriend her knew of her almost morbid attraction to jam, even in jars. Do you remember how she could not contain herself when she saw it with desserts, how she had to caress it even before serving herself? Numerous incidents of this nature should have aroused our suspicion; but, blind that we were, we never understood their profound significance. Her love of jam was in the end but the love of death by jam; and it took the completion of her fatal gesture for us to understand it all. Nonetheless, I shiver at the thought of how her last moments must have been.

Please believe that I share your pain, and approve of your decision to banish jam from your life. This is a healthy reaction and I can only commend it from the bottom of my heart. It demonstrates both your determination, and your courage in overcoming pain, as well as your instinct for self-preservation. I am truly glad that without jam, you do not, indeed, risk letting yourself be compelled to follow the example of your sister.

LETTER FROM MISS LANTERN TO LOHENGRIN

Dear friend,

I have faith in no one but you. You have demonstrated your regard for me too often for me to doubt it, or for me to be other than blindly trusting. Shall I recall the matter of the trees in the squares of Paris, which were found one morning, split along the whole length of their trunks, and which you understand so well how to re-glue? Or else, the cooking of the generals' heads, a feat which no one had performed successfully until you undertook it? Nonetheless, all of that belongs to the past, although in my heart it is very much of the present; and I would abstain from discussing it for fear of offending your friendship had I not, for the past two days, been gripped by horrible anguish because of my scissors. No, I have not lost them! Nor have they fled—as I believed for a moment—at the sight of the Basset hound which you gave me; but since then, they have not stopped snip-snipping and it is awful, unbearable, the relentless hairdresser noise which deprives me of all tranquility and sleep. Not to mention the incredible damage they are doing to my home! I have no more stockings, no more curtains, no more hair, and all my furniture has been reduced to dust. Moreover, I no longer dare leave my room, which is now locked and barricaded for fear of their fury. I was obliged to throw this letter out the window in order to get it to you. This should prove how horrible is my situation. You are the only one who can save me. Help me quickly or I shall die a victim of my scissors.

LETTER FROM LOHENGRIN TO THE
HONOURABLE MINISTER OF DELICATE INSTRUMENTS

Mr. Minister,

Since yesterday I have been in the possession of the four padlocks and the brain of a fossilised calf which you so kindly sent to me in order to demonstrate the effectiveness of the French army. Let me first of all show my gratitude and admiration for the precision of your demonstration. As for speed, I must admit that, if one takes into account the small number of troops engaged in the manoeuvre, it could not have been greater. The minimal number of our losses proves the enemy was terror-stricken by the quantity of medals which decorate the chests of our brave officers, and surrendered without combat. The legendary courage of the regiment was responsible for the rest.

Yesterday, at the cinema, I saw our troops' victorious entrance into the town of Peplum. I felt a lump in my throat, and a flood of tears down my face during the solemn ceremony of the transfer of Clovis' padlocks, stolen during the Hundred Year's War—at the time of the sacking of Feves—by two or three dogs. For so many centuries our hereditary enemies have refused to return them! That we should have taken advantage of this to procure the fossilised brain of the last calf eaten by Charlemagne before his death, is but the fair reward for the inordinate efforts and suffering of our troops and their valiant officers.

Your name is henceforth linked to these memorable exploits, and the resolve which you demonstrated in this delicate affair is forever attached to your person. You have had a carping critic; now you have a firm friend.

LETTER FROM LOHENGRIN TO MISS DEMOLISHED

Madam,

Ignorance of the law is no excuse! I feel obliged to repeat this to you after our conversation of yesterday.

Ignorance of the law is no excuse, not for you or any other person. Consequently, you should be aware that murders are forbidden during times of peace; and that he who commits acts of this nature risks prison—where one lives permanently in the society of enormous rats—and sometimes, the guillotine.

During times of war, the situation is quite different: murder is not only tolerated, but encouraged, and even glorified under the name of heroism. But we are in a time of peace.

There are, by the way, some lovely wartime expressions that indicate that many men have been murdered: "The enemy's losses are very heavy"; or, even better: "The enemy has experienced considerable losses." Fortunately, we are not in this situation, and, at this time, it is not permitted to kill those whom one hates, nor those who detest you.

I remind you of all this in order to warn you one last time of the dangers that you risk if you decide to execute your plan. Regardless of what you might think, you have no valid motive for killing moths. I repeat, they are not your enemies; and they have done nothing to you. Nor do they constitute a political threat to you. Consequently, I cannot understand why you want to kill them. Because they steal, you say. But then, why not flies, beetles, pigeons, etc . . . ?

I beseech you, think seriously before you commit an irreparable act; but, no matter what happens, believe in my sincerest friendship.

LETTER FROM MR. COAL TO MRS. PLASTER

My beauty,

I have just emerged from a terrible ordeal. A murder was committtted by an individual waiting on the edge of the sidewalk.

At last, my aunt Victorine brings me good news: the fresh catch has arrived from Boulogne, and the eggs will be sent postage paid.

In the course of a pleasant walk that I used to take in the disturbing countryside which surrounds the chateau, I once encountered a stag which had a peculiar bearing. He raised his head toward the sky, imploring the help of the first bats. Boulogne was patiently awaiting the moment to infect them with St. Vitus' dance. I am fortunate to be blessed with a better life, more concerned with the vital, economic, and symbolic interests of our beloved country.

Is he white? The cassock of a priest would be able to inflict a considerable injury on him, and I assure you that a trial will be called for immediately.

Well! Donkey! This flag will bring you victory.

Valiant mothers of families, take up your swords again, and may your gazes skim the thunder! May your husbands be tigers bounding like Russian zebras across the unexplored pampas!

Some potatoes have already arrived; but to bury them will, alas, take but an instant.

Noblesse oblige: we still know about housekeeping, and I can assure you that the purse will only be green for boors.

Finally, I hereby present to your eminent person one last sketch done from memory.

Please examine.

LETTER FROM THE WHITE WINE TO THE GATEKEEPER

Dear Sir and friend,

Good debts make good neighbours. The gift of dust that you sent me the other day has indeed arrived; and I immediately remitted it to the proper authority. I hope that he will know how to use it in the next war against France, that country which only knows how to make umbrellas. You must tell everyone that Pasteur died under the following circumstances:

His last experiments having produced no result, Pasteur fell ill. One of his neighbours took a liking to him, nursed him, and cured him. Out of gratitude as much as emotion, Pasteur married her. Thanks to her, he became involved with the broom-seller who had become her lover. Those two wretches, finding him an annoyance, resolved to rid themselves of him by injecting him with shampoo, of which he died after several days.

I think this is some news which will interest the populace. Ask on this same occasion, your employer to send me a few trees—even fruit trees, a golden icthyosaurus, seven metre sugar-tongs for giant cubes, four microscopic faucets, a carriage gate, a low-flying lemon, well squeezed, a large potato pierced by a bullet and a photograph of a decapitated man—located in jar number eighteen on the square desk of his office number 25.

Assure him of my most complete devotion, and believe me, dear Sir and friend, to be sincerely yours.

LETTER FROM THE GATEKEEPER TO MISS DEMOLISHED

My dear child,

The rainy season is over, the organs will soon bloom. How beautiful is the bile flower! And nothing equals the perfume of testicles opening in the evening. Now is the moment to hoe your garden, if you don't, the bile vesicles will perish, smothered by weeds. Above all, do not forget, at sundown, to let out the magic cretins which you have fattened on dust throughout the whole dry season. They will be marvelous during the hunt for dried sausages—which are so harmful to the development of spiral encephalons that the authorities are offering a reward of up to twenty francs per sausage. Certainly you have here a prime source which it would be wrong to neglect, since your garden, being so full of blooms, must be infested with them.

I am sending you the crossbow you requested for protecting the golden crumbs. I chose a fairly large one so that you can also use it to kill the salt crystals which attack the beautiful shrieks on your ornamental lake. Though you certainly did not ask me, I thought it appropriate to send you one hundred octohedric flies with paternal blessings. They will be indispensable to you if you have—which is likely—rainbows sighing in your underbrush. And if, by chance, you don't, they will be useful in a strong wind, for protecting the muslin whispers from the black ideas which would devour them in no time.

I leave at your disposal a magnificent tidal wave which is wonderful against the too ardent rays of the summer sun. I have already used it with great success. I guarantee that these rays are effectively stopped four metres from the ground, and stay there whimpering like a young dog whose owners have left him locked in the house.

I remain, my dear child, your ever adoring one; and wish only to kiss your mignonette hand.

LETTER FROM THE HONOURABLE
MINISTER OF DRIFTING BOATS TO THE WHITE WINE

My dear colleague,

It's not for nothing that I was nicknamed the terror of Sebastopol street. When I pass near the square of Arts-et-Metiers, it stands aside for me, and the department stores lower their metal shutters. You cannot, then, doubt that I exercise a sovereign authority in this neighbourhood that no one dares contest.

I did not write to you for the purpose of receiving advice. I expect something completely different from you: some money. In your interest as well as that of France and other countries, if not, beware! I will not back down for anything. I will not hesitate to replace all the bridges with waste-paper baskets and to root cops there. I will even, if your obstinacy forces me, go so far as to melt all the churches into floods of sticky mud which will flow across the cities so that the inhabitants will be obliged to evacuate via the roofs for fear of being stuck in the streets. I am the emissary of the good wooden god and I can make your happiness just as easily as your unhappiness and that of the whole earth as well, by letting loose the loneliness which will cover everything like a tidal wave.

I will wait for you at the Porte Maillot tomorrow at midnight. I demand that you come alone, otherwise I will let the loneliness loose; and you know as well as I do what to expect from that.

Do not displease me because all the madmen are on my side. I have them in the palm of my hand like a fistful of pepper. Take care that I do not throw them in your face.

Until tomorrow.

LETTER FROM THE WHITE WINE TO THE BEAUTIFUL BLUE DANUBE

Sir,

Last night I saw you at the corner of the Place des Victoires and the Rue Etienne-Marcel. It was after two in the morning. Huddled in the shadows, you were spying on someone—I can easily guess who. You were waiting for Mr. Coal in order to pull out his moustache. Fortunately, at this hour, Mr. Coal was quietly eating screw thread soup with his family; but what would have happened had you succeeded? The victim's shouts at the moment you robbed him of his moustache—I have no doubt your boot hook would have enabled you to do this—would have been, first of all, the rallying cry of all the pigeons in Paris who would then have gathered in the vicinity of the Opera; and secondly, of all the rats in the capital who could have oeverrun the same area, destroying it in the twinkling of an eye. The area round the Opera destroyed, the pigeons would have thrown themselves on the rats which they would have massacred to the last one in no time. And, I ask you, what then would the Parisians have eaten in the event of a siege?

I understand, without sharing it, your hatred of Mr. Coal, who allowed himself, improperly, I admit, to transform your islands into wooden carousel horses, which have attracted perpetual snow, and the accompanying thick concrete clouds, onto themselves. Take revenge on him if you must. Eliminate him, if his death will bring you peace; but do not cut off his moustache, I beg of you. The consequences of the loss of his moustache will be too serious for the tens of thousands of people who are uninvolved in your mutual hostility.

If you kill him, I assure you that I will keep silent. But, if you persist in your current project, you will find me against you, violin in hand; and you know that I will be merciless.

LETTER FROM MR. KINDLING TO THE
HONOURABLE MINISTER OF OVERHOT BATHS

Mr. Minister,

It was with the greatest interest that I noticed the letter, which you were so kind as to bring to my attention, from the rain to the fair weather. To be sure, I cannot but agree with the rain when it states that fair weather "excites the dogs which roam in packs along the highways, roads, and footpaths, barking day and night, so much so that the residents, deprived of sleep, are incapable of going about their regular occupations." I have known this scourge too often in the district which I represent not to wish that everything should be done to avoid a recurrence. I have already suggested, to this effect, that cornbread obstacles be placed in all the main arteries of the infested region. These obstacles should, through various convolutions, form a circle, in such a fashion that well-placed observers will have only to close the entrance to cause the dogs to perish, strangled by the corn. Meanwhile, the rain's proposal to channel all the dogs toward depilatory centres strikes me as dangerous, since everyone knows that a hairless dog attacks barnyard animals, particularly poultry, which it decapitates; the dog's speed— accelerated by depilation—prevents any interference. This certain massacre represents incalculable losses for our agricultural economy, losses which are in no way compensated for by the expected benefits that the sale of dog hair will have for the hat industry. I suspect that it will be necessary to put the dogs, upon their departure from the depilation centre, through a bath of linseed oil in an attempt to sooth their anger.

Otherwise, the rain is displaying very clear signs of sectarianism in accusing the fair weather of provoking the multiplication of granite quarries which destroy the beauty of our landscapes and discourage tourists from visiting our country. No! this evil comes from elsewhere. It comes from the growth of traffic on the waterways. The increase in the number of barges brings with it the necessity of finding them a cargo. And granite is their cargo of choice. The productivity of the old quarters being insufficient to fill the barges, it was necessary to satisfy these new demands. The remedy is thus simple; it is not at all necessary that the fair weather be forced to eat the scrap iron that is usually thrown into the quarries to precipitate their closing. This creates too great a risk of the fair weather attacking the forests which it could, in fact, petrify at leisure.

Have faith, Mr. Minister, in my heartfelt respect.

7. Elephant on Wheels

T THE CINEMA THEY WERE PLAYING A sad film in which the perfect blond heroine—who sold beauty products for a living—cried, sobbed and gasped incessantly, although the script in no way justified this flood of tears. The broom-seller, who was in the audience, was not in the least affected by the sadness emanating from the screen. On the contrary! This unjustified despair inspired in him a harsh strained laugh which scandalised all the other spectators. Absorbed in his laughter, he did not notice that the others were sobbing. Suddenly, the film stopped, and on the screen appeared a sort of full-jowled Quasimodo who was swallowing a live vulture with some difficulty. The latter was battering its wings in his stomach, which was being distorted by the most ridiculous commotions. The audience, quite indifferent, continued to cry with more determination than ever. Indeed, the sobs were flowing so abundantly that the auditorium was flooded completely and people were wading in tears. The spectators' despair redoubled and the level of tears rose. The theatre management began to get worried. Quickly the film was exchanged for another one entitled 'Various ways of preparing snails'. A whisper travelled through the room and the management thought it had won the contest. Alas, the audience was sobbing even more copiously and the seats began to float on the tears and a veritable tempest was now stirring them up, to the point that little by little, the audience—now beginning to add hiccups to its

111

wailing—became stricken with seasickness. Not a single snail had shown up on the screen—which of course added to the audience's anguish. Instead, they appeared all over the room, on the seats, in the men's moustaches, the women's hair and under their dresses, on the walls and even in the orchestra, which was now also afloat. The musicians fought with difficulty against this rising tide of snails. The cornet was blowing forth bunches of them and the violins were sawing them out by the dozen. The situation was becoming untenable and the management resolved to open the doors so that the mounting flood of tears could escape, even if the spectators might be carried off by the current. But this became unnecessary, since the doors gave way under the pressure of the tears which, careering torrentially into the street, swept away pedestrians and cars, like dead leaves carried off by the wind.

The broom-seller had been carried away like the other spectators but, while all the others were crying with sadness and despair, he continued to explode with laughter without even knowing why. Unconcerned by the current dragging him away, he continued to laugh, flopped on his seat like calves' lights. And his thundering laugh made the windows burst as he passed, rustling the leaves on the trees, and even the flood of tears laughed privately to itself. It had good reason to laugh, actually, and if the broom-seller had known what was in store for him, his hilarity would have been dampened. Parked at the bottom of a hill was a huge removal van which the tumultuous flood of tears, although still rising unstaunched, was incapable of carrying off. It was as if the broom-seller and his cinema seat were being thrown toward the removal van. A simple eddy in the flood of tears sufficed to sweep the seat and its occupant into the vehicle, which appeared to be waiting for nothing so much as this moment, for its doors immediately shut and it took off.

The broom-seller did not notice right away that he'd been locked up and kidnapped. It was not until he heard the explicit tones of the van's motor that he calmed down and started to look around him. This was, truth to tell, quickly accomplished, since there was nothing to see, given the total obscurity reigning inside the vehicle. But this simple deduction provoked his first note of worry: "Where am I?" he asked himself. And he had to admit that he was unable to answer this simple question. Then, suddenly noticing that the van was moving at full speed, he felt quite obliged to ask himself: "Where are we going?" and was equally obliged to admit that he had no ideas on this subject either.

Half-floating, half-driving, the removal van continued on its way. It had long since left the town and was driving through a forest which, seeing the flood of tears reaching almost up to the lower branches of its trees, thought its final hour had come. The frightened birds had abandoned their nests and, assuming that the sea was overwhelming the forest, the titmice, the nightingales and the finches felt their feet becoming webbed. As soon as their webs were adequate, they stopped cheeping and landed on the flood of tears and began bathing in it, quarrelling all the while. Then a blackbird did a timid cancan, immediately followed by a finch; and soon the tears were covered with forest birds doing the cancan as best they could.

The broom-seller was pacing like a caged tiger inside the removal van which was speeding on its way. Unable to think of any enemies, he asked himself anxiously why he was being kidnapped, and by whom; he understood nothing at all of what was happening to him. He could stare at the walls of his rolling prison as much as he liked: not the tiniest crack which might allow him to see outside. Little by little a diffuse gleam outlined a rectangle on the back of the vehicle; and on this rectangle, forms, rather vague at first, started to move. A film was being mysteriously projected on the back of the van. He tried to become interested in what was being shown. In vain. It is really quite difficult to become engrossed in a film while it is raining straw. And it was raining down so thick and fast that the broom-seller was soon covered with straw which he found himself struggling in, half suffocated, while strange noises like the screeching of saws and screams, ranging from inarticulate exclamations to incoherent proclamations like "Hot chestnuts!" or "Vive la France!", occasionally rang out.

Fear was catching up with the broom-seller, for whom this scenario was beginning to suggest a forthcoming cataclysm whose nature he was trying to divine:

Would it be a rain of toothbrushes beating down the harvests and reducing the country to famine, a gelatinous tidal wave, or the City of Paris dissolving like a sugar cube in a cup of tea? At any rate, nothing good was to be expected, and it was with the greatest suspicion that the broom-seller observed an opening forming in one side of the van. Nonetheless, he disengaged himself from the straw and approached it cautiously. He leaned his head out and saw nothing, since the night was very black and the horizon was just barely lit by the distant gleams of a great fire. All he could hear was the stream of tears beating on the sides of the van which continued to move along. Suddenly, he made up his mind: what did he have to lose? At least, once out of the van, he would be free to go wherever he wished. He braced himself and leapt as far out of the orifice as possible, in order not to be run over by the van and, to his great surprise, fell into a heap of barbed wire which was emerging from the tears. He rose all bloody and scratched, and resolved to remain there and await the dawn, which was indeed imminent, since the eastern horizon was already becoming stained with a green which was rapidly intensifying. Finally, the sun appeared. But it was green, and even the naked eye could see that it waned and waxed like an accordion. The broom-seller's heart froze with terror. The green sun and the tears—also green—which extended as far as the eye could see, made it perfectly clear what lilypad fate awaited him. He could not resign himself to floating indefinitely on a sea of tears, even if it meant he would bloom with large flowers.

Suddenly the sun yawned like a dog waking up, and breath reeking of garlic polluted the atmosphere. A kazoo came and fell into the heap of barbed wire the broom-seller was tangled in. He grabbed it and blew into it. A long whine and several tears emerged, which burst and expelled lumps of foam all around, which floated on the sea of tears. Delighted, the broom-seller continued to blow into the kazoo, continuing to to produce teary fireworks which burst into foam and settled all about him. Of course, there was the unfortunate whimpering of wounded beasts, but he got used to that. This was a mistake, as they did not get used to him. When the sea of tears was covered over with a thick rug of foam, circumstances changed rapidly for the broom-seller, who had the unfortunate notion of lying down on it. Barely had he stretched out when the kazoo's whimpering became extraordinarily loud. They were no longer whimpers but veritable roars which destroyed his eardrums and slowly dug a tunnel through his head. When the tunnel was completed, a train full of merchandise emerged from the barbed wire heap and plunged into the tunnel from whence it never emerged. Meanwhile the cattle-trucks gave way to platforms full of enormous machines whose function no one could describe.

The broom-seller no longer had the strength to fight against his fate. He was in shock, stupefied by the switchings, the collisions, the shuntings under way in the tunnel in his head. Switching yard! Now he'd become a switching yard! This thought was killing him and yet he continued to blow mechanically into the kazoo, which let out more and more horrifying shrieks, while the sun, overjoyed, burst out laughing and filled the air with a hideous smell of garlic which the foam inhaled with delight. The foam puffed up to the size of a tree-trunk. Suddenly the broom-seller expired like the 'quack' of a bugle and the trunks of foam clashed together in one immense round of applause. But, although dead, the broom-seller was not yet a corpse. This was obvious when he started to rub his hands, first gently and then with a growing vigour, so much so that a high clear flame soon spurted from between his palms which he squeezed and rubbed together at a positively fantastic rate. When the flame had attained a height of a dozen or so centimetres, the broom-seller was seized with convulsive somersaults, and lava started to flow from his hands and then to fall into the tears, where it produced huge jets of reddish steam which soon obscured the sun, even though it was blowing upon it harder and harder. The garlic-saturated atmosphere had become unbreathable, though it began to seem that the broom-seller was slowly coming back to his wits as his hands were already letting out cries of rage which were provoking discombombulated agitation in the sun. The sun folded and unfolded itself endlessly like some immense green accordion and responded to the broom-seller's cries of rage with recommendations to be calm, recommendations which went unheard by the broom-seller since his cries of rage, repeated by the thousands of echoes created by the waves of tears, were filling the air with a deafening thunder, which the foam trunks could not bear without trembling with fear.

The broom-seller's hands were taking on gigantic proportions as was the volcano in full eruption which had formed between his palms. And the lava continued to flow merrily and the clouds of steam were becoming more and more dense, filling the air with the smell of violets, which combined very disagreeably with the stale smell of garlic exhaled by the sun.

The chaos reached its climax. Suddenly, one of the trunks of foam rose up and Mr. Coal emerged from the sea of tears, upright like a sinking ship. He raised his right hand demanding silence and so the broom-seller and the sun quietened down. He then cried out so loudly that a tempest unleashed itself in the sea of tears and nearly carried off the broom-seller: "The nation is in danger!" At that moment violent eddies were produced in the sea and the broom-seller started turning as if his feet were fixed to a moving axle and the sun let out a garlic roar comparable to that of a hundred furious lions. Impassive, Mr. Coal continued to cry at the top of his lungs: "The nation is in danger!" The broom-seller was now turning like half a plane propeller working off a motor at full throttle. Suddenly, the broom-seller spun off his axle, swept the entire field of vision and went to crush himself against the horizon, where he exploded with the noise of spurting steam, all the while projecting immense flames which nearly put out the sun.

Mr. Coal fainted like a dandelion pistil carried off by the wind while pulling along the sea of tears, beneath which appeared a heavy carpet of soap bubbles which burst in the sun. Then the soap bubbless disappeared in their turn and all that remained was the smell of garlic and the victorious sun choking with laughter.

Winter 1922-1923

The Inn of the Flying Arse

, THE UNDERSIGNED, BENJAMIN PÉRET, CERTIFY that these lines were taken down from my dictation, the first section before making love, and the second after.

1. — Before

The man with the wild bollock came down from the tree he had been living in since his first marriage. In each hand he held a sexual organ, from which emerged millions of little larvae which immediately flew off and settled on some large blue flowers. At the larvae's touch, the flowers reared up as if they were made of rubber.

The man was a double male. He advanced toward a rock where a line of vaginas was becoming visible at eye-level. With his finger, he touched one of them, which made a high pitched sound, the second one made an even higher pitched sound, and the third to the touch proved to be as sensitive as an eyebrow. He pressed his thumb on the fourth one with all his might, and the stone gave way. As the stone gave way, two large white arms, and two legs just as white as the arms, appeared and were instantly covered with roses.

The man disappeared, while, in place of the vagina, a long stream of sulphur ran down to the ground. Not far from there, a great yellow flower which was half opened, came off its root, then wound itself around a tree— some kind of magnolia. It stuck itself onto one of the tree's flowers, which

116

then disappeared into its corolla; and a few minutes later, sulphur could be seen dripping from there as well.

From the place where the man disappeared now came the sound of a propeller turning at full speed, and each second, fragments of bone and flesh emerged from the hole through which the man had entered.

Four flies and twò fat spiders started turning silently around the little pile of bone and flesh which itself began to turn as well. Soon a head was formed and then an arm, a leg, a sex, and the entire body of a newborn baby appeared.

The child brought his hand to his sex which was male, the flies and the spiders disappeared through the same hole as the man. The child, his hand on his sex, began to come. The trees, the animals, the rocks began to curl up until they all began to trace the form of a vagina. The child got up, ran to the tree which he tried to grab, but the tree liquified and poured through his hands, he ran toward the rocks and they flew off.

Once again the child touched his sex with his finger and climaxed. A hedge of male organs came up on either side of him, and the child flew off, followed by two breasts, one white, the other black. He landed some distance away, on the bank of a river; and there he saw emerging from the water the man with the wild bollock, his hands full of excrement which blossomed on contact with the air. A small brain fell with a whistling sound and penetrated the child's skull, ensuring his proper mental development.

The man put the child in his belly, and two Spanish girls threw themselves at his feet, kissing his member with passion. Suddenly, they became round, and took on spots like those of a leopard.

The man stiffened as if he were about to die; the girl who at that moment was licking his member stiffened as well. And the two of them, caught in a propeller-like motion, penetrated an electric cloud and fell at the feet of God.

2. – After

The rug merchant stopped in front of the inn and said: Fresh young girls, nice white little boys! Who wants some, Ladies and Gentlemen?

The man with a fishscale navel, who had one hand on his head, woke up from the long nap he had just taken in the company of a negress: the one he had brought back from a country where the plants move around and make love while walking. He took out his revolver and shot at the merchant, but he had forseen the shot and threw himself to the ground, taking more or less the form of a turtle.

By staring at the electric lights, he started to get drunk. The little stargirl came by, and sold her little perfumed stars to all comers, so she was able to get a meal that evening.

The man with the fishscale navel was again the first to awaken. A dove bearing the olive branch fluttered above his head. He opened the window, the air was pure, the sky was blue, the birds were singing, but all the men were eating in the trees with the hens, and the cocks were in the women's beds.

It was the morning of April 2nd, 1922, and the machines were suffering like women in labour. Only the man who had thrown himself to the ground like a tortoise stretched out his head toward the vulva which he could see a short distance away, but for each forward movement he attempted, the vulva made a corresponding movement further away.

A teal, happening to pass between them, understood their agitation, and consented to stretch itself out in order to link them together. With the tip of its beak pressed to the vulva and one webbed foot on the man's head, the teal turned round and round.

The man with the fishscale navel saw them and burst out laughing, saying:

"You really are gluttons for punishment my poor children."

The Condemned Man's Last Night

UST LET ME FIX MY HAIR AND I'LL BE RIGHT with you."

It was me speaking and I was perched on one of the highest branches of a hundred-year old chestnut tree. It was raining hard. Children were playing at the foot of the tree. Inside the trunk, which was hollow and held together only by its bark, a hen was endlessly laying eggs, breaking each one with sharp pecks as it dropped.

The person I was talking to was smoking a big pipe made of blue glass, which was actually a hollowed-out insulator attached to a reed; he was a young farmer from the area, who took off his goatee and put it in his pocket when he was tired, particularily at night.

I climbed down from my tree and, taking my friend by the arm, went off hunting, although the regulations forbade it at this time of year.

. . . .

At that moment, the door of my cell clattered open, and an eight-year old child dragging a small pitch black goat entered at the head of a crowd of people I did not know. Among them was my defence lawyer. He was holding a pair of braces which he was staring at obstinately, and his lips were moving, pronouncing words I could not make out. "Hello, Papa," said the child as he pushed the goat under the bed.

One of the men I did not know came up to me and said:

—Benjamin Péret, you know what is happening.

ME. — No.

119

HIM. – Write what you wish.

ME. – I haven't anything to write.

HIM. – Fine, get dressed.

I dressed, shaved with care, out of habit unplugged my electric light-bulb, read a few verses of the Bible as well as a chapter of Apollinaire's "Eleven Thousand Pricks", and announced that I was ready.

On the way, the conversation never faltered. I told my lawyer about my projects. As soon as I got out of prison, I intended to take up my profession again, since I considered it to be the most beautiful of all. I was planning to rape, and afterwards murder with new and unheard-of forms of torture, a young woman I had met one day on a road near Epinal and who I had followed all the way home—not without declaring that she was the fairest of all, and that if she would allow me to love her, I would be infinitely happy. She smiled slightly and gave me a little bird which had only one leg. I kept it for a long time. It lived in my breast pocket; here, look.

My lawyer was a charming man who knew what life was about and, even as I spoke, I felt him won over to my ideas, my ambitions. Murder, is it not one of the most delicate pleasures given to man?

—You know, I said to him, when I feel a long sharp dagger in my hand and when the dagger plunges into the chest of a young girl or into the face of one of those men who read the evening paper in their shirtsleeves by the window . . .

I sensed that this life tempted him and, as it would have pleased me if the man who had defended me with so much talent at the Assizes were to continue with me in the work I had undertaken, that is, the popularisation of crime, I developed the arguments which seemed to me the most favourable to my proposition. And so, when we arrived in the prison yard after a period of time which seemed to me very short or very long (it is difficult to appreciate time), he was completely disposed to kill one of the people who was accompanying us so that, he said, we could profit from the confusion and escape.

Once in the prison yard I saw the guillotine and found myself, with no noticeable transition, in a state of astonishing sexual excitement. I think, had I had the opportunity, I could have made love to fifteen women in a row. Nonetheless, I mastered myself and, addressing Mr. Deibler, I asked him for permission to have a word with the head guard of the prison.

I told this fine man how sad I was to leave him and what pleasant memories I held of the friendly relations we had established. As a token of my feelings I told him that I would sow, in the sunniest part of the prison yard, a cherry stone; and I made him promise that he would devote the greatest care to its cultivation. When he gave me this promise, I explained how sweet it was for me to think that in a few years, when the seed had become a tree, he would gather delicious fruit. I asked of him only to give a handful to those who would come, like myself, to expiate their crimes, even though I did not think that my crimes deserved any punishment whatsoever. My lawyer murmured agreement— Dear friend—.

Then it was the priest's turn to tell me that I should not die without asking God's forgiveness for my faults. This time I lost my temper and, straightening my shoulders, I told him squarely that I had no faults to be pardoned. He quickly made the sign of the cross and began telling his rosary silently, which greatly annoyed me.

Mr. Deibler came toward me and, with a politeness which touched me deeply, asked if I was ready. Upon my affirmative answer, he prepared me according to the custom* for a condemned man. Once this was done, I walked forward, supported by Mr. Deibler and my lawyer, toward the guillotine, next to which the aides were standing ready. The three of us were singing "Die Wacht am Rhein." In the distance a mechanical piano was grating out Beethoven's Fifth Symphony.

As I was about to take my place on the rocker* I asked to make a telephone call.

—To whom? asked Mr. Deibler.

—It doesn't matter, I just want to telephone.

He did not want to refuse me. I requested a number. It was that of an admiral who, without giving me time to speak, announced that he was leaving Paris to board his ship. He was to take part in naval manoeuvres in the Mediterranean. I hung up. I was thrown on the rocker. I found myself in the same state of sexual excitement as when I first saw the guillotine. Mr. Deibler noticed and enjoined one of his aides to satisfy me.

—Since he is about to die and there are no women here, he said, you may as well satisfy him.

Never in my life had my fulfilment been so complete: it is true that I was about to die. Indeed, a few minutes later, the blade of the guillotine came down on my head. Justice was done, as the old saying goes . . .

One to One

O WAKE UP IN THE BOTTOM OF A CARAFE, STUNNED like a fly, is enough to make you kill your mother five minutes after you get out. That is what happened to me one morning, so it's no surprise that I should have a head shaped like a dandelion and that my shoulders now sag down to my knees. During the first few minutes after I woke up, I imagined that I had always lived at the bottom of a carafe and probably I'd still believe it if I had not seen this sort of bird on the other side of the carafe, pecking furiously at it with his beak. Thanks to this, the fortuitous and unpleasant features of my situation became clear to me and I flew into a rage. I seized a dry leaf by my side and shoving it into my left nostril, cried out: "Is it possible that the dog is the turtle's best friend?" And, from the top of the carafe, a crack in the glass murmured: "Poor idiot! Enemies are not what the dumb masses think. They have beards and their brains are made of celluloid scrapings and potato peelings. Friends have glass heads and bite like transmission belts."

But I insisted: "Is it true that flies do not die on the hands of a clock? Is it true that rice straw is used to make dumplings? Is it true that oranges gush out of mine shafts? Is it true that mortadella is made by blind people? Is it true that quails eat ewes? Is it true that noses get lost in fortresses? Is it true that bathrooms fade away into pianos? Is it true that in dark rooms the song of dreams is never heard?"

Suddenly there was a great noise like a pot falling and rebounding on a stone staircase and a small opening appeared in my prison. Mercifully for me, it did not take long for the opening to grow to the size of a railway tunnel at the entrance of which appeared a small creature which resembled both a sardine and a butterfly. I was no longer alone and consequently I was in less of a hurry to leave the carafe, which I began to find quite congenial. It would not have taken much to have made me ask the sardine-butterfly to live with me, which she probably would not have refused to do, for she seemed quite gentle and obliging. However, I did not risk making the proposition, which many would have found strange, though it is no more extraordinary than throwing a paving stone from the seventh floor into a busy crowded street in the hope of killing someone. But the world is such that living with a sardine butterfly is more scandalous than living alone in a carafe. Consequently I made no proposition to the charming creature who attracted me so much. In fact, as she entered the carafe, her wings fell off, her tail as well as her fins disappeared, a spark followed by a small wisp of smoke escaped from her head and I saw nothing in its place but a signpost on which was written: SCORPION, 200KM 120m. Again I lost my temper, and grabbing the signpost, threw it as hard as I could against the walls of my glass prison. To my great astonishment, the signpost went through the carafe and bounced two or three times upon its outside surface before reducing it to splinters. It was then that I was surprised to find myself stretched out on my back in a field of wheat. When I made a move to get up on my feet, twenty partridges flew out of my pockets where they must have been sitting for quite some time—although I had not been aware of it—for they left a number of eggs which hatched in my hand.

Having recovered from my surprise, it occurred to me that one field was as good as another, at least in the present state of things, and I resolved that from now on it would no longer be so. Not without difficulty, I succeeded in regaining the vertical position to which I was born, and threw jets of saliva to all sides which flew off, followed by the shots of invisible hunters. I climbed into the ditch, taking care not to crush the pretty white moles which had naively come out to enjoy the cool air. It is true, they experienced this pleasure rarely enough! They were so happy that, although I was a stranger to them, they could not restrain themselves from confiding their story to me. It was a very small white mole with dragonfly wings which spoke:

THE WHITE MOLE'S STORY

Just as you see me, I was born in a box of shoe-polish. My father was a chestnut vendor and my mother a sow. How did that happen? I am not sure. My father was a tall man, and thin as a stick, except that his head was easily the largest that could be imagined. He had no nose and his ears hung like the stems of grapevines torn off by the wind. Of course, he was stupid, that is why

123

he was a chestnut vendor. One day, having torn off a sow's tail, he walked through Troyes, shouting: "THIS IS MY BLOOD." Soon the druggists were following his trail, then the solicitors, hardware salesmen, cess-pit cleaners, lacemakers, orthopaedists, justices of the peace, café proprietors, sacristans, herb dealers, amateur fishermen, children of pigs, and finally the clergymen. Then, shaken with fright, he hid the sow's tail in a box of shoe-polish which he put in a mailbox after addressing it as follows:

CLAY PIPE

at IVORY TOWER

near SCURVY (Morbihan)

The letter had its ups and downs. Soon it climbed an iceberg, then descended into a vat, then climbed a tree whose leaves it devoured, causing it shortly thereafter to fall into a well from which a bucket of blue glass extracted it and set it on the right path. Finally, after a thousand changes, it arrived. The place in question looked more like a tulip which had sprung out of a decomposing skull than a well-managed establishment. Indeed, the staircase was laid out like a dead snake in the hall, and the upper stories were reached by means of an arrow which one stuck through one's backside, before being shot up to the desired level by the ground floor. There the letter found its addressee, who paced from one end of the stairway to the other without meeting "a living soul" and asked himself in what desert he found himself without camels or caravans, in what desert populated only by crackling noises and the tinkling of broken glass, in what desert he dragged his feet melancholically like an asparagus which, expecting to be eaten with vinaigrette dressing, is merely sucked at with white sauce. The unknown person was none other than Clay Pipe, famous for duelling with empty bottles.

It was then I came into being.

But perhaps it is worthwhile recounting the marvellous adventures of Clay Pipe and the empty bottles.

Clay Pipe had always believed that virgins lived in broken bottles. But, having found his left eye in one of them, he realised he had been deceived and was quite vexed. Failing to find the young virgins he was after in the broken bottles, he resolved to raise grandmothers, suitably shrivelled by a half century of use, in them instead. Is it necessary to say that his project miscarried miserably? Hardly had the grandmothers been shut up in the broken bottles, than they liquefied and rapidly became a sort of tar used to repair the streets of Paris. All hope of thus obtaining a generation of diminutive grandmothers was lost. But Clay Pipe was tireless. Without becoming discouraged he sowed naval officers in the bottom of the bottles, but that finished him, for naval officers do not smoke clay pipes, but rather the wreckage from ships and sailors' hair, which, as everyone knows is bad for the health of empty bottles. Clay Pipe was not long in seeing the effect on his protegés, and he

124

took his revenge on the naval officers, who he reduced to the state of slugs, molluscs much appreciated by empty bottles, which eat a great many of them especially in the springtime. He was however wrong not to hide from them the origin of their food, because the bottles, despite everything, were much attached to the naval officers, and they became extremely angry. A paper lantern duel ensued and Clay Pipe was beaten, having swallowed only 721 lanterns, while the smallest of his adversaries had devoured at least a thousand. Since that day, Clay Pipe had paced the horizontal staircase from one end to the other in the hope of finding his empty bottles again, but in vain. They had fled long ago, thanks to the spring geranium shoots which grow so frequently on the bellies of pregnant women and instigate premature delivery.

And the little white mole went away as she had come, like a crescent moon. I found myself alone again, desperately alone, my feet attached to a sort of sleigh decorated with a host of little pigs similar to the flag of the United States. This indicated to me that the sleigh was made of acorn potato flour. While I reflected on the insubstantial nature of such a vehicle, it started to move, while the pigs flew away crying:

"Lafayette I am here! . . Over there! . . You don't make omelettes without breaking eggs . . . eggs . . .eggs . . . eggs . . . eggs . . . eggs . . . Negroes have flat feet . . . Swedes eat mussels . . ." And a thousand other things in which the word "hair" was repeated often.

Only one young pig, shiny as a new penny, stayed on the sleigh and when the vehicle stopped near the ear of a naturalised elephant, spoke the following words to me:

—I live in the toolsheds of roadmenders. I eat sleighs. I read Paul Bourget beginning at the end of each line. I play night-table music. I caress the fingers of brides and I keep a well-known politician in the forest of my bristles. What is he and who am I?

But instead of replying, I asked:

—Did you stand in line?

—Sit down, I beg you, he replied. I had a slight cold and now you are saved.

—I understand nothing of all this, I could not help telling him. And now the cauliflowers litter the airless rooms and turn yellow when by chance the little white crystal spiders happen to meet them, playing their customary game of whist in the evening in the deserted squares, although they have long been closed to the public. But this stupid beast would not let me get away so easily, and once again taking me aside, asked:

—Does the gentleman wish me to put on his dressing gown?

Hoping to get rid of him, I replied in the same silly tone he had adopted: "I can't find my bedroom slippers."

Again the pig asked me: "Does the gentleman wish me to comb his hair?"

—Just part it. I can do the rest very well, I replied, exasperated.

For more than a day, the sleigh slid rapidly between a double hedge of porcupines, which gravely contemplated our strange rig and fled as soon as we were out of sight, uttering cries so piercing that frightened birds fell to the ground, where they remined flattened out like a piece of putty on a window. I began to worry. The more so since an indefinable odour floated in the air, something like the smell of artichokes and a well-groomed head of hair. And our speed, which increased steadily! And the pig, which became as large as a church! This animal upset me more than I can say, with his great pale face barred vertically with a sword, and a pistol tattooed on each side of an enormous nose supporting a large stick to which were attached more than fifty children's balloons. To tell the truth, these balloons, whose purpose I did not understand, intrigued me considerably. For most of them contained a bearded man whose chest was decorated with many rusted medals and which opened like a door, revealing inside a rubbish bin overflowing with enormous rats which jostled and crushed one another, drawn no doubt by some alluring rottenness.

The pig observed my troubles and took up his questions again:

—What is he and who am I?

—No doubt the inventor of a cattle car, so-called because it serves for the transportation of playing cards and principally clubs, like clovers, which must be spread out in good season upon green fields, in order that they may acquire the qualities of suppleness and endurance which other cards do not have.

The animal let out a great burst of laughter and murmured disdainfully: "You joker."

Then he began to sing:

On the prairie there is a lock
a lock that I know
It glows and rocks
when the birds fly around

On the prairie there is a camel
a camel with no teeth
I will make him some with a mirror
and his humps will be my reward

On the prairie there is a pipe
where my destiny hides

On the prairie there is a chairman's chair
I will sit in the chair

and the public will be at my feet
It will be warm it will be cold

I will raise centipedes
which I will give to dressmakers
and I will raise chair rungs
which I will give to bicycles

For a long time he continued in this manner, which was far from reassuring to me. Suddenly, as we approached a forest which had barred the horizon for a long time, I saw the forest leave the ground and come galloping up on both sides after bowing respectfully to my companion, who, at this moment, appeared to be filled with unbearable self-sufficiency. They had a long conversation of which I could grasp only a few words, which gave me no idea of what it was about!

—Down there, in that pavilion . . . what can these letters mean: S.G.D. G. . . . What if we visited the naval section . . . provided that we get safely into port . . . , etc.

However, I supposed it had to do with me, and I had no doubt they intended to do me a bad turn, so I prepared to defend myself, but I did not have the chance, the forest grabbed me from behind and immobilised me in no time, then shoved my head into my stomach, pinned my arms against my buttocks, and carried me away, rolling me along like a barrel.
. . . . ? . . . .
And since then I have wandered the world over.

ℑmagine

MAGINE! A FOOT ON THE MOUTH AND THE MOUTH NOT saying no. Not saying yes either. Indeed, who is this mouth anyway? At first glance you can't really tell; it so resembles a boneless sardine that you don't know whether it is one of the whips or one of the huntsmen gored by a wild boar which came running out of the hotel elevator. This boar is a poem in itself. No matter how many mornings it is chased from the blue room where a young woman sleeps who was originally blond, but who, little by little, by dint of staying locked in her room, absorbed the colour of the walls so that finally, having been midnight blue, they are now a shade of myosotis* which makes the door, each time you strike it, say "forget-me-not" every day while the dawn fossilizes the ferns which seize this unique opportunity to drink from the paleolithic bottle with a speed which seems the result of a miracle and a head cold, the boar lunges abruptly from the pillow on which rests the pretty little head of the girl, who at this moment is making an electric arc from the beautiful ornament on the flooded bed. The sleeping girl does not get upset over such a trifle. She is quite accustomed to it. Even the first time she barely consulted an alarm clock and having noticed that the hands made a Kaiser Wilhelm moustache on the wizened face of the old man who is pointed out at all the crossroads in central Paris, smoothed her lap and having noticed that doves were getting ready to emerge from it with the obvious intention of fleeing un-noticed, she wrung their necks with a brisk gesture and a smile. So, the olive branch, late as always, fell on the head of the young girl, thereby showing that the doves' flight was premeditated even

if it is difficult to know if this branch was meant for the lift boy or the ragman who rummages through the hotel's rubbish bins—all the odds favouring
the latter. Nonetheless, you ask yourself what the ragman could do with an
olive branch except maybe feed it to the cows which graze melancholically
under the arches of the Palais-Royal, munching the medals exhibited in a
window over on the left-hand side.

Now the sleeping girl lets things happen. The wild boar leaves, peacefully the doves flee and the olive branch falls to the bedside rug because it
always happens when the doves have already landed on the chimney-stack
across the way where they make pretty holes in the clothing of the chimney
sweeps who pretend that by getting up early in the morning they can keep
night from going to sleep under the bridges with the pretext that there are
draughts and that it could catch cold.

So the young woman sleeps. But when she wakes up it is a whole other
story. With her, from the bed, emerges a great green and white flame so green
and so white that the pine trees under the snow seem like real top hats with
headlights just like a frog in the water of a pond where it has been hiding
for days and days in order to escape the fisherman who has sworn to catch it
because it looks like a portrait of Isabelle of Bavaria which only he knows
about. Actually, he is wrong. His Isabelle of Bavaria is none other than the
corpse of Sarah Bernhardt who every night slides down the seven stories of
her house on her backside in order to go and get drunk at the corner bar. So
much and so well that one day the bar will show her the door because she
mistakes all the customers for L'Aiglon*, and goes and rubs up against them.
And the customers complain because she has fleas.

The flame would quite like to dress the woman but you try to dress a
woman doing Swedish gymnastics. The flame quickly gave up and sat down,
discouraged, at the vanity table. It looks at itself in the mirror. Is it beautiful,
is it ugly? Beautiful or ugly? It asks itself without finding the answer. Only
one way to know: it throws itself into the air and somersaults. Green it is
beautiful. White it is ugly. In one leap it touches the ceiling and sticks there,
and so gets nowhere at all.

Usually at this moment the wild boar throws itself headlong from the
elevator crying "Alfinete! Alfinete!" The girl starts in surprise because she
has recognised her name, which she never hears spoken except under circumstances as strange as these. One day, walking along the embankments she
heard the call "Alfinete! Alfinete!" and at the same time heard a book-
vendor's stall close with the sound of a pipe bursting on the head of an old
man wearing three pairs of bifocals thanks to which he could read the titles
of the books the vendors were selling. He noted these carefully and that night
at home wrote a chapter of his novel using those titles. His novel: The
Geranium at the End of the World Was Nothing but a Heap of Concierge's

129

Gossip where She Had Been Unable to Find or Recognise Her Rooms. They took off the old man's head for now he was nothing more than a miniaturised dolmen and the young girl carried it off. For a while, the dolmen continued to cry out "Alfinete! Alfinete!" but its voice quickly became feeble and finally fell silent. Then all the leaves on the trees in Paris fell in one swoop and the young woman full of suspicion took the dolmen out of her bag and recognised her father whom she immediately threw into the Seine, because, to walk around with one's father in one's handbag is, for a young woman, really too ridiculous. If only it were her lover, that could be understood, but her father! And since that day, to avoid similar misadventures, she has locked herself in a blue room.

Natural History

Illustrations by Toyen.

The Four Elements

HE WORLD IS COMPOSED OF WATER, earth, air and fire. It is not spherical but shaped like a bowl, and is one of the breasts of heaven. The other is to be found at the centre of the Milky Way.

I. Earth

Earth breeds flies, phantoms which are there to watch over it by day and guard it during the warm weather. When it is cold, dried earth shrivels into pumkins and needs no watching over. But during the summer smoke pours out of its ears and, without flies to direct it upwards, this would lie around like bundles of dirty linen.

When thoroughly watered, earth brings forth the following:

1. Lipstick, which is what kisses are made of. There are two kinds of lipstick—wavy lipstick coming in long ripples which, when distilled, produces flags—and light lipstick which bears the flowers that turn into kisses. There are, however, two very distinct ways of obtaining these. It can be done either by drying the blossoms the very moment they burst open, or by crushing the seeds to obtain a perfume which evaporates so quickly that it is almost impossible to hang on to it.

2. Turkish baths, which come from kneading damp earth with yoghurt. These make such a disgusting din that they have been gradually pushed

further and further into the desert .

3. Frogs, which are slowly eating away the earth.

4. Cellos, which are used more and more frequently to cure arthritis and which, when ground down to a powder, are very popular as a detergent which does not spoil the colours of delicate and flimsy underclothes.

5. Spectacles for people with short sight and which come from softening earth with pots of boiling china tea and then simmering it all in a steamer.

Many other things may be obtained also from dampened earth, such as compasses, sausages, boxers, matches, and prepositions that were still used by by our grandparents but which can only be found nowadays in antique shops.

By blowing on earth, i.e. by gently filling it with air, gooseberries are obtained. Tricycles come by blowing hard.

Mechanical methods (whose origins will be explained in greater detail later) permit greater quantities of air to be pumped into the earth, and have brought forth sieves. This is done by taking earth sprinkled with chicken droppings and subjecting it to a powerful stream of air which has been carefully kept at room temperature. Once reduced to dust the loamy earth is enclosed in a receptacle in which the air, agitated by a powerful propeller-fan, goes from freezing point every five minutes to fifty degrees above zero and vice versa, and produces caretakers. These were discovered originally by the Prince Consort, and have since been very much perfected, but do not last as long as they did in the good old days.

In a receptacle containing air at a pressure of three atmospheres and which is subjected to a very low temperature, earth gives us knitting needles. By increasing the pressure and lowering the temperature we also get blackbirds, cradles, green peas and beastly motor-bikes.

Thinly sliced and toasted, earth turns into fish-hooks. Thickly sliced and shrivelled to a cinder it turns into urinals. Rolled into balls that explode in the flames, it produces cockchafers and, if the balls are large enough, moustaches.

II. Air

Air, in its natural state, constantly secretes pepper which makes the whole world sneeze. At ground level this pepper condenses so as to give trinkets in summer and newspapers in winter. These only need to be put in a cool place for them to be transformed into railway stations or sponges, depending on how many pages they contain. Pepper also becomes condensed at two thousand five hundred feet up in space, after which it falls back to earth as such a fine dust that nobody ever notices it. Therefore, when the accumulated evidence of this flagrant futility does eventually begin to make an appearance, the man in the street automatically treads on it and flattens it without showing any signs of conscience. Higher still, pepper is what puts the sparkle into starlight.

When painted blue, air provides undergrowth in dry weather, and bleach when it rains, but it can be dangerous to human beings if taken in large doses as it causes stomach ulcers and blisters, and also rots the teeth. When painted yellow, air is used for making furs and, mixed with cock-chafer powder, it cures lockjaw. When sugar is added, air is used for mending inner tubes, and if salt is added, it makes beds. When warmed between the hands it increases in size until it is transformed into whips. Shredded into mincemeat and doused with red wine, orchestral conductors may be produced, and these are always extremely useful to country folk at harvest time. Dried in the sun and kept throughout the winter in a very dry place, air will provide engagement rings in springtime, but their extreme sensitivity to variations in temperature makes them very fragile and they rarely survive into adulthood.

Kept in a sealed cupboard, air has a tendency to escape. When it succeeds in doing this, it expires at the threshold in the form of mushrooms. These are often used today for smoothing away wrinkles.

Steeped in vinegar, air produces dock-hands who, in windy weather, run like over-ripe cheese. In such cases tender dock-hands are collected, dried, and then carefully ground so that they may be sown in spots well away from direct sunlight. After a month, the moon rises from these spots, forcing its way out of the earth in order to bloom, as it is not a star as so many people seem to think, but merely the pollen of the innumerable female flowers of the tender dock-hands, which rises from the earth every evening, while the male flowers fall back to the earth so that their seed may spring up again. Each morning the moon sinks down into the sea where, bouncing against the waves, it sets up tides until eventually it melts and, as it dissolves, flavours the sea with salt.

III. Water

In the form of rain, water becomes earthworms burrowing their way into the ground. These worms, going to enormous depths, gather in vast masses in the earth's natural cavities and, when they split, produce crude oil. Several varieties of this oil are worth noting:

1. Studded oil, which has a very brief duration period since, once formed, it is immediately eaten away by moths.

2. Seeded oil, which elephants find irresistable because it makes their

135

tusks grow.

3. Unicorn oil, which is completely useless as oil. Only the horn, decomposing under wind pressure, will give marathon runners, who are in constant use when making china for the purification of clay. This has been previously purified of all noxious matters by the application of strong doses of octopus ink.

4. Hoarse oil, which has been given this name because of the disgraceful raucous noises it makes. This is the oil that causes blisters that spread extremely infectious diseases.

5. Hairy oil, which clings to the bark of trees in cold countries and eventually gives, in swift succession, sparrow's eggs, Chinese crackers and hatpins. The crackers and the hat-pins together produce red billiard balls that are a menace to carp. They are so ferocious that within a few days whole ponds which were once full of fish are turned into deserts, after which the red balls expire through lack of nourishment, at the same time producing will-o-the-wisps.

6. Snowy oil, which is only to be found at the tops of the highest mountains of Europe. At a height of two thousand five hundred yards this oil loses all its properties, becomes dull, tarnished and brittle, and when exposed to sunlight, turns into chairs, a species of lemur which looks harmless, but whose extremely poisonous bite can be fatal if not rapidly attended to.

Chickens, whose feathers are keenly sought after for making low gradients, come from river water by moonlight. However, these chickens do not have feathers in summer, and their sprouting quills are like red teeth which are shredded to make candles which are most useful in the country for locating underground lakes. Such underground water is inhabited by multitudes of keys which, as soon as a well is sunk, slip out through the shaft and build nests at the top of the tallest tree with piercing shrieks. As soon as night falls, they gang up in groups to attack dogs who run for their lives when they see them coming, yelping blue murder.

Once it rises to ground level, well-water evaporates, leaving a brilliant emerald residue at the bottom of the well. When warmed, well-water becomes hard, expands and, at a temperature of eighty degrees, acquires great elasticity which makes it liable to turn into kangaroos in two or three days. But these kangaroos are subject to diseases of the respiratory tubes, as well as to tuberculosis, and this plays havoc with their numbers. This is why deadwood kangaroos, which are rather more hardy than the other types, are the choice of rabbit-breeders since, once the rabbits have been in contact with the kangaroos, their fur takes on a soft silky texture which is perfect for making flags. When temperatures fall below zero, well-water is transformed into beggars. Cut into very thin slices, these are used for making grottoes.

Sea water, once it has evaporated, leaves behind a silk whose long life is a source of constant amazement to man. Certain female silks, a thousand years old, and which still produce four litters of brandy glasses a year—each litter comprising at least a dozen glasses—have been quoted. It is obvious that, under conditions such as this, the brandy glass would have become a plague to man worse than locusts, had he not discovered in crutches an even more implacable ally.

Indeed, one single crutch annually devours hundreds of thousands of brandy glasses and, in equatorial Africa alone, crutches, of which at least twenty different species are known, make up endless armies which, after devouring every brandy glass in sight, turn to terrorising the natives whose harvest of calves' livers they completely destroy, thus reducing them to poverty and famine.

Finally, we should mention bearded-water, whose nature is still not very clear (although it may be made into armour which is very suitable for little old ladies who feel the cold rather badly); flying-water, which navigators use to take their bearings; light water, which is the basis of swimming-trunks; hardwood-water, which is indispensible to sweet-makers; dusty-water, which is useful in carpentry; feathery water, which is hunted in December just at the moment when the feathers take on their most brilliant hues; and clinker water, which is mainly used in electricity, but also has many other uses which we shall investigate later.

IV. Fire

Essentially a mineral element, fire dwells in stones and eggs. Trembling stones are the ones which, when damp and exposed to sunlight, give the best kind of fire. This is soft, sweet, velvety and perfumed, and is currently used for burning down churches. But such stones should not be allowed to tremble too much, as, if the trembling is over-pronounced, the fire will melt and turn into a hot spicy sauce whose heat scalds people touching it and stings them with begonia to make them yawn from morn till night. If the trembling is not intermittent, the fire will crackle and spurt out damp moss which will extinguish it, but also serve as a breeding ground for those fleas which are so dreaded by dyers and cleaners because of the mess they make of their colours. Disturbed by these fleas, colours do indeed lose their glittering sparkle and freshness, so that it becomes impossible to maintain a uniform tone. On the other hand, this kind of disturbing action is exactly what is sought by dyers who require marbled or textured effects. Therefore they capture the fleas and put them in equal quantities in sealed jars with the dye and keep the mixture at a fairly high temperature for varying lengths of time, depending on whether they want to achieve an effect of marble or of watered

137

silk.

Left out in the rain for a whole winter, wind-stones produce fierce fires whose life is, however, very short unless great care is taken to plunge them in the sea before using them, i.e. before putting them in those lobster-pots which are ideal for kindling fires. The fires then attract moles which are their main source of nourishment and thus help to extend the length and intensity of their life.

The amount of different fires that are known is considerable. Amongst the most common must be counted tatter-fire from which we obtain bottles which, when plunged into quinine baths, give such ferocious fires that special tools are needed to cut them into the resilient lightweight planks which children use to make their kites. Wellington fire is also not difficult to find, being the result of a mixture of sleeping-cars and wheel-barrows, and it is greatly sought after by composers. Stretched out on soft and well-brushed beds, when it has been lightly sprinkled with salt, it plays symphonies, and when it has been splashed with ink, it sings operas. One of the most common types of fire, stinking-fire, is obtained by soaking bishops in cod-liver oil. It gives off a noxious odour, but this is excellent for the growth of asparagus shoots, as it puts paid to the drawers which nibble at them. We may also give the example of cloudy-fire which stops rats and mice invading empty houses; passage-fire which fizzles out as soon as it is squirted from hypodermic syringes; taffeta-fire, which is essential in pastry-making; ostrich-fire, which every girl slips into her bra when going to her first dance; hobbling-fire, which scares doctors stiff since it starts epidemics (which must be fought off as soon as they appear with an inhalation of leeks); whipped-fire, which prevents villagers from sleeping on the night before the grapes are gathered in; twig-fire; pill-fire; dry-fire; black-and-white-fire; striped-fire; doctrinal-fire; etc.

All these types of fire are frequently encountered in their more-or-less pure states in all parts of the surface of the globe. They can be very easily cleaned, either with fish-bones or by filtering them through blotting-paper which has previously been soaked in vinegar. However, much rarer varieties of fire are also known, such as button-fire which suits blondes so well, or brain-fire which is produced with great difficulty by crushing turkeys with twitch-grass to make a smooth paste which is then put out to dry in the sun after sprinkling it with equal quantities of very fine iron and copper filings. If the filings are not fine enough, the paste will run and produce small change; if it is too fine, birds will come and peck at it, causing it to explode and give out clouds of skin-clinging black dust which can only be got rid of by painting the affected areas with tincture of iodine. After a few days a nut of brain-fire can be discovered on cracking open a pound or two of this paste which has been allowed to dry. One must still be very careful to avoid dropping it on wool as this would be liable to become inflamed. When this brain-fire is crushed and compounded with clusters of heliotrope flowers, which have also been reduced to a powder, it is made into a night-cap for women wishing to acquire beauty spots. Amongst the rarest of the remaining fires we should still note shutter-fire, which rises from volcanic ash long after the eruption has taken place, and which, at the rate of a few ounces per ton of ash treated with cider, makes it very scarce; dewlap-fire, which is used as a decorative motif; flying-fire, which it is strictly forbidden to take into fashion-houses as it stirs up the passions of the needlewomen against the wives of their bosses; rose-fire, which is found at the crack of dawn in the woods in springtime; cross-bow-fire, which is a very rare disease of the horns of cockled snails (one in ten thousand has it); quivering-fire; braces-fire; breast-fire; and, last but not least, crumb-fire, which female penguins some-times secrete when laying their eggs, although it evaporates after a few moments if not gathered immediately and put into fresh cream.

Mexico, 1945

¶he Mineral Kingdom

NCE WATER, AIR, EARTH AND FIRE WERE TIRED OF dancing round and round an ice-cold flame of void, they blew it out. They sat down, worn out, and huddled against one another as they were cold and it was really just to keep warm that they had gone on dancing so long like bears in a cage.

—I am half dead, said fire, wiping his sweat-soaked brow. The sweat was evaporating fast and turning into fine snow which fell on their feet and froze them.

—We really must do something to avoid freezing, said earth and shivered so much that air, who was squashed between her and water, turned into a huge umbrella under which the others sheltered with their teeth chattering.

Water blew on her numb fingers which were as red as coals; the glow from them could have given them light. Something in them went solid and water began to work it mechanically between her fingers like an odd crumb of bread. After a few seconds, they heard a feeble bleat: water was holding a piece of sulphur in her downy hands, which were covered in soft hairs that shone in the gloom like good thick cream. They were all amazed and admired the sulphur which sparkled in the empty night like a sly piece of sun, and they all set out to imitate water. Fire even tried to go one better and clenched both fists, then blew on each in turn till he obtained in his left hand turquoise which instantly ran off howling like a beaten dog, and in his right hand flint, which fell and hit earth on the knee. There was a rumble like a waterfall. A spark flew off and set fire to the sulphur just as a sticky substance was

141

seeping from the air's fingers. This also caught fire on contact with the burning sulphur and brought forth plaster, so that this impalpable dust covered them with an impenetrable layer of white; but it insulated them from the cold and the darkness vibrating like a violin string.

Water, air, earth and fire now began to enjoy themselves so thoroughly that they no longer felt cold. Their hands recovered their natural agility and the game started to be fun; they tried to see who could be the most ingenious or the quickest to invent new minerals. They yelled, blew, whistled, sighed, breathed and sang at their hands, and produced in the process, among other things, copper, which appeared with a pirouette and a bow, and nickel, which cried heart-rendingly, so that they had to set about cheering it up—taking turns at first, and then since this produced no visible result, they all started cossetting it together, and crooning at it affectionately. It was no good, the nickel only ended up sobbing even more miserably. Fire lost his temper and shouted at it, and got so angry he kicked it out of the way. But it still went on moaning and whimpering for a long time; they all got upset and muttered imprecations at the beastly creature, which meant that for a while they could make nothing but boring schists, and lead and zinc and rust and other minerals with no shine to them, and quite without interest; they threw them aside disdainfully and sometimes angrily, as they appeared in their hands.

Air started yelling a rugby song at the top of his lungs, interrupted by the occasional sneeze, to the embarassment of water who blushed and modestly lowered her eyes; suddenly his hands felt so heavy he had to drop them at his sides, and the weight made his arms stretch a good three metres in one swoop, while his neck stretched out like a spring so his head bounced up and dangled on the end of it. Air groaned and some big fat drops which sparkled like tears in sunshine, dripped from his battle-scarred hands, dropping into the black void with a sound like an omelette splatting on the pavement; they then bustled off like thousands of ants abandoning their ant-hill after a rabid pick has dug it open. Mercury had been born. It continued for hours to drip from air's fingers, which were now as long as telephone wires on which swallows rehearse their migrations. Air was completely worn out and just stood there with his arms hanging at his sides. Water, earth and fire were wide-eyed with surprise and overflowed with joy and admiration and praise. Earth held out her hand like a dandelion flower to try and collect a few drops for a closer look, she wanted to slide them gently from one hand to the other. She even took it into her head to blow on them, with such an un-expected result that her jaw dropped and she caught her breath. Numberless crystals in thousands of different colours were fluttering in the hollow of her hands, twittering and tweeting for all they were worth.

They all stared at earth's hands in horror, even air who had gradually reduced weight and more or less returned to his normal weight and size, and recovered the proper fan-shaped use of his hands, and his elder-pith arms. Water now collected a few drops of mercury on her hand, and whistled over it for some time. The mercury meandered unconcernedly with little hops between the life line and the head line, and water absently picked up a pinch of salt and crushed it between her fingers into a fine dust which covered the mercury. The next time she whistled the mercury stuck to her hand like a stamp on an envelope and at the third whistle it appeared to boil. She whistled once more, then shook her hand vigorously and opened it. Snorting and neighing and bucking and leaping to left and right, phosphorous appeared; it came to a halt in front of them and preened itself like a young dog out to please, while humming an incomprehensible tune. They were taken aback and slightly afraid at this curious performance; they cocked their heads to one side and were asking themselves mentally how such an exuberant ingredient could possibly be used, when it made a totally unexpected movement and threw itself at fire. It gave him a nasty bite on the thigh and then ran off giggling and crackling as fast as its legs could carry it, and disappeared into a cloud of rust.

Now they started mixing the minerals they had despised up till then, however they felt like it; they always remembered to add a drop of mercury. There were hoots of laughter and shouts of joy which sometimes winged away at top speed never to be seen again, but often they stayed circling above their heads. Earth was the first to have mica rise from her hands with big black eyes, waddling along like a well-to-do shopkeeper, carefully combed and freshly shaved and wearing its Sunday best; it was so completely absorbed in keeping up appearances that it fell down, falling so badly it ran like over-ripe Camembert. It was earth again who had solemn funereal marble come out of her hands; it greeted them formally and correctly in a cavernous voice which sent such a shiver up their spines they did not even try to hold it back when it walked off, with a stiff, dry, precise little nod, with the head turned just a fraction like an automaton, before disappearing into the distance behind a spout of methylene blue.

Fire brutally crushed two drops of mercury between his fingers producing a cloud of sparkling dust which would not settle anywhere except on them. It gilded them from head to toe. Earth was embarassed and started to scrape herself clean to recover her usual looks but soon she had to give up the thought that she could get rid of this layer of gold; it was settling on her as fast as she could scrape it off. And the dust hung in the air and blocked their eyes and ears, which hampered their efforts considerably. It was getting harder and harder; but then earth and air agreed to try hitting one another's hands, having primed them with a few drops of mercury and a chip of slate. The gold dust fell away like a lid, and in one bound emerald rushed off into the distance, ran back, took a look at them, and roared fiercely; then it threw itself at air, tore him apart with its claws and gobbled him up in a flash, so it was nice and full, licked itself carefully, stretched out and fell fast asleep. The others were dumbfounded; they were appalled and fascinated at the same time, but when they saw the emerald lying there sleeping peacefully at their feet, they were furious. Fire angrily kicked at a block of agate which flew off and bounced from a granite rock onto a spike of rock crystal on which it was impaled with a long, blood-curdling scream. It writhed around spiralling with shock and pain in horrible contortions till they jumped up to the emerald and abruptly strangled it. They squeezed so hard and so suddenly that the emerald's eyes were thrown some distance and lay there shining like two stars of absinthe. Its belly burst open and air stepped out, now bigger and broader, built like a fairground wrestler; he was smiling and smoothing his hair, which was not quite so neat as before his brutal mishap.

—Isn't he lovely, cried earth smiling at him enticingly, he looks like the plume of a hat.

Water had been very upset by air's mishap, and she took umbrage at these words. She frowned so hard that her eyes looked as if they had gone parallel to her nose. She muttered various insults about girls who think they are irresistible, man chasers, and other tramps only good for disrupting marriages. Go and walk the streets! But earth took no notice. She did not even hear, but still smiling, with her eyes alight with desire, she minced towards air, who was already hooked and no longer hiding his feelings. Just when earth was about to throw herself into air's arms, fire gave her a kick on the backside so hard she was thrown for miles, where she fell with a dull thud. She lay there flashing with fury and trembling with rage.

—That'll teach you how to behave, said fire. And as for you, he added to air, I suggest you disappear pronto, or else . . .

He did not have to complete his threat. Screams of pain and fury made him turn his head. He saw earth and air locked in a writhing heap with minerals strewn all around them which burst, broke and fought as if they had gone mad. It was as if the fight between earth and water was the signal for a general free-for-all. Sparks and jets of icy vapour or scalding steam shot out in every direction. The minerals were divided into two camps, one supporting earth, and one water. So earth was clawed apart by coal, and a jet of nauseating acid half suffocated water, without the slightest let-up in the battle.

—Those fools will kill each other, said air with a fatuous smile.

His smile exasperated air more than all that had happened before, and he slapped air so hard he sent him flying flat against the horizon where he was suspended unconscious.

With air out of the way fire turned to the raving viragoes. Earth already had two black eyes and water was almost bald, having been half scalped by tin. Fire grabbed water by the feet and swung her round his head. She quickly unwound and turned into a huge lasso which fire flung at air and let go of the end he was holding. So earth coiled herself round air and started to fray, and the first river flowed out, rushing menacingly at earth who lay in a faint. The threat was so great that fire took fright and hid himself trembling under the earth. The fight between the minerals ceased as abruptly as it had started. There was complete calm and silence which covered everything. They all remained warily in their places. Water was so surprised by the sudden peace she dared not approach her enemy. Fire lay in wait beneath the earth.

And the sun rose for the first time.

Paimpont, 1950

145

The Vegetable Kingdom

HE BLADE OF GRASS, A SPARK RISEN FROM two pebbles clashed together, looked itself up and down and muttered: "I am good looking, but what's the point if I am alone? That must change and people must look at me." And it curled up, tied itself in a knot and undid itself till a tiny bit of it broke off and was blown away by the wind onto a patch of mica. The mica shook itself hard as if it had been stung or burnt, so that the blade of grass was thrown off and fell to the ground— but not without taking with it a chip of mica. A cucumber came up, inflated, then deflated, then reflated. The blade of grass looked at its handiwork and thought: "Well, that's one more sunset done!"

With those words it fell asleep; it was worn out by its first day of life. Meanwhile, while it slept, things were on the move around it. Flints with velvet pupils, solemn quartz, hypocritical marbles, dreaming jades crept up as carefully as Indian hunters to look at this new arrival which was blithely waving back and forth, taking poses, and winking at them without being asked. The jade was the first one who dared touch it—oh so delicately; he thought he recognised one of the family. It was enough to send an electric current through him, which gave birth to the cherry tree; the cherry rapidly lifted itself up on stilts and let its fruit hang lovingly. More boldly, a shard of iron stroked its hand up and down the blade of grass and brought from it immediately a violet coloured glow which ran off with quick little steps and disappeared into the ground a short way off. A few minutes later an artichoke came up from this spot and soon grew ten metres high; then it realised its

147

mistake and prudently came back down to its normal height. Meanwhile an opal threw itself at the blade of grass, and embraced it vigorously with a long kiss on the lips. It still failed to wake it, but an oak tree rose from the ground.

A fine rain began slowly to fall. Every drop that fell on the blade of grass evaporated immediately, but the vapour then condensed to form a new plant. A cabbage fell on its head which it squashed. A poplar tree took fright and tried to hide behind a star which had come out in the night sky, but fled quickly when it saw the tree. The poplar stopped dead in its tracks and wavered just long enough for the wind to change and fix it in its usual proportions for ever. The willow tree did not understand what was wanted of it. It tried to go back into the earth it had just come out of, so it bent down and bumped into the blade of grass. The grass was horrified, and stood groaning as it looked at the object before it; it had thought itself alone. Its whimpering extended to the early hours, though they had not yet come into view over the horizon; the sound seemed to want to meet them and take them by the hand but it made all the stones shiver uncontrollably. Some of them, especially granite, porphry and lava, actually trembled with fear. And they were right; the rain, which was now falling steadily, when it touched them, wove multicoloured crowns which dissolved very quickly to form seeds which germinated immediately. That is how the marshmallow came into being. It sobbed and frowned severely at the unconsolable mignonette: "Pull yourself together, will you!" At the same time the elm, still a boy, was hopping around looking for somewhere to fix its roots, chased by the hateful ivy, which shouted: "You will not escape, I'll get you yet."

Disorder reigned under the cover of the night. The honeysuckle came from nowhere zigzagging to escape a pine which was tilting at it and threatening to impale it. A pansy was sitting astride a heliotrope pulling out its hair in handfuls, and a magnolia freshly sprung from the earth could not escape rape by a bamboo which first tried to seduce it with a lullaby. Elsewhere an iris was comfortably settled at the top of a beech tree, but its triumph was short-lived. The beech shook vigorously and the iris was thrown quite a distance so that it skewered into the waterlogged earth, and was imprisoned there forever. On the right a walnut tree was bombarding a rosebush which shrewdly put out thorns to protect itself. To the left a marguerite daisy was stripping off its own petals to show how it loved the chervil which was hovering around it. Straight ahead the ash tree was furiously cracking pebbles. Behind it the vine was drunkenly singing a bacchic refrain in a syrupy voice. The whole place was an appalling free-for-all, an incredible orgy. The laurel bush assaulted the lilac which then took it out on the boxtree. The box turned shy and it took a long time for it to get over the ordeal, but no one can be sure it ever really forgot.

The tourmaline was frothing with rage in a corner while blushing to the roots of its hair with shame. "This really cannot go on," it resolved. It walked up determinedly to some stinging nettles, grabbed a clump, and began to whack at the vegetation. As it had already grown quite big, the greenery retorted: "Mind your own business you puritanical idiot, you fraud who cannot even work out what colour to be." The peach tree gave it a kick which sent it flying, then scratched the ground and pulled out the bramble, which surrounded the plants with an apparently impenetrable hedge. But the tourmaline did not give up. The peach tree's kick had knocked off a bit of its sparkle and it threw this over the bramble hedge; a thousand different sorts of cactus sprang up, all crammed against each other so that the plants had to keep completely still to avoid being pricked all over.

Calm appeared to have returned, but only precariously. The vegetation momentarily powerless, was only waiting for an opportunity to rebel. It was the storm that set things off. A tempestuous wind had followed the rain and in no time turned on its head the unstable order achieved by the tourmaline. The prickly pear was suddenly squashed up against the jasmine, which screamed so loud it scared the virginia creeper. The creeper was all set to climb over a rock but the jasmine's screams made it lose all its leaves at a stroke. But the jasmine recovered and shook off the prickly pear, a bulb at a time. What did the wretched things care! The bulbs laughed at the groaning jasmine, and each one stuck itself into the soil and multiplied then broke off and multiplied again so that soon the whole area was covered with prickly pears, till once again no one could move an inch. But their immobility did not last long, as the wind started blowing even harder. In one blast it carried off the potato, the turnip and the onion, which were methodically getting drunk at the top of an oak tree, and buried them. The same blast dragged the plum tree into a deserted corner with the sycamore and the chestnut, which flattened everything in their path, and started a bloody fight in the course of which the carrot was flayed alive and thrown into a hole, and the plane tree was so badly beaten up it was covered in bruises for ever.

Now thunder began to rumble in the distance, and then lightning ran across the sky. The clematis rushed forward trying to catch a streak of lightning. It finally succeeded, until then it had been a great tree, but the lightning carried it off, stretched it out and broke it, so the clematis ended up thread-like, and the lightning went away with a bit of it and threw it in the sea where it gave rise to seaweed. The seaweed multiplied rapidly in spite of the storm which tore it out in armfuls, which the waves washed up on the shore; they were crushed brutally against granite rocks, which turned them into reeds bristling with terror. Here and there the lightning whistled a waltz as it struck a flint which burst into a hawthorn bush, or a rock-crystal lightning conductor which dissolved to engender the tulip or the apple tree,

149

depending on whether the lightning struck the tip or whipped across the stem of the conductor. If the lightning struck an ordinary bit of limestone, it split open obsequiously to let the laurel spring out. The lightning was now coming down on every side, bringing out the mango tree, the raspberry cane or the lettuce here, the broom, the bracken and the vanilla orchid there, or the coconut palm, the sugar beet and the elder tree, all in a frightening state of chaos. So a lettuce more than eight hundred metres high bore raspberries, while a coconut palm bushier than an oak tree dropped plums at its foot, and the bracken had tomatoes hanging from its spores. All the vegetation was in this state and every plant complained. The elder was no bigger than a radish and groaned: "When will they be able to make reed-pipes from my stems?" The broom sighed: "Give me flowers, please, some flowers for pity's sake," and looked at its long, straight, dry trunk.

Everywhere you looked there was desolation and it was miserable to see the growing havoc—mistletoe coming out of the earth with cornflower blossoms, while roses bloomed in the pear trees. Nothing was in its place! And with the storm blowing for centuries, the chaos only went on getting worse. A willow was seen with flint arrowheads hanging from its branches and a black pebble gave off a heady whiff of garlic. There seemed to be no remedy and the flora seemed condemned to drift from species to species and had to get used to the most peculiar couplings. It was quite common for the flowers of a turnip weighing several tons hanging in mid-air to be fertilised by a wallflower, or for nuggets of obsidian to drip from faded peonies. Suddenly, when there was nothing to suggest that harmony would reign one day, the sky began to clear, and the storm moved on, and through the still heavy clouds a ray of sunshine was seen and the rainbow glistened with all its jewels over the spellbound earth. The vegetation understood at once and without protesting every plant quietly returned to the spot for which it was meant: the strawberry came down from the trees where it had been living as a parasite and lay flat on the ground, the plum tree which was creeping along the earth, stood upright, the vine which was as stiff as a cavalry officer, slackened and laid itself out to dry upon a rock and the other plants folllowed their example. There was nothing more to add.

Paris, 1958

The Animal Kingdom

HE VENUS FLY-TRAP YAWNED: "NOTHING to put in the pecker!" It looked all around and rolled its eyes ferociously, growling and grumbling against the cruel fate that had given it such a large appetite. Above it, the flame tree waved its long pods with a sound like castanets, as if just to taunt the fly-trap. A seed fell out of one pod and began to fly around back and forth, but it met another seed with which it coupled and soon thousands of flies and mosquitoes were criss-crossing the air. The fly-trap was very relieved; it would not die of hunger; from now on it could be sure of getting enough to eat. Even better, the flies and mosquitoes multiplied so fast that the fly-trap could not keep up; it was getting flushed, and was on the point of turning apopleptic. It stopped eating and fell asleep.

The trees and flowers and all of nature was now invaded by flies and mosquitoes and everywhere there was a feeling of disgust, almost nausea. "Who will get rid of these revolting objects?" asked a blooming rose, and shivered. Its shivering made its petals drop and drift away on the air. The wren, the blue-tit and many other birds emerged from them and sped off after the insects, whose debris piled up on the warm ground mixed with fragments of plants. The mixture rapidly fermented and soon the soil was swarming indescribably: ants had been born in their thousands and without delay they attacked the vegetation, which screamed with terror. "Have pity!" pleaded the sweet pea; "Help me!" moaned the plum tree; "Save me!"

squealed the walnut, but the ants did not pause for one moment. They sawed, they chopped, they snipped away, they laid waste all in their path. "That is quite enough," said the agave, "I am going to get this sorted out. And with one of its leaves it gave a prod to a briar. Out tumbled an anteater, curled up in a ball out of fear; then it realised that no one meant it any harm, and the smell of ants made its mouth water, so it set to work methodically and drove the ants to earth.

The agave was rather proud of this; encouraged by this first success it prodded with one of its thorns a pebble which was sunbathing beside a dried-up river bed. The pebble yelped with pain, and was immediately covered with a dark pelt and ran off moaning, having turned into an otter. Once out of reach of the agave it spotted a pond and dived in to cool its wound. The agave laughed and a grasshopper sprang from its mouth, and went and hid beneath stone. The agave, increasingly pleased with itself, took a handful of salt and threw it at the calyx of a gladiolus, and out jumped a cod, looking rather surprised. At the same time it spat at an oak tree whose bark soon rang with the rat-a-tat-tat of a woodpecker's beak. This time it went really wild. It squashed a clump of borage and produced the mole, which dug its way into the earth in search of a cheese or a piece of gingerbread. Then it picked up its violin. It tuned the strings, and waves of worms came out. Then it started playing a waltz and a pig hopped out of the bow with a grunt, followed by a horse which was upset by the pig's grunting and ran away. "That's enough music!" shouted the rhododendron with a snort, which gave birth to several kangaroos. The agave was annoyed by this protest and walked away, saying: "We need some life around here. I shall shuffle the cards until the king of spades is an ace again and soap bubbles release turkeys when they burst, and pheasants and ducks and squirrels, which at the moment mope around in Turkish baths. And now my pipe has gone out! Little robin, come and give me a light." The robin meekly appeared from the agave's pipe and lit it before flying off. As it went on its way the agave thought, "Where shall I find a vanilla hair broom to make a lion with a beautiful mane? All I need is an ordinary syllogism, even a rickety one, which I could scratch with a beetle's wing-case to bring out a giraffe. And what could I not obtain from that? In white sauce the male giraffe produces the cormorant while hot, and the ibis when cold; cut it into thin strips and one can turn it into prawns and sea-urchins. When soaked in grease the giraffe will make a sparrow or a frigate bird, depending whether the sun is shining or there are clouds in the wind. And as for the female giraffe . . . My shoelace has gone and broken!" The agave bent down to re-tie its shoe-lace. It picked up the now useless end and threw it away without caring where it went. It was a primrose that started wriggling and struggling till out popped a dog the size of one's fist. It had a thin, thread-like tail, two or three metres long and hobbled around on three legs, with the fourth one tucked up behind its head to make a sort of crest. But it barked with more strength than one would have expected from such a small creature. The agave picked it up by its cranial leg and rubbed it with sandpaper. The dog grew visibly, and wagged its upper leg for joy. Now it was normal size, but it still had that tail and that leg! The leg was quickly dealt with; the agave snapped it off with a quick movement, took one of its biggest thorns, poked a hole in the dog's skin and stuck the leg back where it should have been. The animal whimpered and the agave was upset and punched it so hard its face was smashed in. "Right! You can be a bulldog!" it said; but there was still the tail to deal with. The agave grabbed a synonym and cut the tail clean off—the animal came and licked its hands. "This will be enough for me to make a thousand breeds of dog," said the agave, and chopped the tail into little bits. It put one bit in a keyhole, and a Dachshund came out the other side. A second crumb of it, rolled in sugar, gave birth to the Sheepdog and a third piece was thrown into a drawer, where it mixed with the dust to make a Pointer. By mixing and combining the pieces with all kinds of ingredients—trapezes, litotes, sneezing powder, king and country, soldiers' cockades, etc.—the agave succeeded in producing all the dogs from the tail of the first one, but none of them barked except the first; so it picked up an alexandrine and started to beat the pack with it. The dogs soon began to bark and growl as if they had never done anything else.

"That's all right," said the agave, "now let's go on." It picked up a rule of proportion and dropped it in vinegar which began to fizz and swear, and then to laugh inanely, while at the same time turning as black as pitch. The monkey appeared and scampered off to bathe in the nearest river, making sharp little cries. The agave was as happy as could be. It sang, shouted, waved its arms and chattered, seized with a senseless exultation: "If one boils a candle and then rolls it in prepositions, it will give a kingfisher. Take one feather from the bird and stick it into the buttocks of a vaseline-coated moth-eaten square root, and the result will be the scorpion. And what about the shark? I can already see in it a pureed half-compass left out in heavy rain. Everything is possible: I shall extract the zebra from a smoked laundry-shed and the toad from a thimble of flowers; but I shall have to work in the moon-light so as to keep it apart from the flea. I shall crush the flowers of rhetoric to dust with crumbled diagrams until all the humming-birds fly out. And the devil if I do not find a dried flower between the pages of a psychology book which will make a very presentable ass when mixed with Prussian blue."

A lifebelt covered in moss lay in his path. He picked it up, brushed off nearly all the moss and said, "Come along, lizards." Nothing happened, but the lifebelt seemed to have difficulty breathing, so the agave slit it open on the spot and a wave of lizards hopped out.

The agave went on, "I know all the cetacians: the blue whale which is extracted from grilled incense powdered with circumflex accents, the sperm whale made from a pine cone used as a fishing rod which breaks when you catch a block of sealing wax made furious by the cruel ill-treatment to which it has been subjected; and the dolphin born from the copulation of a loft with a haybox oven. And I know the felines too: the tiger which you find sleeping in a pocket where you have stuffed kissed hands, a paperclip, some jelly beans and an address book. It will only wake up if I decorate it with a delicately embroidered necklace of magnetic iron. Then there is the panther which was green at first when it leapt from a bugle bubbling with beer-froth. Several kinds of panther are known to science. Liquid panthers which rumble in mimosa woods in early spring and evaporate with the first storm; buttered panthers which were used to make fingers for monkeys; bivalve panthers which the wind makes sing out of tune; bearded panthers which can sometimes be found in shaving foam—they give it its special quality (without them shaving foam would just be a sort of liquid manure). Not to mention the terrible knife-blade or dumb-founded panther, which lurks in stations at night and eats up the points. And I can also see coming from a grain of sand which has been driven by the wind three times around its starting point, the floppy owl. It is covered in soft fish scales and it is trembling because it is about to dive into a river of warm milk to escape from an imaginary danger. When nothing happens it will come back up looking dishevelled, and blink. And over there is the toucan which I started making with the beak, which I cut from a sausage tree fruit, but I made a mistake and before I had time to put it right it flew off and started making an infernal racket in the back of a cupboard. Too bad for it!

"I put together a tortoise from a liquidised Archimedes principle with red tomato sauce folded into it; but what a circus that was! First it got mixed up with a caterpillar because the Archimedes principle evaporated just when I had got it out of the hollow of my hand. I had to rub it vigorously with a metal brush to give it a bluish shine, then feed it up with proverbs for several months and finally dip it in copper filings to give it a presentable shell, but it is so heavy the animal can no longer run, let alone fly as I had wished.

"I took a whipped sophism and made all sorts of pelicans: the pelican on springs which makes the colour yellow, the soapy pelican you boil to use in carpentry, the dead-wood pelican for unblocking taps, the legless pelican which sits on hen's eggs till the eggs lay more, and the horned pelican from which pipe-cleaners are made. But none of them had either plumage or a fleece, so they shivered in the cold. They were not complete pelicans. It was only after I extracted from white-hot flypaper the helical pelican— the one which shears sheep and lives on the wool—that I thought of soaking the next one in cod-liver oil. I marinated it for some time and it emerged just as we see them today. The rhinoceros was quite simple; it was born

155

unaided from a puff-ball. It was no bigger than a may fly, but then it grew like everyone else and when it thought it was big enough, it stopped. The same went for the elephant which worked its way out of a coconut thanks to its tusks, but it had no skeleton and slithered wretchedly around on the ground like a legless man, trumpeting with pain, for its delicate skin was scratched by the smallest pebble. It was so flat you would have mistaken it for a carpet. I took pity on it and made it a skeleton out of spider's thread which it swallowed. A moment later it stood up on legs eight metres long, as slender as a giraffe's, and with four knees, so that it kept falling down. I had to cut, fill out and shape its legs to give it a bearable existence.

"If I had to tell you everything, I would never get to the end. I had to spread speech around here and there, but it was still a mess. The starfish whined till it got on everyone's nerves, and the mouse croaked hoarsely in a language with no r's or s's. It argued endlessly about trivial nonsense with a fluty-voiced heron; though I suspect they barely made themselves understood as they were continually on the point of hitting each other. That is why I decide to cut man out from a prune. He was still tiny, but I felt sure that time would let him grow—it had promised it would. Man had barely started breathing when he stood up on his legs and yelled, "So where's the wife, then?" I said: "It's up to you to find her." So he collected some honey which was oozing out of a hive and shaped it to make his wife.

Paris, 1958

rose: Collaborations

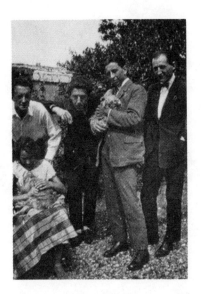

Paul and Gala Eluard, Breton, Desnos and Péret in 1924.

Calendar of Tolerable Inventions from Around the World

ALMANACH SURRÉALISTE

DU

DEMI-SIÈCLE

Tronc de soldat

LA NEF

ÉDITIONS DU SAGITTAIRE

1	S
2	M
3	T
4	W
5	T
6	F
7	S
8	S
9	M
10	T
11	W
12	T
13	F
14	S
15	S
16	M
17	T
18	W
19	T
20	F
21	S
22	S
23	M
24	T
25	W
26	T
27	F
28	S
29	S
30	M
31	T

CARNIVAL MASK.* — To avoid being recognised during her gondola escapades, the daughter of the Doge, Filippo Mani, consecrated the use of velvet and lace masks.

LADDER. — One of Rameses III's gardeners, having observed the continuous upward movement of a tree frog along the trunk of a eucalyptus, noticed the evenness of its jumps and had the idea of compensating for the human paws' lack of adhesiveness by means of horizontal bars maintained between vertical rods.

BIRDHOUSE. — Shelter designed by Elie Bonjour, colonel in the National Guard, to allow birds to await the return of fine weather.

KISS-CURL.* — Sported for the first time by Lola de Valence after she had been applauded with paper streamers.

DIVING SUIT. — It was Robert Houdini who created the human bottle imp.

161

1	W	**SNAIL FORK.** – During the dinner hosted by von Moltke to celebrate the surrender of Paris in 1871, his aide-de-camp, exasperated by not being able to extract a single snail from its shell, broke two prongs off his fork on the edge of the table.
2	T	
3	F	
4	S	

5	S	
6	M	
7	T	
8	W	**BILLIARDS.** – Ordered for the purpose of a demonstration by Pico della Mirandola, who wanted to establish that human dialogue depends on nature and is only opposed (not insurmountably) by the sun.
9	T	
10	F	
11	S	

12	S	
13	M	
14	T	
15	W	**VENETIAN BLIND.** – At Goa, Mohammed Askia had the windows of his palace garnished with leaves in order to filter the ardour of the sun.
16	T	
17	F	
18	S	

19	S	
20	M	
21	T	
22	W	**DECALCOMANIA.*** – During a costume ball given in 1854 at the court of Napoleon III, Seymour appeared disguised as a prowler, his forehead covered with false tattoos reproducing the portrait of Gabrielle d'Estrées with the Duchess of Villars.
23	T	
24	F	
25	S	

26	S	
27	M	
28	T	

1	W
2	T
3	F
4	S
5	S
6	M
7	T
8	W
9	T
10	F
11	S
12	S
13	M
14	T
15	W
16	T
17	F
18	S
19	S
20	M
21	T
22	W
23	T
24	F
25	S
26	S
27	M
28	T
29	W
30	T
31	F

VEIL. – Made fashionable by Madame Sabatier on her return from a trip to Algeria.

KITE. – Conceived by Lao Tsu to demonstrate the meagreness of man's powers beside those of a paper fish.

MANNEQUIN. – Brought back, in about 1860, by Francisco Lazcano from the Carolina Islands, where they were worshipped by the natives under the name of *tino*.

DRAWER. – Tabernacle-shaped excavation carved into a piece of furniture in which the Grand Master of the Knights Templar kept his seal. Identified and vulgarised by the church, the drawer was furnished with an annulling button.

1	S
2	S
3	M
4	T
5	W
6	T
7	F
8	S
9	S
10	M
11	T
12	W
13	T
14	F
15	S
16	S
17	M
18	T
19	W
20	T
21	F
22	S
23	S
24	M
25	T
26	W
27	T
28	F
29	S
30	S

SPRINKLING-ROSE.* – Derived from a habit of one of Philippe-August's archers: of using a rust-gnawed sallet*, which he had found abandoned on the battlefield of Bouvines (1214), to water his salads.

CUCKOO CLOCK. – It was the Duke of Baden who imposed, by decree, the use of this timepiece to protect agriculturally useful birds by trapping the female cuckoo.

SPINNING TOP. – Eleanor of Aquitaine, to test knights suspected of dishonouring their pledges of love, enjoined them to spin tops shaped into silver hearts pierced with a golden arrow, upon their shields.

KALEIDOSCOPE. – The young son of a Portuguese sea captain introduced into a tarnished spy-glass feathers plucked from the parrot his father had brought back from Brazil.

1	M
2	T
3	W
4	T
5	F
6	S
7	S
8	M
9	T
10	W
11	T
12	F
13	S
14	S
15	M
16	T
17	W
18	T
19	F
20	S
21	S
22	M
23	T
24	W
25	T
26	F
27	S
28	S
29	M
30	T
31	W

RED EGGS. – At the turn of the century, eggs given to the Mayday demonstrators by shopkeepers posted along the parade route.

INVISIBLE INK. – Chamisso de Boncourt obtained it by distilling the shed skin of a variegated snake.

FALSE EYELASHES. – "When I have lashes like those, I'll be all yours," said Cléo de Mérode, passing in front of a hairdresser's dummy modelled after her features. The next day, the acquaintance she had been addressing affixed fragments of the tail-feathers of a lyre-bird to her eyelids.

MUSTARD. – Produced in 1165 at the request of the Anti-pope Guido da Crema, who was looking for anti-honey.

1	T
2	F
3	S
4	S
5	M
6	T
7	W
8	T
9	F
10	S
11	S
12	M
13	T
14	W
15	T
16	F
17	S
18	S
19	M
20	T
21	W
22	T
23	F
24	S
25	S
26	M
27	T
28	W
29	T
30	F

ELECTRIC SIGN. – Modern version of an idea of Arlini's, the famous 18th century artisan, who presented to the court at the Palais Royale, gloves with glow-worms attached.

CORNET. – Through popularisation of the arum bouquet, one flower of which could, in the 12th century, contain an engagement ring.

CUP-AND-BALL. – Having seen, during a Sabbath, her black billy-goat balancing a death's head on the point of one of his horns, the witch Alips de Mons invented this game, which was originally divinatory in nature.

ESCALATOR. – Invented by Maurice Legendre, night-watchman in a furniture warehouse.

PERSPECTIVAL FURNITURE. – Invented in 1943 by a Mexican cabinet-maker who had been given a picture from a department store catalogue, and asked to build a mirrored cupboard from this model.

1	S
2	S
3	M
4	T
5	W
6	T
7	F
8	S

ATTIC. — The idea of removing it from dwellings goes back to Caius Gracchus' favourite slave. She hoped in this way to keep the swallows nesting in the roof from leaving in the autumn.

9	S
10	M
11	T
12	W
13	T
14	F
15	S

SEQUIN. — The appearance of stonecutters coming from work with chips of mica in their hair was the origin of the decoration of certain costumes for the Bal des Ardents.

16	S
17	M
18	T
19	W
20	T
21	F
22	S

HAMMOCK. — Anacaona told the officers of the 'Pinta' that his ancestors, looking to build their nests by means of a shuttle, had obtained the hammock.

23	S
24	M
25	T
26	W
27	T
28	F
29	S

BACKSCRATCHER. — Substitute for the sceptre used by Nago chieftains to dispense justice and which, during difficult cases, could be used to scratch the spinal column.

30	S
31	M

1	T
2	W
3	T
4	F
5	S

6	S
7	M
8	T
9	W
10	T

11	F
12	S
13	S
14	M
15	T
16	W
17	T
18	F
19	S
20	S
21	M
22	T
23	W
24	T
25	F
26	S
27	S
28	M
29	T
30	W
31	T

ANAGLYPH. – Lacepède obtained it by deducing the relationship linking the mimetic range of the chameleon with the rotary movement of its eye.

CAFE TERRACE. – Tortoni bequeathed this to Alfred Tattet, a friend of Musset, so that he could "benefit from the air of the boulevards."

JACK-IN-A-BOX. – A gadget of which the wooden Jack-in-a-Box is a scaled down replica, was placed by a mysterious hand next to Catherine de Médicis' prayer stool, two days after the Saint Bartholomew massacre.

SOAP BUBBLE. – It was the accidental escape of such bubbles above the tubs in his mother's wash-house that determined the young Montgolfier's vocation.

1	F
2	S
3	S
4	M
5	T
6	W
7	T
8	F
9	S
10	S
11	M
12	T
13	W
14	T
15	F
16	S
17	S
18	M
19	T
20	W
21	T
22	F
23	S
24	S
25	M
26	T
27	W
28	T
29	F
30	S

LACE. – Created especially for Laure de Cléry who had desired a 'glade-coloured' nightshirt.

BEAUTY SPOT.* – Armido di Parma, having dismounted in front of a blacksmith so his horse could be shod, was touched on the temple by a spark which was right on target, and according to his followers, it lit up his face in an extraordinary fashion.

BALCONY. – Drawer open onto the street where the Genovese beauties could, on feast days, show themselves in all their finery.

MAYONNAISE. – Was indeed brought back to France by the soldiers who occupied Port-Mahon in the Balearics in 1756, but which had originally been conceived by the Minorcans when they heard the gulls sneezing above the seaside olive groves.

1	S
2	M
3	T
4	W
5	T
6	F
7	S
8	S
9	M
10	T
11	W
12	T
13	F
14	S
15	S
16	M
17	T
18	W
19	T
20	F
21	S
22	S
23	M
24	T
25	W
26	T
27	F
28	S
29	S
30	M
31	T

SANDWICH. – Prepared by his cook for Lord Sandwich (1718-1792) who, absorbed for weeks on end playing patience, had no time to sit down for meals.

BINOCULARS. – Suggested to his lord by the Comte de Permission as an imitation of snail's horns, which allow one to see everything without leaving home.

REVOLVING DOOR. – Built at the request of the owner of the Café Anglais who, to honour Evans upon his return from Crete, reduced the labyrinth to its simplest expression.

SEWING THIMBLE. – The needle used to sew the Druid's ceremonial vestments was forbidden, under any circumstances, to prick the finger, which was therefore protected by the cup of an acorn.

STILTS. – Originated in the hallucination of a witchdoctor from the Marquesas islands who, in gusting winds, felt himself pass from the top of one coconut-palm to another.

NOVEMBER

1	W
2	T
3	F
4	S

5	S
6	M
7	T
8	W
9	T
10	F
11	S

FUNNEL. — The steward of Philippe de Beaumanoir's vineyards used a shepherd's horn in casking his wine.

12	S
13	M
14	T
15	W
16	T
17	F
18	S

MONOCLE. — Toulouse-Lautrec's watchmaker wore a monocle to compensate for the contraction of the eye muscles resulting from using a jeweller's glass.

19	S
20	M
21	T
22	W
23	T
24	F
25	S

COFFEE MILL. — Derived from the primitive goat mill the Abyssinians used to grind coffee (Everyone knows that goats are the source of the discovery of coffee.)

26	S
27	M
28	T
29	W
30	T

CARAVAN. — Little is known except that a raft of nomads, ran aground in 1550 at Saintes-Maries-de-la-Mer, the crew transformed the sail into a tarpaulin, attached wheels, captured some wild Camargue horses, and continued their wandering ways.

1	F
2	S
3	S
4	M
5	T
6	T
7	W
8	T
9	F
10	S
11	S
12	M
13	T
14	W
15	T
16	F
17	S
18	S
19	M
20	T
21	W
22	T
23	F
24	S
25	S
26	M
27	T
28	W
29	T
30	F
31	S

ZIPPER. – Was not invented, as is popularily believed, by a Swiss doctor, but rather by W. Landolph, author of *The History and Prehistory of Horsetail Grass* (1892), *Horsetail Hinges in the Treatment of Saint Vitus' Dance* (1906), *The Horsetail in the Works of Paul Klee* (1923).

FRENCH FRIES. – Brébant, during the siege of Paris, came up with the idea of frying new potatoes to accompany camel cutlets.

ATOMIZER. – Built to please the Khmer king who had the idea of squeezing the peel of a tangerine into a flame.

TOBOGGAN. – Lulu the sea-elephant's games gave this idea to the clowns of the Loisset circus in 1877.

BUTTON. – Made fashionable by Isabelle of Bavaria, who secured her blouse with snowdrops.

The Child Planet

HE CHILD PLACED HIS TONGUE ON THE EGG SO lightly that the bird didn't think to fly off. The cloister away in the mist opened the express counter to all comers. A marvellous wrestler took on the destruction of the twisted columns which supported the walls. The child was blond, with a tongue as thick as a table. Arithmetic sums covered the tombstones and the monks multiplied magnetic gazes in the cuneiform flowerbeds, palm trees fell from monkey skulls in the shape of Artemisia. "Oh!" exclaimed a witness of these tragic events, "have the dead no other hope than the clenching hearts of strong wits in the ports of wild cards and diamonds."* A chair on a table signals in semaphore and the customs agent separates the waves into three main movements: the heart, the hand, and the hoof. The echoes answered with base maxims the sermons of those who sang to the lyre of the mysteries of the sky smokey with arti-chokes. The car's right rear wheel would stick going up the hill. A hair on a card is reason enough for the violets which are no longer hungry. Banners ignited the barns and scandalised married women. The child looked through the world at eyeglasses and smiled at the nude young woman who was touching his pink little finger. As for the favourite horse of the heroes of the great war, it vomited its jockey at the feet of the unkown woman. She was Russian and loved snow like a wing-collar loves a neck. She only took off her mask the minute before the explosion. She opened her blouse and grasped one of her breasts which was hollow and contained a tiny vanity kit. Her eyes, two volcanoes, abolished the transit of the heavenly bodies. Her foot-

173

prints remained in the wall at shoulder height. After washing the winds, she discovered her white hip on which was tattooed a negro head with the left eye missing. Ridicule can certainly kill you, you others, as long as the lovely railway which encircles my hope doesn't collapse in the dumbstruck fear of the blood-soaked peasants. The whole thing was circled with this inscription: God and the King. The wireless is capable of minor experiments which are nonetheless dangerous to the public. She cut off the hand of a blue-arsed monkey which laughed in her face while cutting a broom-stick into thin slices destined for mysterious ends: putting out the candles in the neighbouring church. Pay no heed to the miracle of the sideboard and the holy riches of the rivers, dig your heels into the evening tides of chloroform planet.

Prose: Polemical

Drawing by Matta for the cover of "A Word from Péret."

𝕬𝖚𝖙𝖔𝖒𝖆𝖙𝖎𝖈 𝖂𝖗𝖎𝖙𝖎𝖓𝖌

HO AMONG THE READERS OF THIS journal* has not been struck by the strange poetry which comes from our dreams! Who has not during his sleep lived one or many thrilling, tormented lives, in every way more real and gripping than the miserable life of everyday? Have you not been astonished, while you were plunged into that sort of reverie before sleep and dreams, at the ideas and images, phrases which come to mind and reveal the preoccupations which during your waking state you had been unaware of? You must also have noticed that this same phenomenon is produced as soon as you let your mind wander randomly. It is here that consciousness is abolished or almost so. Reason has gone back into its kennel to gnaw its eternal bone.

It will suffice, then, to chase away this bitch reason, to write without stopping, without minding the crush of ideas. No more need to know what an alexandrine is or a litotes. Take in your hand paper, ink, and a pen with a new nib and settle comfortably at your table. Forget all your preoccupations, forget that you are married, that your child has whooping-cough, forget that you are a Catholic, that you are a shopkeeper, that bankruptcy looms, forget that you are a senator, that you are a disciple of Auguste Comte or Schopenhauer, forget antiquity, forget about literature from any place in the world and any period in history. You no longer want to know what is logical and what is not, you do not want to know anything except what you are about to be told. Write as fast as possible so that you lose none of the secrets about

177

be told. Write as fast as possible so that you lose none of the secrets about yourself being confided in you; above all do not reread anything. Soon you will notice that, little by little, as you write, the sentences come more quickly, more audibly, more vividly. If by chance you find you have suddenly stopped, do not hesitate to force the door of the unconscious and write the first letter of the alphabet for example. The letter A is as good as any other. Ariadne's thread will come back by itself. This said, let me begin.

A league of asparagus which wasn't quite seven exhausts itself trying to cut out a rainbow in a jar of boot-blacking. The rainbow runs along the beach looking for a sea foam pipe*. It hears the sea in the hollow of its hand and becomes, after years of study on an island of quicksand, captain of a ship. This is when the king of some country or other gives it a soup tureen as a gift. It places turtle's eggs inside; and at the new moon the tureen flies off like the last sigh of a consumptive. Yet the night was very fine and the stars, after losing heavily at baccarat, went off trout fishing with car headlights. All this would have gone quite well if the Grand Duchess Anastasia had not, that day, eaten a large sheet of emery paper. In no time at all the Grand Duchess having broken the bank, lost her head. The rest of her body followed quickly and soon only the toenails were left, and they went off to draw themselves a neon sign in a dark corner full of the noise of jaws opening and closing to the tune of *"au clair de la lune, mon ami Pierrot . . . "* For the wretched spectator of this scene there was nothing to do but to swallow a big glass of very black ink. He did so without too much repugnance though the high temperature had made pens sprout in the ink. After this, he closed the window shutters and went to sleep like a saucer no one had remembered to dress with a coffee cup. But if coffee rains down the sleeper's neck, he is quite obliged to shout fire to call the firemen. They arrive like red herrings and here they are with shouldered arms, unable to find the barrel of their gun and putting cartridges in their noses, pulling the concierge's ear, eating the parrot's seeds, putting leaches in the boss's safe, eating fried mosquitoes, and pulling the devil by the tail so as to be taken quickly and cheaply to their grandmother's. The poor old lady is nothing but skin and bones. From time to time she sells a piece of her skin to make a drum which she sends to one of her grandsons on his birthday. It is rather touching, but somewhat stupid because when she is reduced to the state of a skeleton she will have no other recourse than to live in haunted houses, since her landlord hates the cracking of joints in stairways which are already thoroughly worm-eaten.

Time passes and the earth turns, flies fly, water runs under the bridges which no longer know what to do with their arcs since the death of Noah who is so good and dead that the fleas which nested in his ear took refuge on dogs, the dogs which give their hair to the cats at cockcrow. The beetroot spring could easily dry up and salpeter cover the pope's nose before acanthus leaves take the bit between their teeth. Such is not the case with the lady-birds which the authorities have straitjacketed in total disregard for justice. But justice only wears old shoes worn down by avarice and its scales have weighed so many rotten potatoes that they tell the time like an old cuckoo clock. Cuckoo! Cuckoo! Here's the little soldier with the frozen feet. He goes one two . . . and down he rolls to the foot of the stairs and crashes his head into the letter box. Another pane broken. But the glazier can do nothing because he is, for the moment, very busy cutting himself trousers out of an old factory chimney. His trousers had flown off on the Fourteenth of July. They had taken themselves for a captive balloon and wanted to get free. They even succeeded. I wish them good luck. His glazier, the landlord, was not interesting. He had eyes made of rye bread and on Sundays he mooed while watching the bicycles go by, which was not very seemly. Sometimes the bi-cycles took their revenge by throwing lighter flints at him with their free wheels. As he had no flintlocks he cooked flintstones with laundry boat jam. This is how he came to think of opening a restaurant and made his fortune. He is now the finance minister and rich as a hot sauce. He wears all sorts of weeds, good and bad, and this wins him the blessings of the vines and the vintners. The wine is neither better nor worse, but the vintners are drunker than ever. They can be seen everywhere even on the rooftops where, during, their moments of lucidity, they replace the tiles and help drain off the rain-water which they swallow without hesitation. Whatever the weather, they stroll around and sharpen their teeth on their daggers or vice versa. Their teeth are useful to them, either for eating apples or killing time. And their heart-shaped mouths swallow four-leaved clovers all day long, but luck is uncertain and a four-leaved clover cannot always protect itself from a hay-maker* which has five like a potpourri masking a yellow cat. If it is yellow, that's because it has been roasted and the four digits of the clover multiplied by the five of the haymaker will have no effect. Such is misfortune. It has a fork in its left hand and a pair of tongs in its right. With one flick of the wrist it can pull off an upstart's nose, grabbing it on the end of a fork and leaving it to be held at the Poste Restante. The nose itself doesn't get upset over such a trifle. It knows its time will come and that it will get its revenge when the cherries ripen, but in the meantime it must be on its guard, and rip out, as soon as they appear, the long hairs which are trying to smother it. Otherwise the neighbourhood wigmaker would take it for a wig and put it on his bald wife's head.

Letters

PEN LETTER TO THE BRAZILIAN LEAGUE*

To the comrades of Brazil. To the comrades of the Paris area. To the Executive Council. To the International Secretariat.

Paris, 19 March, 1932

Dear Comrades,

I lived in Brazil for several years. I participated in the founding of the Communist League of Brazil and, since its beginnings, I was an activist in its ranks. I was even honoured with the trust of the comrades of Rio de Janeiro, who appointed me to the post of Regional Secretary. We were engaged in completely illegal activities. Many of us were deported, imprisoned or are now being pursued. I myself was imprisoned and then expelled from the country; I arrived in Paris two months ago. As soon as I arrived, I wrote to comrade Naville*, to put myself at the disposal of the C.L.* which, through comrade Naville's agency, has asked me to make a report on the present Brazilian situation. This report has now been in the hands of the Executive Council for more than a month, along with a letter from me which protests at the distance being created between myself and the C.L. Finally, on the 27th of February, I was able to meet with comrades Naville, Molinier, Treint,

180

and three others who told me they were the Executive Council. I then found out that it would be impossible for me to belong to the C.L. because I had links with the Surrealists! As can be imagined, I am still astonished. In Brazil, where I defended Surrealist ideas publically, and in print, I was also a militant, working illegally with the C.L. And nobody saw anything incompatible between these two attitudes. And if I am told that the situation is different in Brazil to that in France, I can easily reply that the only difference existing between the two countries is that, in Brazil, there is more precision, more logical precision, and that this precision was not incompatible with my affiliation to the Surrealist group. It is even less necessary now because, since my return from Brazil, my Surrealist friends have evolved, allying themselves purely and simply with the principles of dialectical materialism. Under these conditions, it seems impossible for me to accept the injunction I am put under, i.e. to abandon all Surrealist activity and to denounce the movement in *Vérité.** This makes no sense to me, and to demand this of me is to show proof of the same sectarianism we condemn, and rightly so, in the Stalinists.

The issue is self-evident: what is Surrealism? I answer: "Pure psychic automatism by which one proposes to express, either verbally or through writing, or in any other manner, the real functioning of thought. Dictated by thought, in the absence of all control exercised by reason, outside of all aesthetic or moral preoccupations (André Breton, *Manifesto of Surrealism*, Paris, 1924). This definition describes the relationship of art to thought for those who claim to be members. Besides which, it is obvious that the artist is conditioned by the society in which he lives. Nonetheless, he still has the ability either to accomodate himself to society or to revolt against it, and this is precisely the point. Regardless of all the mistakes and weaknesses for which one can reproach the Surrealists, one cannot deny that they maintain, with more rigor and force than ever, an intellectual position that is strictly revolutionary. It should suffice to note that this position has resulted, for one of them, in three months imprisonment*, for another, the loss of his post as professor*, and for a third, the banning of his film by the police*. I know that certain Surrealist members of the Communist Party have as a result, taken a position against us, but this opposition has never been expressed in our magazine *Le Surréalisme au service de la révolution*, which is a cultural organ that does not participate in political discussions that are situated, from a philosophical point of view, in the domain of dialectical materialism.

Naville told me, and he wrote to the Executive Committee of the Brazilian Communist League, that several manifestoes against the left opposition and Comrade Trotsky, have appeared bearing my signature. I asked him to show them to me. Naturally he was unable to do so, because these manifestoes do not exist. All this is nothing but slander and intriguing by Comrade Naville. Enclosed, by the way, are the manifestoes I did sign

181

during my stay in Brazil. One can see that the leftist opposition is never in a single instance, criticised; their objectives are completely different. Moreover, I have been censured for having signed the manifesto concerning the lawsuits being brought against Aragon*–a manifesto which Naville describes, I don't know why, as 'liberal' (in passing I must point out that Aragon no longer has anything in common with the Surrealist group). I am not, of course, in favour of the poem that instigated all these lawsuits; but, because I am not in favour of it, must I also find the lawsuits completely justifiable? I imagine that not one comrade could answer this question in the affirmative.

Having stated my case, I strongly protest against the attitude of the Executive Council, which refuses my admission to the C.L. without giving me a hearing–since no discussion on the subject ever began. And I also ask the comrades if they believe that an affiliation with the C.L. is incompatible with an attachment to a Marxist group which, as a group, has no political activity, and if so why? I add, that on my part, I do not see any incompatibility in exercising these two activities simultaneously. And finally, as I have already stated both verbally and in writing, to the comrades of the Executive Council, I remain at the disposal of the C.L. for any task which might be assigned to me, or for any explanations which I might be asked to furnish; but I maintain the right, which ought not be refused, to participate in the elaboration of our political stance.

With communist greetings,

Benjamin Péret

2 Rue Livingston, Paris.

BENJAMIN PÉRET TO ANDRÉ BRETON

Barcelona, 11 August (1936)

My very dear André,

If you could see Barcelona as it is now–adorned with barricades, decorated with burnt-out churches, only their outside walls standing–you would be, like me, exultant. Indeed, as soon as you cross the border, it starts. The first house you see on Spanish soil, a huge villa surrounded by a park, has been seized by the Worker's Committee of Puigcerda. As you arrive in this village there is the sound of thunder. It's from a church that the workers, not satisfied with setting fire to it, are dismantling with a rage and a joy which is wonderful to see. All over Catalonia, all along the route of the horrid little train which I took from Puigcerda to Barcelona, you can see churches which have been set on fire, or whose bells have been taken—it was a magical trip. In Barcelona, no more police. The Red Guard drives around in cars requisitioned by the F.A.I.* or the P.O.U.M.* and the P.S.U.C.* It's not a good idea to be lacking the right papers because you end up in a cellar, shot without trial. The anarchists are practically the masters of Catalonia, and their only opponents are the P.O.U.M. The ratio between them and us is about three to one, which is not excessive under the present circumstances, and could change quite easily. We have about 15,000 armed men and they have about 40-50,000. The Communists, who have merged with three or four small parties are a negligeable force. In their newspaper, they declared last Friday that the issue is not the proletarian revolution, but rather to uphold the republic, and whoever tried to make the revolution would find themselves facing them and their militias. So, they are announcing their intention to sabotage the revolution, but I don't think they have the power to do so.

News from the front is excellent. Among other things, 30 aeroplanes arrived yesterday and tanks are expected. In which case it will be time to attack Saragossa definitively; and the experts think it will fall within 48 hours.

I will try to write at greater length in the days to come. The mail plane is leaving soon.

My regards to all and excuse me to my friends for not writing, but I have not had the time. In the next few days, I must leave for the front on a political mission.

Benjamin.

Valencia, 26 August (1936)

My dear André,

I am only passing through here, stopping between trains. I'm on the way to Madrid and the Somosierra front. I've already been to Aragon. Things are dragging because of the French government, which is holding up the shipment of arms to Catalonia and Madrid in every way possible. Otherwise, the enthusiasm of the militiamen is magnificent, even though, among the anarchists the most incredible chaos reigns. In the course of my trip, I travelled over 1,000 kilometres and saw over 60 villages. There are these kind

183

soviets set up all over the place, but as they are not called that, nobody realizes this and the Generalitat* of Catalonia has its work cut out to keep people in their ignorance. In Valencia, the Madrid government is completely powerless. The workers' parties, allied with the middle class, are governing. Every day I think about writing at greater length, but I am taking care of a million things for the P.O.U.M. and the P.O.I.* I hope I'll have more free time when I return to Barcelona and I'll be able to write then. I am planning to stay in this wonderful country for several months.

Benjamin.

Barcelona, 5 September (1936)

My dear André,

I have had no news from anyone, and I don't know if you have received any of my letters or postcards (I've written to everybody), as the mail here works as well as it is able and seems—going by the rare letters received by my fellows—to follow strange routes, since letters take three weeks to get from Paris to Barcelona.

Here things are quietly returning to a more bourgeois order. Everyone is slowly letting up. The anarchists have become kissing cousins with the bourgeois of the Catalan left, and the P.O.U.M. makes eyes at them endlessly. There are no longer armed men in the streets of Barcelona, as there were when I arrived. The Generalitat (i.e. the bourgeoisie) has taken everything in hand—though they are trembling hands still—and the revolutionaries of the 19th of July are collaborating loyally with them, hence breaking the duality of power which had been established following the insurrection. So, for the moment, in both the political and economic domains, the revolution is being shelved.

As for military matters, the recruits are betraying us all the way down the line, and when they aren't betraying us they are so stupid and ignorant that it amounts to the same thing. But the enthusiasm of the militiamen is wonderful. Nonetheless, you should expect *serious defeats* in the days to come. Largo Caballero's* government, by the way, was only put together in the panic which resulted from waiting for these defeats, because, in Madrid— where I came from yesterday—the only visible trace of the revolution consists of charming militia girls and posters announcing *incantando por* . . . ('seized by . . .'). All of Madrid looks like Passy, a Passy where the marquesas have stopped wearing hats and their husbands have given up neckties and bowlers.

Until the past few days the military situation, according to the general opinion, has been quite favourable. However, it's true, you only needed to spend a little time at the front, as I did, to discover that the soldiers have ruined everything.

Yet this is no reason to despair. The fascists have, according to all the eveidence, received important reinforcements, both technicians and armaments, while on our side we've had only insignificant aid, for the French government puts all possible obstacles in the way of sending arms etc. to Spain, and especially to Catalonia, which represents the most advanced elements.

Nonetheless, our losses are small (or at least they have been up till now) as the fascists shoot very badly. For example, I was going along a road under bombardment. The shells were falling hundreds of metres away from it. The road was intact. The village where we were going had been shelled for a week. Only a few houses had been destroyed. There hadn't been a single casualty, not one wounded. Coming out of the village, people were fighting—machine-guns and rifles. The battle lasted all night and started up again the next day. It lasted all morning. Not a soul was wounded.

I have just learned that you made a speech against the Moscow trials.* Can you please send me a copy immediately *by airmail*. I will see to having it published here. I hope you have added my name to this protest as well.

There are so many things to say about the situation here. I would never finish if I tried to set everything down.

I am at present the P.O.I. delegate in charge of liason; consequently, at least for the time being, I cannot go to the front as I had intended, and I don't know how long I will be here.

Another thing, if you write to me, do not allude to the contents of this letter, because the firing squad is a matter of almost nothing here and I have told you things I ought not to have said. In other words censorship is severe. If you have anything special to tell me—you never know—write with lemon juice between the lines and send it on paper with a cafe letterhead so that I know I have something else to read.

This letter is coming to you by means of a friend who is going back to France.

Also, can you please let Man Ray know that comrade Jean Rous* is coming to him on my behalf. He is looking for X-ray plates of 30 by 40 format for the hospitals here, which they lack totally. If Man can help him find some in good condition, it would be excellent. One other question, can you take on the responsibility of selling some precious metal items from old churches (for the benefit of the revolution, of course!) and give me the answer with a simple *yes* or *no*, but *urgently*, please.

Benjamin.

Barcelona, 15 October (1936)

My dear André,

I have written you several times and sent you the issue of *Batalla* in which the text of your declaration appeared,* but I am without news from you and am feeling completely isolated here.

Miravittles* asked me some while ago to draw him up a list of all the people in the cultural domain who might make up a sort of front, for the support of revolutionary Spain. I gave him a list of all our friends as well as their addresses, and suggested he appoint you as the delegate for France for this kind of work. I proposed Nezval* for Czechoslovakia. If you have any ideas for other countries, write them to me, including addresses, and I will forward them to Miravittles.

I wanted to write to you about the political situation here, but I have no one to send this letter back with, and the censor will not let this kind of thing pass.

Militarily, the situation in Catalonia remains good. This is the real centre of the fight. Madrid is far behind. Politically, the revolutionary momentum has slowed quite a bit. The petty bourgeois of the Catalan left have regained a considerable amount of ground and the workers' parties are following behind.

I am working here for the P.O.U.M. and my job is with the radio where I—now don't laugh so!—take care of broadcasts in Portuguese. I find it unbelievably uncomfortable to talk in front of the sausage-like microphone. Besides this, I am getting together a collection of revolutionary posters. I already have some, but the Spaniards are so indolent that the slightest request requires a considerable amount of time. Tomorrow I am returning to the Huesca front, where I expect to participate in the assault on the town. As for photographs, it is incredibly difficult. Several different people have made promises, but I have seen nothing as yet. In any case, I wouldn't be able to send them because I am certain that they would never arrive, and as I am obliged to stay here, I am not getting over anxious. Moreover, there is a love interest in my life here* and I cannot leave until the young lady is able to accompany me back to Paris. So I cannot say anything about my return.

I have also written a few poems which I unfortunately have not had time to copy out. I will send them to you upon my return from the front.

I recently saw in the newspapers that Gracia Cabrera* was sent to a concentration camp in Africa by the fascists, as well as Inocencio (de Puerto Cruz).

It may happen that I find myself back in Madrid quite soon. Can you tell me if Bunuel will be there, and what his address might be?

186

I have met up with Miro two or three times. Nothing to write home about, naturally.

Benjamin Péret

P.S. Here is a manuscript I signed in the name of "the Surrealist artists and writers in Paris". Was this a mistake?

29 October (1936)

My dear André,

I am back from the Aragon front where the situation remains much as it was in August. The fighting spirit hasn't diminished in the slightest, but organization on the anarchists' part has improved, while in the other organizations it seems to have become bureaucratized. Huesca ought to fall rapidly if only we had enough ammunition for a large scale attack. And the fall of Huesca—with the immediate threat to Saragossa which this would bring— would result in the fascists being obliged to loosen their stranglehold on Madrid. But the government of Madrid is very wary of that of Catalonia, which represents the most advanced elements in Spain, and consequently sends arms and munitions in parsimonious quantities. This is the reason, in fact, for the stagnation on the Aragon front.

Naturally, there's a lot more to be said on this subject, but I can't write it here.

Yesterday I saw a manifesto, or rather a telegram of congratulations to the USSR which I am happy to see you did not sign because to do so would have been to uphold the whole policy of bluff, intrigue and cowardice of the Communist International. Let Eluard and Max Ernst sign it right next to Aragon, Desnos, and Tzara (the latter is speaking here tomorrow, I shall go and see that). Here the communists are making a great fuss over two 3,000 ton boats filled mostly with butter and beans, which have been sent from the USSR to Spain. But it happens that almost no butter is consumed in Spain! If that's a reason to congratulate the USSR, why not! Mexico has done much better. They have sent officers, cannons, machine-guns, and a few planes. Under the circumstances, that's rather better than butter and beans.

I have been thinking of coming home soon, but it is only an idea as I *literally* haven't got a sou, and my lady friend neither. I think I can find the means to make the trip as far as Perpignan; but beyond that I don't see how. If you see a sponsor anywhere, I ask you with all my heart to do your best to

187

extract some money and let me know about it *without sending anything here*. In turn I shall tell you when I expect to leave and will ask you to send it to Perpignan, to the *Poste Restante*. A thousand pardons for burdening you with this especially as you must have enough to think about in your own circumstances, but I did have this vague recollection that when I left you had somewhat authorised me to.

I received a letter from Marcel Jean* telling me Oscar* was now back in Paris and with news of our friends in the Canaries. Can you make my excuses to him for not writing today—I have a million things to do—and ask him to let me know exactly the situations of each of our friends in Tenerife.* I will have a note published in the papers here. If Oscar could send me a detailed letter on this subject, it would be even better, but I need it *right away*. In Lerida I saw a man who makes very interesting drawings and sculptures. He's a cabinet-maker. Unfortunately, he had no photos but he's going to take some and I will get them next week when I go through Lerida to the front to Durruti. There are also two young people in Lerida who are not uninteresting.

Otherwise, how are you? What's going on? We have no news from France because the papers don't get here.

I have seen Penrose and Gascoyne*. No news worth mentioning. They translate from dawn to dusk.

Benjamin.

1st Company, "Nestor Makhno" batallion
Durruti Division
Pina de Ebro
Aragon front

7 March (1937)

My dear André,

Apart from the postcard I sent I haven't written because there was nothing of interest to communicate. Since the first days of my return it has been clear that any collaboration with the P.O.U.M. is impossible. They are quite willing to accept people to their right, but not to their left. Otherwise nothing to be done because of the ultra-fast bureaucratization of all the organizations and the scandalous civil servant mentality which is developing. Moreover, as a result of Stalinist pressures, the revolution is steadily going downhill and if this isn't halted it will lead directly to violent counter-revolution. Under these circumstances I have decided to sign up with an anarchist militia, and now here I am at the front—at Pina de Ebro—where I will stay as long as nothing more interesting takes me elsewhere. This sector —which I did not choose—is perfectly calm: we are separated from the fascists by the entire breadth of the swollen Ebro, i.e. by a good kilometre of water. And not a cannon shot, not a bullet, nothing. It's too calm to last. I would like to tell you of all the low tricks of the Stalinists, who are *openly* sabotaging the revolution with, obviously, the enthusiastic support of bourgeois of all varieties. There are so many things, so many supremely disquieting signs, which I cannot write about here. I am going to try to take advantage of the free time I have here in order to write. First I am going to write some poems so that I can finish a book which will contain *Immortelle Maladie, Dormir, dormir dans les pierres, Je Sublime* and these new poems. Perhaps this will work at the NRF. Write me a bit—to let me know if you've received this letter. Needless to say, I have no news of anything happening in Paris. What has become of you? The only thing I know is that you have spoken against the Moscow trials; and that's all.

Benjamin.

31 March 1938 (Paris)*

My dear André,

At the meeting yesterday, Maurice Heine brought a whole pile of documents extracted from *Le Temps* showing that Negrin* refused an offer from the French Government to send troops to Catalonia. For this reason it was no longer possible to ask for 'protection for Catalonia' and this made us consider modifying the very sense of our manifesto.* We are going to draw up a manifesto demanding the constitution of a 'single military front' against that holy alliance, war and fascism, calling for revolutionary defeatism in case of war. We are preparing the manifesto for Sunday and will submit it to general discussion on Monday or Tuesday. As soon as it's done, I'll send it to you. We are asking for signatures outside of Surrealism. This will be a kind of re-edition of *'Appel à la lutte'*, addressed to all the political or trade union organizations (a certain number of unions have created a 'centre for action against the war' and the holy alliance) who have demonstrated in this way. What do you think?

Benjamin.

Durruti's Egg Will Bloom

VERHEARD ON THE MORNING OF 20th OF MAY LAST, IN
a half sleep shot through with jumbled images of the Aragon front, which I
had left three weeks before—this sentence woke me with a start.

I had always seen Durruti as the most revolutionary of the anarchist
leaders, the one whose attitude was most violently opposed to the capitu-
lations of the anarchists who entered the government, and his assassination
had moved me profoundly. * I thought that the teachings which had made up
Durruti's life would not be lost, that—to take up the old cliche—the seed (the
egg) which he had sown would rise up (bloom) very soon.

My beloved inclined toward anarchist attitudes and admired Durruti.
She was not entirely with me, she wasn't born to my life, but I hoped that
she would make up her mind soon, that she WOULD BLOOM.

A Word from Péret

T CANNOT BE DISPUTED THAT THE INVENTION OF language, an automatic product of men's need for mutual communication, worked in the first place to satisfy the need for human relationships. It is nonetheless true that men began to express themselves in fully poetic forms as soon as they had succeeded, albeit quite unconsciously, in organising their language and adapting it to their most pressing needs, so that they can begin to feel all the possibilities it has to offer.[1]

1. A clear case in the present day and in our highly evolved society, of a poetic language being rebuilt before our eyes, not at high social strata but among pariahs and outcasts, is *argot*. *Argot* reveals among the popular masses that create and use it, an unconscious need for poetry which is not satisfied by the language used by other classes, as well as a basic, latent hostility towards those classes. It also shows there is a tendency among working people, who in France all have their own professional *argot*, to form a separate social corpus with its own language, behaviour, customs and morality. New words are constantly arising from the language of these disinherited classes; it is possible that this slang is repeating at a higher level the whole process of the development of language once it has satisfied man's primary needs. The whole process can be roughly traced, from onomatopoeia (*tocante* — tick-tock, for 'a watch'), to more developed poetic images (*balancer le chiffon rouge* — to wave the red rag, 'to speak'). Indeed Victor Hugo saw in it "spontaneous words, created whole, no one knows where or by whom, with no etymology, no analogy, no derivation, solitary, barbarous, sometimes hideous words, with exceptional expressive power . . . One of these words may be like

191

Even the most backward of so-called primitives has these days lost sight of the distant time when language was invented. At best a fragment of legend here and there remains as a poetic reminder of that discovery. But the wealth and variety of cosmologies invented by primitive peoples go to show the vigour and freshness of their imaginations. They clearly have no doubt that "language was given to man to use in a Surrealist way," which coincides with the fulfilment of their desires. In fact man in ancient times did not know how to think other than poetically, and in spite of his ignorance it may be that he sees intuitively further into himself and into nature, from which he barely differentiates himself, than does the rationalist thinker who dissects it from the standpoint of book learning.

(. . .) Some definition of poetic wonder is probably expected of me; that is the last thing I propose to give you. Poetic wonder is so luminous it

---

a claw, the next like a dulled, bleeding eye."
Here are a few words and expressions taken at random from a quick browse through a small dictionary (Jean de la Rue: *Dictionnaire d'argot et des principales expressions populaires*. E. Flammarion, edit. Paris):
Badigeonner la femme du puits: (to colour a woman out of a well) to lie.
Blanchisseuse de tuyaux de pipes: (pipe-stem laundress) prostitute.
Prendre un boeuf: (get a bull) get angry.
Casser des emblèmes: (smash a few emblems) get angry.
Casser la gueule à son porteur d'eau: (smash the water-carrier's face) have periods.
Fée: (fairy) girl.
Cerneau: (green walnut) girl.
Cloporte: (woodlouse) concierge.
Débâcler son chouan: (unbolt your owl) open your heart.
Décrocher ses tableaux: (take your pictures down) pick your nose.
Déchirer son tablier: (tear your apron) die.
Diligence de Rome: (stage-coach from Rome) tongue.
Escargot: (snail) tramp, policeman.
Fonds de pêche: (peach bottom) navel.
Fremillante: (quiverer) meeting.
Lait à broder: (sewing milk) ink.
Pape: (pope) imbecile, glass of rum.
Étrangler un perroquet: (strangle a parrot) drink a glass of absinthe.
Philosophe: (philosopher) old shoe.
Polichinelle: (Punch) eucharist.
Porc-épic: (porcupine) blessed sacrament.
Pape d'orient: (oriental pope) diamond.
Sanglier: (wild boar) priest.
Seminaire: (seminary) prison.
Symbole: (symbol) head, hat, credit at the wine shop.
La vaine louchante: (the vain woman with a squint) the moon.
Cinq et trois font huit: (five plus three makes eight) someone who limps.

does not suffer from competing with the sun. It drives back the shadows and sunlight dampens its brilliance. The dictionary of course gives only a dry etymology in which the marvelous is as unrecognisable as an orchid in a herbarium. I will simply try to suggest what it is like.

Dolls made by the Hopi Indians in New Mexico sometimes have heads that look roughly like a medieval castle. I shall try to take you inside this castle. There are no gates and its walls are as thick as a thousand centuries. It is not in ruins as one might be tempted to believe. Since the roamntic period the crumbling walls have been rebuilt, and re-cut like a ruby; but they are as hard as that stone, and now that I strike them with my head, they have all the ruby's limpidity. They part like high standing grass through which an animal is carefully picking its way. And by some osmotic process I find myself within, amid a play of light like the aurora borealis. Sparkling suits of armour standing guard in the hallway, like a row of snow capped peaks, greet me with raised fists whose fingers moult to make an endless to and fro of birds—or are they shooting stars which couple and mix their primary colours to make the delicate nuances found in the plumage of humming-birds and birds of paradise. Though apparently alone, I am surrounded by a crowd which blindly obeys me. They are beings fuzzier than a speck of dust in a sunbeam. In their root-like heads, their will o' the wisp eyes wander back and forth and their twelve clawed wings allow them to move as quickly as the lightning flash they carry in their wake. They eat from my hand the eyes of peacock feathers and if I squeeze them between my thumb and forefinger I roll a cigarette which drops between the feet of a suit of armour and quickly turns into the first artichoke.

The marvelous meanwhile is all around us, hidden to vulgar eyes but ready to burst out like a time bomb. The drawer I open exhibits among the cotton reels and compasses an absinthe spoon. Through the holes in the spoon a squad of tulips is goose-stepping towards me. In their flowers stand professors of philosophy discovering the categorical imperative. Each word they say is a worthless penny which breaks on the ground bristling with noses which throw them back into the air to form smoke rings. As they dissolve slowly they generate tiny splinters of mirror which each reflect a blade of wet moss.

But why open a drawer if the scorpion which has just dropped from the ceiling onto my bed is speaking: "You should recognise me, I am the old lamp-lighter. Of course I left my wooden leg on a wasteland beside the crumbling remains of a factory long since burnt down, where the tall chimney still stands and now knits bright coloured shawls. My wooden leg has come some way since then. Look at its ministerial belly, the "Sam Suggy" hat on its head, all that gold, all that . . . But you easily recognise a pope quickly hiding a monocle in his left hand, which could have been simply a poisoned communion wafer, while making a backward sign of the cross in the air with

193

his right hand. At this gesture the chimney split from top to bottom like a mussel, so that we could see the sixteen floors on which naked ballerinas no more substantial than a cloud of pollen, were practising lascivious, complicated steps, in a tiger's eye." With this the scorpion stings itself and is incorporated into my table top, leaving an ink-stain in which I can read in mirror-writing: "Executioner hair."

The marvelous, I say again, is all around, at every time and in every age. It is, or should be, life itself, as long as that life is not made deliberately sordid as this society does so cleverly with its schools, religion, law courts, wars occupations and liberations, concentration camps and horrible material and mental poverty. And yet, I remember, it was in Rennes prison where they had locked me up in May 1940, because I had committed the crime of thinking such a society was my enemy, unless it was simply because it had forced me like so many others to defend it twice in my life when I felt nothing in common with it.

You know what these places are like: a poor imitation of a bed which one is forced by the regulations to fold against the wall during the day, so that one has to stretch out on the floor; a table fixed to the wall opposite the bed with a stool next to it bolted onto the wall so that the prisoner will not be tempted to yield to the obsessive compulsion of using it to hit his gaoler over the head (I cannot understand how a man can become a gaoler. Apart from the ignominy attached to such a "profession," the gaoler has to live inside the prison too.)

One morning the glass in the windows beyond my reach, was painted blue. I spent a good part of the day on my back on the floor with my head turned to the window, through which the sun no longer shone. And in the glass a moment after it had been painted, I saw the face of François I, as I remember it from school history books. In the next pane was a rearing horse. Beside that was a tropical landscape rather like a Rousseau painting, and in its bottom right hand corner was a fairy. She stood there so charmingly throwing butterflies with a light, peaceful movement of her hand above her head. In the last pane I read the number 22 and knew immediately I would be let out on the 22nd. But the 22nd of which month and which year? This was the first week of June 1940. The charge against me in those days carried a heavy penalty and I assumed I would be in prison for at least three years. But still, against all probability, I was immediately convinced that I would soon be freed.

Almost every day the images changed, without there ever being more than four on the eight panes of glass. Francois I became a ship ploughing through the waves, the landscape with the fairy a complicated machine, the horse became a cafe, etc. Only the number 22 stayed there obstinately until the day a bomb fell nearby and made the gaolers disappear for a whole day, and most of the glass at the same time. The only unbroken pane, although it was cracked, was the one where I could still see the number 22 in its usual spot—though it had once or twice disappeared from this pane and appeared elsewhere.

And whether you like it or not I left Rennes prison on 22nd July 1940 after paying a ransom of a thousand francs to the Nazis.

I hardly need add that once free, being delighted with my "discovery" I painted panes of glass blue and green, and red, etc, but never, alas, saw anything on them but a more or less even patch of colour. This was a fundamental mistake. No chemical formula will help you create the marvelous. It grabs you by the throat. You have to be in the right state of "vacancy" for the marvelous to deign to visit you. You may say "There you are! I thought so, it was only an illusion you experienced." The prisoner who daubed paint on the glass obviously could not have painted the images I saw later. But they were so real I could not doubt for one moment I had seen them. So how come my own painting did not reflect any images?

In prison I was in the state of "vacancy" I spoke of, I was one of "Those whose desires have the shape of clouds." (Baudelaire, *Le Voyage.*)

All the images I had seen the first day (I refer only to these, as I do not remember the others well enough—and they were expected each day, whereas the first ones had been a surprise), revolved around a violent thirst for freedom only natural in the circumstances. François I immediately suggests school where I first saw this king; he tends to be depicted in history books as a friendly and liberal monarch who supported Renaissance artists and poets. His position is ambivalent in the context of school itself. For children school means subjection; it is a sort of prison from which they are freed every evening, but how infinitely preferable to the one in which I was. The teacher foreshadows the gaoler, but is of course more benign than those I had to deal with day and night.

The rearing horse symbolised my impotent protest against my captivity and also reminded me that during the first world war I had been in contact with the Ist cavalry regiment, a real penitentiary where all the officers addressed the other ranks with nothing but the grossest of insults, followed by threats of punishment. It was just like prison, with the slight difference that the soldiers enjoyed a few hours of freedom each day, which meant that, however wretched their military life, it was better than being in prison.

The Rousseau-style tropical forest with the fairy and butterflies: Rousseau was in the expeditionary force sent to Mexico by Napoleon III and his memory of that country inspired his tropical vegetation. Before this war I was convinced it was imminent and that I was therefore likely to be arrested, because of the military dictatorship it would mean in France, and I had tried

195

in vain to come to Mexico, which I had long wanted to visit, and where I am now a refugee. The fairy immediately calls to mind my girlfriend, of whom I had no news at the time, and whose fate worried me even more than mine. I knew she was threatened with internment in a French camp, or expulsion from the country, which would result in her being thrown into a concentration camp by Franco. I could not forget the terrified expression of distress I had seen on her face a week or ten days before on the platform at the Gare Montparnasse in Paris when I had been bundled onto the train for Rennes in chains, with an impressive escort of gendarmes. The fairy was throwing out all these black thoughts, these "black butterflies." On the glass the butterflies were pale, but she was always scared of insects and even butterflies. I had often joked about her fear and said: "What will become of you if we ever go to Mexico? In tropical countries there are real clouds of butterflies." Her presence in this exotic landscape indicated my desire to see her free, out of reach of police dogs, and throwing out real, colourful butterflies. That would be so much better for her than chasing away the black moths that must afflict her day and night. So, if we managed to reach Mexico, we would be free, and then what would a cloud of butterflies matter? I should add that I have lived in Brazil, a tropical country where I was imprisoned for the same sort of reasons as on this occasion, but conditions in the prison in Rio de Janeiro, though they may have been more sordid than Rennes gaol, were generally less brutal and a great deal more bearable.

The number 22: when I was a child this number was very popular, at least among children who shouted it to warn of approaching danger. In the situation I was in it was a reminder of ever present peril and the insistent way it imposed itself on me underlines the seriousness of the threats I had to live with.

But as soon as I saw the number I knew it was the date on which I would be freed; it was an illumination. I cannot explain it, but I knew quite clearly and without any doubt. I was immediately relieved by the knowledge, which is absurd because it could have meant the 22nd of any month in any year, but my conviction helped me to bear the uncertainty of my fate. This conviction was revived every day by the figure's reappearance, while the uncertainty was made much worse by hearing one day, to my amazement, that the Germans had occupied Rennes—I knew nothing about the military situation. So the certainty given to me by the number 22 compensated symbolically for my obsession with freedom and my ambivalence about the dangers around me—my awareness of how great was the danger conflicted with my hope of escaping.

The succession of four images was like a speeded up film of my life. Childhood: François I; youth: the 1914 war represented by the rearing horse; my time in Brazil and the present (then): the tropical forest with the fairy;

and the future: the enigmatic and absurdly optimistic number 22.

In *L'Amour fou*, Andre Breton examines a case of prophetic revelation; he performed physically the itinerary covered in a scarcely reduced way by a poem[2] he had written eleven years before. The lines by Breton which are the epigraph to this preface show another illumination which he has probably not yet noticed.[3]

It would be hard to maintain that when he wrote the poem or that sentence Andre Breton meant to prophesy the future. Consciously, of course, he knew nothing about it. But I, when I saw the number 22, knew that contrary to appearances it marked my imminent freedom. But I resisted this belief and told myself firmly that it was absurd. The 22nd of June went by without my belief being weakened, but my inner opposition to it was briefly reinforced. I do not know if I am managing to give a flavour of the conflict inside me. It was really like an argument between two people with opposite points of view. In fact the one who maintained I would be freed on the 22nd had no arguments to bring against the other, who heaped him with good reasons why imminent freedom was impossible. And yet the first one was right. He could definitely "see," while the other understood and criticised.

The number 22 in this account is, whether we like it or not, a poetic instance of clairvoyance which I am far from being the first person to report. Even apart from Andre Breton to whom I have referred, poets in every age have noticed and felt this phenomenon. "What I say is the oracle," said Arthur Rimbaud. "The man who really thinks is the seer," Novalis had said before him. He considered the seer to be the real poet. In a parallel way Rimbaud confirmed the poet as seer. Romantics in every country spoke, albeit sometimes incorrectly, of their "visions" and poets have always more or less suspected this fault which is part of their make-up as poets.

I will not contest the fact that this sort of "seeing" was in my case favoured by unusual material conditions. Mystics all over the world whose visions and ecstasies attain poetic status, when they are not fools, have practiced rigorous fasting. It may be that the undernourishment to which I was subjected in prison helped me to see the images hidden in the windows. The tension aimed at the recovery of freedom which racked my whole being, combined with the habit of writing poetry, would in that case have fleshed out my violent desire for freedom in the form I have described.

As we know, anyone who claims to be a poet is automatically thereby placed on the margins of society—to an extent directly proportional to how

2. *Tournesol*, in *Claire de Terre*, Paris, 1923.
3. These pages had already been written when I read in no. 2/3 of *VVV* that he had noticed it and referred to it in an article entitled: "The situation of Surrealism between the wars."

truly he is a poet. The recognised category of *poètes maudits* ("damned poets") makes this clear. They are damned because they place themselves outside a society which in the past condemned their predecessors, the sorcerers, through the church, for the same reason. The sorcerers' intuition undermined the religion which dominated medieval society, and poets today combat through their "visions" the intellectual and moral postulates which modern society would surreptitiously like to dress up as religion. Their visionary capacity means they are liable to be thought mad by ordinary people. Madmen in primitive societies are sent from heaven, or are messengers from the underworld; at all events their supernatural powers are not disputed. One has to admit therefore that there is a common denominator between the sorcerer, the poet and the madman. But the madman breaks off relations with the outside world and drifts around in the wild ocean of his imagination, so we are scarcely able to see what is before his eyes. The common denominator linking the three can only be magic. This is the flesh and blood of poetry. In fact, in the days when magic was the sum of human knowledge, poetry could not yet be distinguished from it, so one is in no danger of being wrong in thinking that primitive myth is largely composed of illuminations, intuitions, and presages confirmed in the past so powerfully that they penetrated instantly to the deepest level of these peoples' consciousness.

(. . .) Even without getting lost amid hypotheses which leave one wandering around the domain of utopia, one can entertain the idea that man may one day be freed from his current material and moral constraints and attain a period of freedom—I mean not only material freedom but also mental freedom such as it is difficult for us to imagine.

Primitive man does not yet know himself, he is still searching for himself. Present day man is lost. The man of the future will first have to find himself, and become aware of himself with all his contradictions. He will have the means to do so. He may already have them without knowing how to use them, as he is not free to think beneath the dust which smothers him. Man in the past when he knew no limits to his thought except those of desire, was able in his struggle with nature to produce these marvelous legends; how much more will the man of the future be able to create, if he is conscious of his nature and increasingly dominates the world with an obstacle-free mind.

These myths and legends are the collective poetic production of societies where inequalities of status were still not large and had not led to noticeable oppression. Poetry cannot conceivably be practiced at a collective level except in a world free of all oppression, where poetic thought has again become as natural to man as looking or sleeping. This will be the "progressive universal poetry" envisaged by Frederick Schlegel nearly 200 years ago. This poetic thinking developed without constraint will create exalting myths of pure wonder, for the marvelous will not upset people as it does today. These myths will not be tied to any religious consolation, as that will have no place in a world turned to the pursuit of the provocative, tempting chimera of perfection which is forever inaccessible.

We cannot conclude that the whole population will take part directly in poetic creation, but poetic creation will no longer be the preserve of a handful of individuals, but the life and way of thought of large groups of men, with the support of the whole population. For poets will have re-established the connection with them which was broken so many centuries ago. The miserable existence to which society currently reduces the majority of the population cuts it off from any kind of poetic thinking, though the aspiration to poetry remains latent. The popularity of stupidly sentimental literature—adventure stories etc, is a symptom of this need for poetry. But the world which offers jewellery for sale costing a few pence a piece, can only offer the masses poetry that is cheapened in the same way; and it is served with the prisoner's dry bread, while the masters eat tasty morsels and some-times take a fancy to real poetry. Only sometimes, of course, for their style of life makes them no more inclined to flights of poetry than their slaves. These days poetry has become the almost exclusive preserve of a tiny number of individuals who are the only ones left who feel more or less clearly that it is necessary.

(. . .) Poets—I do not mean just any sort of entertainer—can no longer be recognised as such, unless they show by total non-conformity their opposition to the world in which they live. They stand against everyone, in-cluding revolutionaries who by working only in the field of politics, arbi-trarily separate politics from cultural movement in general, and advocate subordinating culture in order to achieve the social revolution. There is no poet or artist aware of his place in society who does not think this urgently-required, indispensible revolution is the key to the future. But I find it as reactionary to wish to subordinate poetry and all of culture dictatorially to the political movement, as it is to exclude it completely. The "ivory tower" is only the other side of the obscurantist coin from so-called proletarian art, or vice versa—what does it matter. The reactionary camp try to make poetry in-to the equivalent of religious prayer, while the revolutionary side all too easily confuse it with propaganda. A poet these days must be either a revolutionary or not a poet, for he must endlessly launch into the unknown; one step taken one day does not let him off the next step taken the next day, because every-thing has to be started afresh each day (. . .) Only at this price can he be called a poet and aspire to a legitimate place at the apex of the cultural movement where neither praise nor laurels are to be won, but he must work with all his strength to pull down the constantly re-growing barriers of routine and habit.

199

The Dishonour of the Poets

F ONE LOOKS FOR THE ORIGINAL SIGNIFICANCE OF poetry, today concealed by the thousand flashy rags of society, one ascertains that poetry is the true inspiration of humanity, the source of all knowledge and knowledge itself in its most immaculate aspect. The entire spiritual life of humanity since it began to be aware of itself is condensed in poetry; in it quivers humanity's highest creations and, land ever fertile, it keeps perpetually in reserve the colourless crystals and harvests of tomorrow. Tutelary god with a thousand faces, it is here called love, there freedom, elsewhere science. It remains omnipotent, bubbling up in the Eskimo's mythic tale; bursting forth in the love letter; machine-gunning the firing squad that shoots the worker exhaling his last breath of revolution and thus of freedom; gleaming in the scientist's discovery; faltering, bloodless, as even the stupidest productions draw on it; while its memory, a eulogy that wishes to be funereal, still penetrates the mummified words of the priest, poetry's assassin, listened to by the faithful as they blindly and dumbly look for it in the tomb of dogma where poetry is no more than delusive dust.

Poetry's innumerable detractors, true and false priests, more hypo-critical than the priesthood of any church, false witnesses of every epoch, accuse it of being a means of escape, a flight from reality, as if it were not reality itself, reality's essence and exaltation. But incapable of conceiving of reality as a whole and in its complex relations, they wish to see it only under its most immediate, most sordid aspect. They see only adultery with-

200

out ever experiencing love, the bomber plane without recalling Icarus, the adventure novel without understanding the permanent, elementary, and profound poetic inspiration that it has the ambition of satisfying. They scorn the dream in favour of their reality as if the dream were not one of the most deeply moving aspects of reality; they exalt action at the expense of meditation as if the former without the latter were not a sport as meaningless as any other. Formerly, they opposed the mind to matter, their god to man; now they defend matter against the mind. In point of fact, they have brought intuition to the aid of reason without remembering from whence this reason sprang.

The enemies of poetry have always been obsessed with subjecting it to their immediate ends, with crushing it under their god or, as now, with constraining it under orders of the new brown or "red" divinity—the reddish-brown of dried blood—even bloodier than the old one. For them, life and culture are summed up in the useful and the useless, it being understood that the useful takes the form of a pickaxe wielded for their benefit. For them, poetry is only a luxury for the rich—the aristocrat and the banker—and if it wants to become "useful" to the masses, it should become resigned to the lot of the "applied," "decorative," and "domestic" arts.

Instinctively they sense, however, that poetry is the fulcrum Archimedes required, and they fear that the world, once raised up, might fall back on their heads. Hence the ambition to debase poetry, to deny it all efficacity, all value as an exaltation, to give it the hypocritical, consolatory role of a sister of charity.

But the poet does not have to perpetuate for others an illusory hope, whether human or celestial, nor disarm minds while filling them with boundless confidence in a father or a leader against whom any criticism becomes a sacrilege. Quite the contrary, it is up to the poet to give voice to words always sacrilegious, to permanent blasphemies. The poet should first become aware of his nature and place in the world. An inventor for whom a discovery is only the means of reaching new discoveries, he must relentlessly combat the paralyzing gods eager to keep humanity in servitude with respect to social powers and the divinity, which complement one another. Thus he will be a revolutionary but not one of those who oppose today's tyrant, whom they see as baneful because he has betrayed their interests, only to praise tomorrow's oppressor, whose servants they already are. No, the poet struggles against all oppression: first of all, that of man by man and the oppression of thought by religious, philosophical, or social dogmas. He fights so that humanity can attain an ever more perfect knowledge of itself and the universe. It does not follow that he wants to put poetry at the service of political, even revolutionary action. But his being a poet has made him a revolutionary who must fight on all terrains: on the terrain of poetry by appropriate means and on the terrain of social action, without ever confusing the two fields of action under penalty of re-establishing the confusion that is to be dissipated and consequently ceasing to be a poet, that is to say, a revolutionary.

•

Wars like the one we are undergoing are possible thanks only to a conjunction of *all* forces of regression, and they signify, among other things, an arrest of cultural expansion, checked by the forces of regression that culture threatens. This is too obvious to be gone into. From this momentary defeat of culture fatally ensues a triumph of the spirit of reaction and, above all, religious obscurantism, the necessary crown of every reactionary movement. One must go back very far in history to find a period when God, the Almighty, Providence, etc., were so frequently invoked by heads of state or for their benefit. Churchill hardly makes a speech without assuring himself of the Lord's protection; Roosevelt much the same; de Gaulle puts himself under the aegis of the Cross of Lorraine; Hitler daily invokes Providence; and from morning to night metropolitans of all kinds thank the Lord for the blessing of Stalinism. Far from being an unusual demonstration on their part, their attitude consecrates a general movement of regression at the same time that it reveals their panic. During the preceding war, the clerics of France solemnly declared that God was not German, while on the other side of the Rhine their counterparts proclaimed his German nationality. And never have the churches of France known so many faithful as since the commencement of German hostilities.

Where does this renaissance of fideism come from? First, from the despair engendered by the war and general misery: people no longer see a terrestial solution for their horrible situation—or they do not yet see it— and they look to a fabulous heaven for consolation of their material ills, which the war has magnified to unheard-of proportions. For all that, during the unstable period called peace, humanity's material conditions, which gave rise to the consoling religious illusion, subsisted, even though attenuated, and imperiously demanded satisfaction. Society was presiding over the slow dissolution of the religious myth without being able to find a substitute except for civic saccharin: fatherland or leader.

Faced with this ersatz, some people, thanks to the war and the conditions of its development, remain bewildered, without any recourse but a return to religious faith pure and simple. Others, finding these substitutes insufficient and old-fashioned, have tried either to replace them with new mythical products or to regenerate the old myths. Hence the great apotheosis in the world—on the one hand, Christianity; on the other fatherland

and leader. But fatherland and leader, like religion—which is at the same time their brother and rival—can nowadays dominate minds only by coercion. Their current triumph, fruit of an ostrich-like reflex, far from signifying their brilliant renaissance, presages their imminent demise.

This resurrection of God, fatherland, and leader has also been the result of people's extreme confusion, engendered by the war and its beneficiaries. Therefore, the intellectual ferment created by this situation, to the extent that one is carried away by it, remains entirely regressive, affected by a negative coefficient. Its products remain reactionary, whether they are the propaganda "poetry" of fascism or anti-fascism, or religious exaltation. An old man's aphrodisiacs, they restore a fleeting vigour to society only to better strike it down. These "poets" in no way participate in the creative thought of the revolutionaries of Year II or Russia 1917, for example, or in the thought of the mystics or heretics of the Middle Ages; for they are destined to provoke a factitious exaltation in the masses, while revolutionaries and mystics were the products of a real and collective exaltation that their words translated. They expressed, then, the thoughts and hopes of an entire people imbued with the same myth or animated by the same spirit, while propoganda "poetry" aims to restore a little life to a myth in its death throes. Civic hymns, they have the same soporific power as their religious patrons, from whom they directly inherit the conservative function; for if mythical then mystical poetry creates the divinity, the hymn exploits this divinity. Just as the revolutionary of Year II or 1917 created a new society while the patriot and the Stalinist of today takes advantage of it.

To compare the revolutionaries of Year II and 1917 with the mystics of the Middle Ages does not in any way amount to situating them on the same plane: but in trying to bring the illusory religious paradise down to earth, revolutionaries do not fail to exhibit psychological processes similar to those of mystics. Still, one must distinguish between mystics, who, despite themselves, tend to consolidate myth and involuntarily prepare the conditions that will lead to its reduction to religious dogma, and heretics, whose intellectual and social role is always revolutionary because it brings into question the principle on which myth relies to mummify itself in dogma. Indeed, if the orthodox mystic (but can one speak of an orthodox mystic?) conveys a certain relative conformism, the heretic, on the other hand, expresses opposition to the society in which he lives. Only priests, then, are to be considered in the same light as the current supporters of fatherland and leader, for they have the same parasitic function in regard to myth.

I could want no better example of the preceding than a small pamphlet that recently appeared in Rio de Janeiro: *L'Honneur des poètes* [The Honour of the Poets], which contains a selection of poems published clandestinely in Paris during the Nazi occupation. Not one of these "poems" surpasses the poetic level of pharmaceutical advertising, and it is not by chance that the great majority of their authors has believed it necessary to return to classical rhyme and alexandrines. Form and content necessarily maintain a very strict relation to each other, and in these "verses" they react on each other in a mad dash to the worst reaction. It is rather significant that most of these texts strictly associate Christianity and nationalism as if they wished to demonstrate that religious dogma and nationalist dogma have a common origin and an identical social function. The pamphlet's very title, *The Honour of the Poets*, considered in regard to its content, takes on a sense foreign to all poetry. All said, the honour of these "poets" consists of ceasing to be poets in order to become advertising agents.

In the case of Loys Masson the nationalism-religion alloy contains a greater share of fideism than patriotism. In fact, he limits himself to embroidering on the catechism:

> *Christ, grant my prayer to draw strength from deep roots*
> *Let me deserve the light of my wife at my side*
> *That I might go without weakening to the people in jail*
> *Whom she washes with her hair like Mary.*
> *I know that behind the hills you are striding closer.*
> *I hear Joseph of Arimathea crumbling the ecstatic wheat over the*
>   *Tomb*
> *and the vine singing in the broken arms of the thief on the cross.*
> *I see you: As it touched the willow and the periwinkle*
> *spring settles on the thorns of the crown.*
> *They blaze:*
> *Firebrands of deliverance, travelling firebrands*
> *oh! may they pass through us and consume us*
> *if that is their road to the prisons.*

The dosage is more equal in Pierre Emmanuel:

> *O France seamless gown of faith*
> *soiled by traitorous feet and spit*
> *O gown of soft breath ferociously ripped*
> *by the tender voice of revilers*
> *O gown of the purest linen of hope*
> *who know the price of being naked before God . . .*

Accustomed to the Stalinist censer and amens, Aragon nonetheless does not succeed as well as the preceding "poets" in alloying God and country. He meets the first, if I may say so, only at a tangent and obtains a text that would make the author of the French radio jingle "Levitan's furniture is guaranteed for life" turn pale with envy:

There is a time for suffering
When Joan came to Vaucouleurs
Oh! cut France to pieces
The light had that pallor
I remain king of my sorrows

But it is to Paul Eluard*, the only author of this pamphlet who was ever a poet, that one owes the most finished civic litany:

On my gourmand and tender dog
On its pricked-up ears
On its clumsy paw
I write your name.

On the springboard of my door
On familiar objects
On the tide of holy fire
I write your name . . .

It should be noted, incidentally, that the litany form appears in the majority of these "poems" doubtless because of the idea of poetry and lamentation it implies and the perverse taste for evil that the Christian litany aims to exalt with a view to deserving heavenly bliss. Even Aragon and Eluard, formerly atheists, feel obliged, the one to evoke in his productions the "saints and prophets" and "Lazarus' tomb," and the other to return to the litany, no doubt in obedience to the famous slogan: "The priests are with us."

In reality, all the authors of this pamphlet proceed, without admitting it even to themselves, from an error of Guillaume Apollinaire's, which they further aggravate. Apollinaire had tried to treat war as a poetic subject. But if war, considered as combat and separate from any nationalist spirit, can at a pinch remain a poetic subject, the same cannot be said for a nationalist slogan, even if the nation in question is. like France, oppressed by the Nazis. The expulsion of the oppressor and the propaganda to this end falls within the realm of political, social or military action, depending on how one envisages this expulsion. In any case, poetry does not have to intervene in this debate by other than its own means, by its own cultural significance, leaving poets free to participate as revolutionaries in routing the Nazi adversary by revolutionary means—without ever forgetting that this oppression

205

corresponded to the wish, whether avowed or not, of all the enemies—first the national, then the foreign—of poetry understood as the total liberation of the human spirit. For, to paraphrase Marx, poetry has no homeland because it belongs to all times and all places.

Much more could be said about the freedom so often invoked in these pages. First, which freedom are we talking about? Freedom for a small number to squeeze the entire population or freedom for this population to bring this small number of priveleged people to their senses? Freedom for the believers to impose their God and their morality on the whole of society or freedom for this society to reject God, his philosphy and his morality? Freedom is like "a breath of air" [*"un appel d'air"*] said André Breton; and to fulfill its role this breeze must first sweep away all the miasmas of the past that infest this pamphlet. As long as the malevolent phantoms of religion and fatherland, in whatever disguise they borrow, buffet the intellectual and social air, no freedom is conceivable. Every "poem" that exalts a "freedom" wilfully left undefined, even when not adorned with religious or national attributes, first ceases to be a poem and then constitutes an obstacle to the total liberation of humanity, for it deceives in presenting a "freedom" that dissimulates new chains. From every authentic poem, on the other hand, issues a breath of absolute and active freedom, even if this freedom is not evoked in its political or social aspect: in this way the poem contributes to the real liberation of humanity.

Mexico, February 1945

The Heart of the Comet

LL MYTHS REFLECT THE AMBIVALENCE OF man in the face of the world and himself; this ambivalence is the result of the profound feeling of alienation that man experiences, and which is inherent to his nature. He sees himself as weak and disenfranchised with regard to the natural forces which dominate him. He has the intuition that he could live a less precarious existence and feel happier. But he cannot see the path to happiness in the conditions of life which nature and society have imposed upon him, and he consoles himself by situating this happiness in a golden age or in an unearthly future. The importance then, of myths, resides in the hope for happiness which they embody, the belief in its possibility and the obstacles which lie between man and his desire. Briefly, they express a feeling of duality in nature which man participates in and which he does not imagine can be resolved during the course of his own existence . . .

Until now humanity has only conceived of one myth of pure exaltation: sublime love, which, taking off from the very heart of desire, aims at its total satisfaction. It is the cry of human anguish undergoing a metamorphosis into a song of joy. With sublime love, the marvelous also loses its supernatural, extraterrestial or celestial character which, up till then, all myths possessed. The marvelous must in some way return to its source in order to discover its true direction and inscribe itself within the limits of human existence. Using the most primordial hopes of an individual as a springboard, sublime love offers a means of transmutation which will result in

207

the reconciliation of flesh and spirit, tending to melt them together into a better unit where one cannot be distinguished from the other. Desire has the responsibility of fostering this fusion, which is its ultimate justification. This is the ultimate goal that humanity now can hope to attain. It follows that sublime love is opposed to religion, particularily Christianity. This is why a christian can only condemn sublime love, a love which is intended to deify the human individual . . . Although it is rare for a human being—particularily the male—to abandon himself to desire except in so far as it brings him back to his most primitive state. In sublime love, the human caught in its vertiginous grasp, has only one aspiration, to let himself be carried off as far as possible from this state. Desire, while retaining a link to sexuality, now sees itself transfigured. It incorporates, with its appeasement in view, all the benefits which its earlier sublimation, even the most complete, had procured for it and which provoke a new state of exaltation. Beyond sublime love the sublimation of desire carries with it, in some sense, its disincarnation, since, in order to be satisfied it must lose sight of the object which provoked it. This is why in man a state of duality is maintained, which keeps flesh and spirit opposed. On the other hand, with sublime love this sublimation is only possible with the carnal object as go-between and tends to re-establish in man a cohesion which was earlier non-existent. Therefore, desire in sublime love, far from losing sight of the flesh and blood person which inspired it, tends in the long run, to sexualize the entire universe.

In our day Surrealism has taken up the revindication of romanticism with new vigour, without hiding the obstacles which the world puts in the way of this revindication. Better than anyone else, André Breton recognised that love is the explosive centre of human life, that it has the power to bring light or shadow into life, that it is the beginning and end of all desire; that it is, in a word, the single and only justification of life. The Surrealist revolt was caused in a large part by conditions that man and the world had imposed on love; moreover, the protest has fed upon these conditions as it amplified and gained ground in other domains. Even if the Romantics implicitly recognised the fusion of heart, spirit and flesh in sublime love, this flesh often retained the traces of the indignities foisted upon it by Christianity. The rehabilitation of the flesh, without which the very notion of sublime love dies, and its recognition in all its splendour, is indeed one of the great tasks which Surrealism set itself. And so the grimacing ghost of sin is dissolved by the light cast by a woman's beauty.

Even if love, in the widest sense of the word, directs all of human life, it must, in order to finally elevate itself to sublime love, eventually prune the exuberant tree of desire, beginning with its lowest branches. Deprived of the innumerable shoots it had sent out in all directions, the tree will then be able to nourish itself with the sap of the earth and grow even higher toward the only star which incites metamorphosis. The expression "Two full hands don't embrace too well" has never made more sense than when taken literally. After all, man only has at his disposal a limited amount of affection, which is all the more effective if it is attached to a single object. Sacrifice is indispensable for whoever wants to embark on the quest of sublime love. Don Juan never had more than one breath of love to blow into each one of the objects of his desire. He who resists a thousand temptations to abandon himself to one alone has achieved the maximum sum of the possibilities belonging to each one, and in passing it from one to the other, it is multiplied to the highest power, by neglecting fractions and aiming for the most complete whole number that their sum can attain.

Notes

Biographical Introduction. Since biographical information on Péret is scarce, particularily in English, the introduction takes this form, rather than being a critical analysis. English readers should consult J.H.Matthews book on Péret for this (see bibliography). The numbers which follow in these notes are page numbers.

7   **Guy Prévan:** In his *Trajectoire politique d'un révolutionnaire poète* in *Benjamin Péret*, ed J.M.Goutier, 1982.

8   **Early poems:** Péret did not exactly publicise the existence of these early poems, they were discovered by chance only recently.

8   **Courtot:** In his book *Introduction à la lecture de Benjamin Péret*, 1969.

8   **SIC:** Important avant-garde review edited by Pierre Albert-Birot.

8   **Rabourdin:** From his essay *Les premiers poèmes de Benjamin Péret* in *Benjamin Péret* ed. Goutier, op. cit.

8   **Jacob:** Letter to Francis Picabia.

8   **Desnos:** From *Nouvelles Hebrides*, Gallimard, 1978. This story is immortalised in a slightly different version in Breton's *Nadja*.

10   **Barrès trial:** Essentially, Breton et al accused Barrès' effigy of repudiating the Anarchist tendencies of his youth (he had been a Socialist and had, by 1921, become a Boulangist member of the assembly as well as an anti-Dreyfusard), out of self-interest, ambition and nationalism.

10   **Comoedia:** Review dated 15 May, 1921, quoted in Marguerite Bonnet, *L'Affaire Barrès*, Corti, 1987.

10   **La Liberté:** 16 May, 1921, op. cit.

10   **Naville:** From *Le Temps du surréel*, Galilee, 1977

11   **Desnos:** Op. cit.

11   **Soupault:** In a review in *La Revue européen*.

11   **First automatic text:** Indeed, one of his only authentically automatic texts if one considers lack of punctuation and illogical syntax to be essential proof of "pure psychic automatism," as Breton later described it.

11   **Tristan Tzara:** Tzara joined the Surrealists a few years later, after the death of Dada was confirmed.

13   **Daybook:** Published in *Archives du surréalisme*, Vol. I, Gallimard, 1988.

14   **"Appel aux travailleurs":** "Appeal to worker-intellectuals," defined in this manifesto as "writers or those who in some way or other exert an influence on opinion."

14   **"Chiens écrasés":** "Squashed dogs."

15   **Naville:** Op. cit.

17   **Thrown out of Brazil:** The *Cahiers Léon Trotsky*, March 1986, contains an article *Benjamin Perét au Brasil*, which gives details on this.

17   **Reservations:** This is not entirely true! Thirion's remarks should not be taken entirely at face value, for his political affiliations were somewhat at odds with those of Péret.

17   **Thirion:** From *Révolutionnaires sans révolution*, Laffont, 1978.

19   **Aid to Spain:** The reasons for the ban were complex. In part it had to do with the British government's fear of spreading Communism, which caused them to put pressure on the French. The french, fearing invasion by Hitler, gave in to it.

19   **POUM:** See note to p. 183.

20   **Andrade:** Letter to the editor of *Arts*, December, 1962.

21   **"For an Independent Revolutionary Art":** This manifesto was originally only signed by Breton and Diego Rivera, but this was a measure of prudence to protect Trotsky.

21   **Péret's dislike of priests:** It was his normal practice to spit upon and otherwise
ins   insult any cleric unfortunate enough to cross his path. David Gascoyne describes such an incident in his introduction to *Remove Your Hat & Other Works* (by Péret), Atlas Press, 1986.

24 **Surrealist games:** Among others, the Surrealists invented their own pack of cards during this enforced wait. The four aces are illustrated below. Their symbols and suits are as follows—Dark Star (Dream), Flame (Love), Lock (Knowledge) and Wheel & Blood (Revolution).

24 **Varo:** He married her in 1943, upon the death of Elsie Houston. However, she stayed in Mexico when he returned to France in 1948.

28 **Anthologie des mythes:** A collection of South American texts edited by Péret, he also translated the *Livre de Chilam Balam de Chumayel*, a Mayan myth cycle, at this time.

29 **In English before:** Except part of "Natural History", an early version of which appeared in *Atlas Anthology Three*.

29 **Small editions:** A part of *La Parôle est à Péret* appeared in *Anti-Narcissus*, and versions of "The Dishonour of Poets" appeared in *Radical America* and as a pamphlet from No Starch Press (an early version of the present translation).

Poetry

1. Selections from "Je ne mange pas de ce pain-là." Literally: "I will not eat that sort of bread", idiomatically: "I'd rather starve." or "I won't stand for it." This collection of Péret's political poetry was published in 1936 by *Editions Surréalistes*, illustrated by Max Ernst in an edition of 249 copies. The poems were written between 1926 and 1934 and appeared in *La révolution surréaliste* and *Le Surréalisme au service de la révolution*.

33 **The "Young Guard":** Communist youth song, also "between the arse and the shirt-tails" is a French expression denoting two things so similar to each other as to be indistinguishable. The poem comments on Gide's belated affiliation to the Communist Party.

34 **Foch:** French general. When this poem was first published the literary critic of *La Liberté* (!) called for its author to be shot.

34 **Calf's lung:** Péret's obsession with "mou de veau" probably derives from the notorious invention of Raymond Roussel: the statue which runs on rails made of calf's lungs in his play *Impressions d'Afrique*.

38 **The Sixth of February:** On the 6th of February, 1934, there was a huge riot in Paris occasioned by an attempted right-wing coup in which the Stalinists were implicated. The Surrealists had only recently parted company with them.

38 **Stilettos:** In French "cannes-gillettes", probably homemade weapons, sticks with razor blades ("gillette") inserted in the end.

38 **Burning crosses:** The "croix-de-feu" was a veteran's organisation which took part in the riots—no connection with the American KKK.

38 **Firing post:** French capital punishment customs require the victim to be tied to a post, which the firing squad then shoots at.

39 **The Fourway Pact:** On the 15th of July, 1933, France, Italy, Germany and England

signed an agreement to create an alliance between the European powers.

39 **Worm-shaped corridor:** Allusion to the Danzig corridor, the eventual pretext for the German invasion of Poland.

40 **The heroic death of Condamine de la Tour:** This poem first appeared in *La révolution surréaliste*, no. 6, 1926, with this note: "The *Academie Francaise* has proposed "the heroic death of Condamine de la Tour," who was killed last year at the head of his battalion of sharpshooters in Morocco, as the subject for the 1927 Poetry Prize. Our contributor, Benjamin Péret, inspired by this explosive action, is already able to present the jury of the *Académie* with the following poem, which so precisely captures the true value of the military prowess of his compatriot."

40 **Strumpot:** In French "Gidouille", a word invented by Jarry to describe the magnificent and repulsive dimensions of the stomach of Père Ubu.

2. Selections from "Je Sublime." Literally "I Sublime." Published in 1936 by *Editions surréalistes*, in an edition of 241 copies, with four frottages by Max Ernst. The poems were written in 1935.

3. Selections from "Un point c'est tout." Literally "A Full Stop, That's All," but idiomatically: "That's Final." Originally published in the periodical *Les 4 Vents*, Paris, 1946.

A Lifetime. Written for a collection edited by Marc Eigeldinger, *André Breton: Essais et temoinages*, Neufchatel, 1950.

54 **Fleecing will be free:** see note to p. 80.

Death to the Pigs and the Field of Battle: In French "Mort aux Vaches et au champ d'honneur", literally "Death to the Cows and to/on the Field of Honour", however, "Mort aux Vaches" in 1920's street slang meant "Death to the Cops", and "vache" also has the meaning of "idiot". Incidentally, the word "pig" to denote a policeman, or law officer, goes back to early nineteenth century English.

The book was originally published in 1953 by *Editions arcanes*, although Péret wrote it in the Winter of 1922-23. Chapter 5 had already appeared in *La Révolution surréaliste*, no 4, 1925.

61 **1. Look Smart.** In French "A pieds joints", literally "Feet Together."

61 **The last Abencerage:** A character from a novel of the same title by Chateaubriand— a vibrant Oriental love story. The last Abencerage is the last member of a Moorish family in Grenada.

80 **3. No Charge for Fleecing:** Literally "Here the Shave is Free," but during the 1920's and later the expression "Demain l'on rase gratis" was used by unbelieving voters when faced with preposterous electoral promises.

80 **The Speaker:** The character who, in French is called "M. le President" fulfilled a similar role in the French Assembly as does the Speaker of the House in the British Parliament. He should not be confused with the character who appears later "M. le President de Conseil", here translated as "The Prime Minister."

89 **4. Loser Takes All:** In French "Qui perd gagne", literally "Who loses wins."

90 **5. The Parasites Abroad:** In French "Les Parasites voyagent", literally "The Parasites go on a Journey." If this is a French catch-phrase of the period it is now totally obscure. This chapter consists of a text full of made-up words which Péret has footnoted and assigned meanings to. The words which do have slang meanings ("rond" for example, note 2), are not assigned their usual meaning. ("Je n'ais pas un rond" meant "I've not got a cent.") Occasionally Péret will invent a word such as "bruleur" (note 49) which almost means "something which burns", and in his note he defines this as "sun", and the association is obvious. This does not, how-

ever apply to most of the other invented words.

Péret's interest in slang is perhaps partially explained in this section of *La Parôle est à Perét*: "Slang is proof, in the people who create and use it, of an unconscious need for poetry which is not satisfied by the language of other classes, and also demonstrates a fundamental and latent hostility to those classes." Here is an evident connection between Péret's politics and his literary works.

103 **6. Lovely Stories Continue but Don't Stay the Same:** In French "Mes belles histoires se suivent mais ne se ressemblent pas", literally "My beautiful stories follow one another, but do not resemble one another," based on a familiar expression, still in use today "The days follow one another, but they're never the same."

111 **7. Elephant on Wheels:** In French "L'Elephant à billes," literally "Elephant with ball-bearings." The phrase which inspired Péret remains obscure to the translator.

The Inn of the Flying Arse: First published in *Littérature*, No 3, May, 1922. Despite the first sentence, the story is not signed at the end.

The Condemned Man's Last Night: First published in *La révolution surréaliste*, No 7, June, 1926 and then in *Main Forte*.

121 **The custom for a condemned man:** In other words, a shave and a haircut. M. Deibler (next sentence) was a real person, one of a line of official executioners who handed the job down, father to son.

121 **The rocker:** The condemned man does not kneel at the guillotine, he is strapped, lying down, to a board, which is tilted horizontally until his head is beneath the blade.

One to One. In French "Corps a Corps" meaning hand to hand combat, but this expression also assumed the meaning of a "One-to-one relationship." First published in no. 9/10 of *La révolution surréaliste* in 1926.

Imagine. First published in Vol. 3 of Péret's Oeuvres Complètes, where it was given the first word of the story as title.

128 **Myosotis:** Type of forget-me-not, thus the next line.

129 **L'Aiglon:** Sarah Bernhardt's most famous role was as the transvestite hero of Edmond Rostand's *L'Aiglon*.

Natural History. Originally published, in a "hors commerce" edition of 273 copies, by Jehan Mayoux, in Ussel, 1958. The first section had already appeared in the periodical *Les 4 Vents*, no. 8, Paris, 1947. The texts were written in Mexico and France between 1945 and 1958.

Prose: Collaborations

Calender of Tolerable Inventions from Around the World. First published in the *Almanach surréaliste du demi-siècle*, La Nef, Paris, 1950.Even more than Peret's other texts, this piece is full of puns and word-play, some of which require notes.

161 **Carnival mask:** In French "loup," usual meaning: "wolf."

161 **Kiss-Curl:** In American: "Cow-Lick."

162 **Decalcomania:** Surrealist painting process invented by Oscar Dominguez, based on smearing paint between two sheets of paper, separating them, and seeing what results.

164 **Sprinkling-rose:** In American: "sprinkling-head."

164 **Sallet:** A medieval helmet, in French "Salade," thus its function here.

169 **Beauty spot:** In French "mouche," usually meaning "fly," and to "faire mouche" is to "hit the target" or "bullseye."

172 The extra day in the first week of December is present in the French original.

213

The Child Planet. It was thanks to Youki Desnos that this collaboration was first published in Péret's *Oeuvres Complètes*, Vol. 4. It was accompanied by the following note: "This Saturday, the sixth of May, we each composed a poem simultaneously, without corresponding. We amalgamated them and gave the whole, as a title, Péret's first word and Desnos' last: the Child Planet. Each page was signed by its respective author, and the whole jointly signed."

173 **Strong wits in the ports of wild cards and diamonds:** In French " les esprits forts dans les rades de manille et de carreau," a phrase full of double meanings. "Esprits forts" can mean "free thinkers" or "strong spirits," "rade" is a "port," or in slang a "bar," and "etre en rade" means "to lack something". "Manille" is a wild card, also here a pun on the port of Manila.

Prose: Polemical.

Automatic Writing. This text, dating from 1929, first appeared in Vol. 4 of the *Oeuvres Complètes*. It was intended for the Brasilian magazine *Diario da Noite*.

177 **This journal:** i.e. *Diario da Noite*.

178 **Sea foam pipe:** In French "une pipe en écume" is actually a "meerschaum pipe," but this sentence, and the pun-laden one before seemed to need a more literal rendition. In context, the "seven" of the previous sentence is an allusion to the "seven league boots" of fairy-tales.

179 **A haymaker:** An American boxing expression here employed to make some sense of this passage which, again, has several meanings. Briefly, Peret writes "les quatres feuilles du trèfle multiplies par les cinq de la giroflée n'y font rien," "giroflée" is a "stockflower," and a "giroflée a cinq feuilles" has the figurative meaning of a slap that is so hard that the mark of five fingers remains on the adversary's face.

Letters. The first, to the Brazilian League, was published in *A Propos de Péret*, by the *Association des amis de Benjamin Péret*, in 1987. The letters to Breton appeared in *Introduction a la lecture de Benjamin Péret*, by Claude Courtot, Le Terrain Vague, 1965.

180 **Open Letter to the Brazilian League:** As explained in the introduction, the Brazilian League was the Brazilian sector of the Communist League of the Left Opposition.

180 **Naville:** Pierre Naville, ex-Surrealist, an editor of *Clarte* at this time.

180 **The C.L.:** Here Péret is refering to the French Communist League.

181 **La Vérité:** French left weekly newspaper.

181 **Three Months imprisonment:** Georges Sadoul received this for writing the celebrated "St. Cyr Letter" to a commmandant at the military academy there. It read: "Dirty swine, you're hiding your game, you've just been made 61st in your class at the Saint-Cyr Military School. I know how greatly you admire armies, you fistulous and grimy officer. If you do not hand in your immediate resignation to the Commander General, then you're nothing but a pile of refuse and a garbage can full of shit. Furthermore you can go and eat shit, with your fancy white gloves, you dirty Saint-Cyrien. DOWN WITH YOUR SHAKO PLUME! We'll manage to kick you out and hang you high, clip your Marshal Joffre's tail, the master of your young years, fuck off you dismal Cyr, you dirty little creep. Signed. The Unknown Soldier."

181 **The professor:** Gaupenne was implicated in the above affair.

181 **The banning of his film:** Bunuel's *L'Age d'or*.

182 **Aragon:** The "Aragon affair" had its origin in Aragon's trip to the USSR, where he denounced Surrealism at the Kharkov writers' conference. Upon his return to Paris, he denied his move away from Surrealism, and published *Aux Intellectuels révolutionnaires*, in which he defended the psychoanalytic method which he had just denounced as "idealistic". His new poetry, however, followed the Party line, and included *Front Rouge*, a worthless piece of propaganda, which provoked the government to put him on trial for "incitement to murder." Nonetheless, Breton and the Surrealists signed a manifesto in his favour. Aragon, a few days later,

anounced in *L'Humanité* that he disassociated himself from this manifesto and "disapproves of the totality of its contents" because of its attack on the Communist Party.

The Communist League replied to Péret's letter, in part stating: "It is evident that one cannot be at the same time a participant in these publications [i.e. Surrealist manifestoes] and a member of the opposition. It is not just that the comrade [Péret] has criticised "trotskyism," but also he has shown serious deviations with regard to the Bolshevik-Leninist line of the Left Opposition, which is even more serious." They concluded that in order to be re-admitted, Péret should make a clear repudiation of these Surrealist texts and a public affirmation of the correctness of the political line of the Left Opposition.

183 **F.A.I.:** Federacion Anarquista Iberica, the Iberian Anarchist Federation, a far left group, mostly made up of peasants from Andalucia.
183 **P.O.U.M.:** Partido Obrero de Unificacion Marxista, Workers' Party of Marxist Unification, leftist revolutionary party formed by Nin and Maurin from two oppositional Communist parties. Their policy was to fight the war for the revolution, not for democracy, but for workers' control.
183 **P.S.U.C:** Partido Socialista Unificado de Catalunya, the Socialist Party of Catalonia. Since it was affiliated to the Third International, more Communist than Socialist. Their policy was to win the war for democracy and the republic, then worry about the dictatorship of the proletariat.
184 **P.O.I.:** Parti Ouvrier Internationaliste, International Workers Party, of which Péret was a member.
184 **The Generalitat:** The Catalonian government, which only had limited powers.
184 **Largo Caballero:** Prime Minister of the government of the Republic.
185 **The Moscow Trials:** The Surrealists were among the very first, on the left, to denounce the Moscow show trials.
185 **Jean Rous:** delegate from the International Secretariat.
186 **La Batalla:** The POUM's daily newspaper, published in Barcelona.
186 **Miravittles:** Jaume Miravittles was chief of propaganda in Catalonia.
186 **Nevzal:** Czech Surrealist.
186 **Love interest:** Péret met Remedios Varo in Spain.
186 **Garcia Cabrera:** Founder of the Tenerife Surrealist group and an active Socialist.
188 **Marcel Jean:** French Surrealist artist and writer.
188 **Oscar:** Oscar Dominguez.
188 **Our friends in Tenerife:** There was an active Surrealist group in The Canaries during the thirties, centred round the review *Gaceta de Arte*.
188 **Penrose and Gascoyne:** English members of the Surrealist movement, painter and poet respectively. They worked for Radio Free Catalonia as translators and broadcasters.
189 **(Paris):** Breton was now in Mexico with Trotsky.
189 **Negrin:** Minister in Largo Caballero's government, he had also entered into secret negotiations with the Nazis.
189 **Manifesto:** It is unclear which manifesto this was.
189 **"Appel à la Lutte":** A manifesto of 10th February 1934, in which the Surrealists and others, reacting to the attempted right-wing coup of February 6th, called for a united front against the right.

Durruti's Egg Will Bloom. Published in the "Dream" issue of *Cahiers GLM*, March 1938, edited by Breton. Durruti was the great Spanish Anarchist and their most successful military commander.
190 **Durruti's death:** At the time this was thought to be an assassination, but it is now generally accepted that Durruti was killed by a stray bullet.

A Word from Péret. In French "La Parole est a Péret," a literal, but incorrect translation would be "The word belongs to Péret." The actual meaning of the phrase is "It's Péret's turn to speak." First published by *Editions surrealistes* in New York, 1943, although intended as an introduction for his anthology of South American myths.

The Dishonour of the Poets. First published in 1945 in Mexico City. This text attacks the celebrated *L'Honneur des poètes* published during the occupation by *Editions de Minuit*. Immediately after the war it was republished, but in Belgium, because the only publishers to have paper available in France were those that had collaborated with the Germans!

205 **Eluard:** Once Péret's closest friend after Breton within the Surrealists, this attack must finally have ended this friendship. The "name" in the poem quoted, which only appears at the end of the last verse, and there are many verses like those given here before it, is "Freedom."

The Heart of the Comet. More literally "The Comet's Nucleus." This essay was written to preface Péret's *Anthologie de l'amour sublime*, published in 1956. It contains 56 extracts whose theme is love. A glance at the table of contents reveals little to shock the sensibilities of any graduate of the liberal arts. One wonders how it is possible that this anodyne collection could have been compiled by one of the most mordant and stubborn Surrealists who, moreover, wrote some of the best love poems of his time.

Bibliography

Most of Péret's books were published in extremely small editions (some in less than one hundred copies) and have been unobtainable until The Association des amis de Benjamin Péret began publishing his Oeuvres Complètes. Four volumes have now appeared, the first two containing his poetry, the last two his prose fiction. Volume 5, political writing, is due out in Spring 1989. All contain precise bibliographical information. In this list certain publishers are indicated by initials (E.S. = Editions surréalistes, T.V. = Le Terrain vague, E.L.= Eric Losfeld), and all the books in French are published in Paris unless stated otherwise.

I. Books by Péret in French.

Poetry
Le passager du transatlantique, Collection "Dada," 1921.
Immortelle Maladie, Collection "Littérature," 1924.
Dormir, dormir dans les pierres, E.S., 1927.
Le Grand Jeu, Gallimard, 1928.
De derrière les fagots, E.S., 1934.
Je ne mange pas de ce pain-là, E.S., 1936.
Je Sublime, E.S., 1936.
Trois cerises et une sardine, Editions GLM, 1937.
Dernier malheur, dernière chance, Editions de la revue "Fontane," 1945.
Air Mexicain, Librairie Arcanes, 1952.

Prose: Fiction
Au 125 Boulevard Saint-Germain, Collection "Littérature," 1923.
152 Proverbes mis au goût du jour, (with Eluard), E.S., 1925.
Il était une boulangèrie, Editions du Sagittaire, 1925.
Et les seins mouraient, Les Cahiers du Sud, 1928.
Au paradis des fantômes, Collection "Un Divertissement," 1938.
Les Malheurs d'un dollar, Editions de la Main a Plume, 1942.
Main Forte, Editions de la revue "Fontane," 1946.
Feu central, Editions K, 1947.
La Brebis galante, Les éditions premières, 1949.
Mort aux Vaches et au champ d'honneur, Editions Arcanes, 1953.
Les Rouilles encagées, E.L., 1954.
Le Gigot, sa vie et son oeuvre, T.V., 1957.
Histoire Naturelle, privately printed, Ussel, 1958.

Prose: Polemical, Art criticism, Translations etc.
La Parôle est à Péret, E.S., New York, 1943.
Le Déshonneur des poètes, Poésie et Révolution, Mexico City, 1945.
Toyen, (with Breton & Heisler), Editions Sokolova, 1953.
Le Livre de Chilám Balám de Chimayel, Denoël, 1955.
Anthologie de l'Amour sublime, Editions Albin Michel, 1956.
Anthologie des mythes, légendes et contes populaires d'Amérique, Editions Albin Michel, 1960.
Pour un Second Manifeste Communiste, (With Munis), T.V., 1965.
Les Mains dans les poches, Léo, Montpellier, 1968.
Les Syndicats contre la Révolution, (with Munis), T.V., 1968.

II. Books & Articles about Péret in French.

BAILLY, Jean-Christophe, " 'Au-delà du langage': Une Etude sur Benjamin Péret," E.L.,

1971.

BEDOUIN, Jean-Louis, "Preséntation," in "Benjamin Péret," Seghers, 1961.

BENAYOUN, Robert, "A Plus d'un titre . . ." in rep. of "La Grand Jeu," Gallimard, 1969.

BRETON, André, "Benjamin Péret," in "Anthologie de L'Humour noir," Sagittaire, 1940.

CARROUGES, Michel, "Sur Benjamin Péret," in "Preuves," no. 106, Dec. 1959.

CHENIEUX-GENDRON, Jacqueline, "Benjamin Péret: une écrire 'ultra-metynomique',"
in "Surréalisme et le roman," L'Age d'Homme, 1983.

COURTOT, Claude, "Introduction à la lecture de Benjamin Péret," T.V., 1966.

COURTOT, Claude, "Benjamin Péret et l'automatisme," in "Pleine Marge," no. 7, June
1988.

ELUARD, Paul, "L'Arbitraire, la contradiction, la violence, la poésie," in "Variétés," no.
for June, 1929.

ELUARD, Paul, Prière d'insérer for "De Derrière les fagots," 1934.

FAUCHEREAU, Serge, "Le vrai visage de Benjamin Péret," in "La Quinzaine littéraire,"
no. 90, march 1970.

GOUTIER, Jean-Michel et al, "Benjamin Péret," Henri Veyrier, 1982. Contains essays by
Durozoi, Schuster, Courtot, Rabourdin, Prevan and Debenedetti.

GOUTIER, Jean-Michel, "D'Entrée de jeu . . ." in "Pleine Marge," no.7, June 1988.

NAVILLE, Pierre, "Benjamin Péret," in "La Revue européene," no. 26, April 1925.

NAVILLE, Pierre, "Benjamin Péret vous parle," in his "Le Temps du surréel," Galilée,
1977.

MAYOUX, Jehan, "Benjamin Péret, la fourchette coupante," in "Le Surréalisme, meme,"
nos. 2 & 3, Spring & Autumn, 1957.

PRIGIONI, Pierre, "Conte populaire et conte surréaliste," Argalia Editore, Urbino, 1970.

PIERRE, Jose, "Une dimension populaire du surréalisme," in "Le Monde," no. 7804,
February 1970.

SABATIER, Robert, "Benjamin Péret," in Péret's "Oeuvres Complètes," IV, Corti,
1987.

SCHUSTER, Jean, "Péret de profil," in his "Archives 57/68, batailles pour le surréalisme," E.L., 1969.

The Association des Amis de Benjamin Péret have published two collective works to
vindicate Péret against various attacks:
"De la part de Péret," re: "the Hugnet affair," 1963.
"A Propos de Péret," re: the LeBrun affair," 1987.

III. Works by Péret in English Translation.

1. Books (apart from the last, all entirely poetry).

"Remove Your Hat," translated by David Gascoyne & Humphrey Jennings, Contemporary Poetry & Prose Editions, London, 1936. An earlier version "A Bunch of
Carrots," was censored and withdrawn before sale.

"Péret's Score," trans. J.H.Matthews, Lettres Modernes, Collection "Passeport" No 10,
Paris, 1965.

"Four Years After the Dog," trans. Paul Brown & Peter Nijmeijer, Arc, 1974.

"From the Hidden Storehouse," trans. Keith Holloman, Field Translation Series, Oberlin
College, Ohio, 1981.

"A Marvellous World," trans. E.Jackson, Louisiana State University Press, 1985.

"Irregular Work," trans. Paul Brown, Actual Size, London, 1984.

"Remove Your Hat and Other Works," trans. David Gascoyne, Humphrey Jennings,
Martin Sorrell, Atlas Press, London, 1986. Reprints first book in this section, with
three stories added.

2. Books containing selections from Péret's poetry.

"Surrealism," ed. Levy, Black Swan Press; "The History of Surrealism," Maurice Nadeau,

Penguin; "A Short Survey of Surrealism," David Gascoyne, Cobden-Sanderson; "Selected Verse Translations," David Gascoyne, OUP; "These are also Wings," ed. Brown & Nijmeijer, Transgravity; "The Autobiography of Surrealism," ed. Marcel Jean, Viking; "The Poetry of Surrealism," ed. Michael Benedikt, Little, Brown & Co.; "The Random House Book of 20th Century French Poetry," ed. Paul Auster.

3. Magazines containing selections from Peret's poetry.
Contemporary Poetry and Prose; This Quarter; Arsenal; London Bulletin; New Directions; Radical America; Rebel Worker; View; Mothers of Mud; Headline; Brooklyn Review; Los Angeles Weekly; Sulfur; Second Aeon; Free Union Libres; Kayak; Field; American Poetry Review ; Durak; New Honolulu Review; Pocket Pal; Seneca Review.

4. Prose: Fiction.
"At 125, Boulevard Saint-Germain" no trans. in "This Quarter," Surrealist number, 1932.
"In a Clinch" trans. Jolas, in "transition," 12, Paris, 1929. Rep. "transition Workshop," Vanguard, 1949, & "Remove Your Hat & Other Works," Atlas, 1986.
"The Thaw" in "VVV," no. 1, June 1942. Rep. "New Road," Grey Walls Press, 1943, "Radical America," IV, no. 6, August 1970, "The Custom-House of Desire," (see below).
"A Life Full of Interest," "A Very Fleeting Pleasure" & "The Thaw" in "The Custom-House of Desire," ed. & trans. J.H.Matthews, California University Press, 1975.
"The Flower of Napoleon" in "The Autobiography of Surrealism," ed. & trans. Marcel Jean, Viking Press, N.Y., 1980.
"The Misfortunes of a Dollar" trans. M.Sorrell in "Atlas Anthology Two," Atlas Press, London, 1984, rep. in next entry.
"The Misfortunes of a Dollar," "Death by a Leaf" & "At 125 Boulevard St.-Germain" trans. anon. & M.Sorrell, in "Remove Your Hat & Other Works," Atlas Press, 1986.

5. Prose: Polemical.
"Magic: the Flesh and Blood of Poetry" part of "La Parôle est à Péret" in "View," IV, no. 2, 1943, rep in "Antinarcissus: Surrealist Conquest," no. 1, 1969.
"Thought is ONE and indivisible" in "Free Unions Libres," no. 3-4, London, 1946. Rep. in "Surrealism and Revolution," Solidarity, Chicago, 1966 & Simian—Son of Coptic Press, London, n.d.
"Notes on Pre-Columbian Art" in "Horizon," XV, no. 89, 1947.
"Remembrance of Things to Come" in "Trans/formation," no. 1, 1952.
"The Dishonor of the Poets," "The Factory Committee: Motor of the Social Revolution" & "Poetry Above All" in "Radical America," IV, no. 6, 1970.
"A Note on Slang" & "Against Commercial Movies" in "Surrealism and its Popular Accomplices," ed. F.Rosemont, Black Swan Press, Chicago, 1982.
"The Poets' Dishonor" trans. James Brook, No Starch Press, Berkeley, 1985.

IV. Works about Peret in English.

BRETON, André, "Benjamin Péret" trans. S. Schwarz, in "What is Surrealism: Selected Writings of André Breton" ed. F.Rosemont, Pluto Press, London, 1978, and trans. W.Partington in "Atlas Anthology Two," Atlas Press, London, 1984.
CAWS, Mary Anne, "Péret's 'Amour Sublime'—just another 'Amour fou'?" in "The French Review," XL, no. 2, 1966.
GASCOYNE, David, "Introduction" to "Remove Your Hat and Other Works," Atlas Press, 1986.
MATTHEWS, J. H. "Benjamin Péret," Twayne, 1975.
ROSEMONT, Franklin, "An Introduction to Benjamin Péret" in "Radical America," IV, no. 6, 1970
SOLSONA, S. "Incidents from the Life of Benjamin Péret." Special issue of "The Alarm," no. 8, Summer 1981.